Advance Praise for *Ways of Leaving*

"A standout novel about going home, where old girlfriends, awkward funerals, deeply buried parental secrets and naked, drunken, nocturnal escapades irritate a man like scabs of his squandered youth and misspent adulthood. When Chase returns to his hometown in the Poconos, his father has just died, his wife has left him, he lost his job as a journalist, and his sister wastes away in a mental institution. He's grappling with addictions to sex and alcohol as well as, closer to the surface, a problem with rage, most frequently expressed with dripping sarcasm. It's that sarcasm that gives this bleak, sometimes violent book its surprising levity. Jarrett (*More Towels*, 2002) seamlessly combines dark comedy with real tragedy and pathos, a hat trick comparable to that of certain movies with similar themes—Zach Braff's *Garden State*, for instance, or Diablo Cody's *Young Adult*. . . . Ruthlessly brilliant writing brings grace to a story smoldering in pain."
—*Kirkus Reviews*

"It's official: Grant Jarrett has created the most entertaining, existential antihero since Tony Soprano. Whether you're laughing out loud or wincing in recognition, *Ways of Leaving* will impress you with its raw honesty, keen writing, and ultimately, its big heart."
—Jess Riley, author of *Mandatory Release* and *Driving Sideways*, a Target bestseller

"Grant Jarrett's vividly drawn characters, dark humor, and empathetic voice build bridges that transport the reader through this intergenerational story of parents and siblings in which the desire for salvation is challenged by the equally powerful impulse for destruction. *Ways of Leaving* depicts a seemingly familiar world that becomes freshly discovered and understood in Jarrett's intricate telling."
—Jon Reiner, author of *The Man Who Couldn't Eat*, an *L.A. Times* "Top Pick"

"Chase Stoller is a beautifully mangled all-American mess. Jarrett's ability to paint a picture of the tedium of small-town America and then to drop a character into this who's right out of a Wyeth painting, well that sealed the deal for me. With pitch-perfect dialogue and writing that felt like a perfect Indian summer day, *Ways of Leaving* was that rare book that when I read the last word on the last page, I went back to page one and read it all over again."
—Paul Hoppe, author of *The Curse of van Gogh*

ways *of* leaving

SparkPress, a BookSparks imprint

A division of SparkPoint Studio, LLC

ways *of* leaving

A Novel

GRANT JARRETT

Copyright © 2014 by Grant Jarrett
All rights reserved, including the right to reproduce this book or portions thereof in any form whatsoever.

Published by SparkPress, a BookSparks imprint,
A division of SparkPoint Studio, LLC
Tempe, Arizona, USA, 85281
www.sparkpointstudio.com

First American Edition, 2013
Second Edition, 2014
Printed in the United States of America.

ISBN: 978-1-940716-41-1 (pbk)
ISBN: 978-1-940716-40-4 (ebk)

Cover design © Julie Metz, Ltd./metzdesign.com
Cover photo © Millennium Images UK

This is a work of fiction. Names, characters, places, and incidents either are the product of the author's imagination or are used fictitiously. Any resemblance to actual persons, living or dead, is entirely coincidental.

To what purpose is this waste?

—Matthew 26:8

*And as she looked around, she saw how Death the consoler,
Laying his hand upon many a heart, had healed it forever.*

—Henry Wadsworth Longfellow
Evangeline, Part the Second, V

1

Just a bit more pressure on the accelerator and a snap of his wrist, a minimal effort, and he'd careen across the median and into the gleaming chrome grille of a fully loaded Kenworth. Presto, dead guy! If he did it right now he could beat his father to the finish line. But no, somehow he'd screw it up. The car would stall out on the median and he'd have to sit there waiting for a tow truck while passing drivers snickered and gawked. Or worse, instead of crashing into a tractor-trailer, he'd be the lone survivor of a perfect head-on collision with a perfect family of five. His guilt, shame and incompetence would be plastered across the front pages of every newspaper in Pennsylvania:

Loving Family Snuffed Out by Reckless Lunatic

—

Madman Sole Survivor in Deadly Crash

—

*Psychopath Responsible for Killing
Lovely Family of Five Survives:
Satan Suspected*

Shortly after one o'clock on Saturday afternoon, according to State Police Sergeant Hugh G. Mandible, an expensive European vehicle traveling west at an estimated ninety miles an hour crossed the median onto *the eastbound lanes of Rte. 80 between Exits 23 and 24 and collided with an inexpensive American vehicle operated by Reverend Al Goode, resulting in the horrific, bloody deaths of Reverend Goode, forty-three; Bea, his wife of twenty-two years, who was beheaded in the collision; and their three beloved children: Rose, nine years old; Timmy, twelve, an "A" student in spite of his disability; and M'gubu, their darling handicapped adopted eleven-month-old baby. Chase Stoller, the shady, unemployed thirty-four-year-old operator of the offending vehicle, suffered only minor injuries and was released on his own recognizance. Though Stoller apparently has no criminal record, the few people who would admit an acquaintanceship with him, including his poor dying father, agreed that he did not deserve to live.*

Oh well. It wouldn't really be fair to deprive his father of what might be his final opportunity to disseminate the potent brand of discouragement and disappointment that made him such a joy to be around. Most likely he wasn't even that sick.

Five years ago, when his father had been dying the first time, it was Chase who'd had the honor of escorting him to the emergency room. After several years of stubborn resistance, Chase had finally yielded to his wife's increasingly frantic, almost obsessive desire to meet his family, something he'd successfully avoided with every woman he'd dated since his second year in college. Probably Jennifer had begun to recognize what a disaster her husband was becoming and was searching for some insight into the root of his problems. Or perhaps she was hoping the experience would transform her growing anger into something more akin to sympathy. When the doctor finally strolled into the emergency room that day and explained that the symptoms were nothing more menacing than indigestion, his father immediately became agitated and eager to leave. They were still waiting for the discharge nurse when a platoon of hospital staff propelled a stretcher past the doorway, a grim-faced civilian unit trailing closely behind. There was a rush of activity outside the room where Chase and his father were waiting, and then everyone seemed to disappear. About ten minutes of relative silence preceded a series of agonized howls. It was a horrible, nauseating sound, like someone being tortured or the detonation of some unspeakable grief. A few minutes later a nurse stepped into the room. Her face was the color of chalk and she was trembling. An accident victim had just died, his wife standing next to him, watching. It would be another few minutes. Chase's father sat down, shook his head, sighed and said, "Just my luck."

When Chase's brother Aaron called this time he sounded overwhelmed and agitated, as he did whenever someone was inconsiderate enough to have a desire, a need or a minor request of which he was not the primary beneficiary.

"Do you understand what I'm saying, Chase? Dad is on his deathbed."

Chase was unable to restrain himself. "If I were as old and sick as he thinks he is, I wouldn't get anywhere *near* a deathbed."

When Chase called back it was Sarah who picked up. "I don't think Aaron wants to talk to you right now."

"Hey, how is that adorable sister of yours?"

"Look, Chase, your father is dying and Aaron is having to handle everything by himself. I just don't think that's very fair."

"Okay...."

"And it's not very nice for you to joke about it. It's just not very nice."

"No, it's not." His hauteur was deflating. "And I'm sorry."

She sighed.

"Is he really *that* sick?"

"Do you think Aaron would be this upset if he wasn't?"

" Well . . . I don't know. He does tend to overreact."

"Why don't you call and tell him that after the funeral? I'm sure he'll find that a great comfort in his time of need."

Unemployed and in the early stages of a divorce, Chase could neither unearth nor devise a defensible excuse not to go.

Unfortunately, there was no bright side to this journey, nothing to look forward to, no one he wanted to see—not since his sister's final headlong descent into madness, his frustration and discomfort with which were comprised of equal portions of grief and envy. She'd crossed a line—a line that had somehow eluded him in spite of his occasional gravitations toward its odd, elliptical orbit—and left him behind to make his way alone in the world. No fair.

He'd just put behind him the strip mall-infested outskirts of Stroudsburg when he saw the sign approaching: *Bartonsville Exit One Mile Ahead.* He signaled and took his foot off the gas. "Goddamn it." He turned off the signal and stomped on the accelerator.

For years, Chase's relationship with his sister had been a refuge for him and, though he hadn't quite realized it until much later, for her. Their bond had enabled them to construct a safe haven from their father's bland indifference and the simmering rage their mother masked with a smile, a smile that in her angriest moments was accompanied by an all but imperceptible twitch of her left eye, or maybe it was the corner of her mouth; he never looked at her for too long. Perhaps the bond he and Hannah shared was simply a product of necessity, an integument that evolved as a natural response to the nameless dangers that seemed to engulf them. It could be argued that there was no danger, and in a way that was true—there were few spankings, none of them severe, and they'd never been locked in closets or forced to ingest cleaning solvents—but somehow the threat of terror was always present, an unrelenting brittle tension that might rupture any minute. It was like living under a massive sheet of plate glass, already stressed to the limit of its flexibility, susceptible to any misstep: an imprudent comment, a glance in the wrong direction or an incautious thought. What if they can read my mind? Beatings might have been easier to take; they certainly would have been less stressful. Neither of them felt safe without the other. They didn't have the power to change things, but together they could sometimes laugh about them.

Often at the end of a particularly difficult evening they would get together in one of their rooms and perform a mutual debriefing.

"How long do you think Dad's been dead?"

"He's had a sort of sour odor for weeks, but I think I heard him exhale last Tuesday."

"Sometimes corpses fart."

"I guess he's got all the symptoms, but then so do you."

"Girls don't fart, Chase." Eyelashes fluttering like a butterfly's wings.

"Then I'm pretty sure you shit your pants."

"I have no idea what you're talking about." Here she would roll her eyes. "Was there smoke coming out of Mom's head at dinner?"

"It was coming from her left ear."

"One of her eyes almost popped out when Aaron dropped his fork."

"Her head was expanding, too."

"What do you think is in there?"

"Nuclear winter?"

"Knickknacks."

"Cutlery."

"Dry ice."

"Drano."

"Evil clowns."

Laughter.

But it wasn't only humor that they shared. There was also deep affection. Although they tried at times to bring him into their world, Aaron wasn't interested in what apparently seemed childish to him, which was nearly everything his brother and sister said or did. It wasn't that Aaron had assessed his siblings' interests and activities and judged them unworthy based upon their merits or lack thereof; it was simply that they were not his, and were therefore trivial and irrelevant.

Chase was nearly past the Bartonsville exit when he jerked his steering wheel to the right. A blaring horn, headlights. A fender inches away from the passenger window. He backed off, sighed and sat back. A burst of white, then red, red, red. "Shit." At the end of the exit ramp he pulled over, extracted his wallet from his back pocket, and waited.

"License and registration, please."

He slid the cards from his wallet and handed them out the window. Just say nothing. No stupid excuses. Let it play out. That's what Jennifer would say and, although he might not admit it in the heat of the moment, she would be absolutely right.

"Just wait in your car, Mr. Stoller. I'll be back in a minute."

Already he could smell the toxic breath of the truck stop just north of the exit. "Officer?"

"Sir?" Eyebrows up.

"My father's sick."

"Excuse me, sir?"

"I . . . my father is very, very sick and I'm coming, well—"

"Sir?"

"Could you maybe just not give me a ticket? I'm usually very careful." *I mean, you know, when my father's not dying.*

"Just wait in your car, sir."

"Fuck."

"Sir?"

"Nothing."

Fuck.

It probably wouldn't have been terribly difficult to dismiss the childhood wounds Aaron had inflicted and the festering resentments they'd engendered if the attitude and behavior hadn't remained, even intensified, through adulthood. Whenever they spoke on the phone, an increasingly rare event, Aaron dominated the dialogue. And he would never ask a question. If Chase inadvertently let slip some tidbit of news about his own life, he immediately sensed Aaron's distress, his urgent need to get back to what really mattered. "I think Jennifer is going to leave me."

"Yeah. Well anyway, I'm working on an invention that counteracts the effects of cell phone waves on your brain."

"I was fired last week and I guess that was pretty much the clincher for her."

"Uh-huh. So did I tell you that after not touching my bass for like five years I decided to put a band together?"

"Blue flames are shooting from my ass."

"And Kirk's playing keyboards again."

"I just bent over and boiled the goldfish."

"We're doing a lot of the old originals and also writing some new stuff. Plus I'm really getting into the trampoline. I mean, I got it for the kids, but—"

"Mr. Stoller?" The officer was holding Chase's license, registration and insurance card in his hand. "I'm going to let you off with a warning this time."

"Thanks. Thanks a lot." Chase reached out for his papers. The officer gripped them. "Thank you, really." Still the officer wouldn't let go. "I appreciate it."

"But I am going to ask you to watch your language."

"Excuse me?"

"That kind of talk might impress folks where you come from, but we don't take kindly to it around here."

Chase stared up at the hulking officer. He had nothing against this man, and he wouldn't intentionally cause pain or injury to anyone. He really wouldn't. And yet the thought of striking repeated blows against the officer's ankles with a crowbar produced in Chase an undeniable feeling of jubilation.

"You mean you don't cotton to it," he mumbled, and grinned. *Thwack.*

By this time Jennifer would be fuming, emitting huffs and puffs, squirming in the passenger seat, belching uncontrollably, waiting with giddy anticipation for the opportunity to excoriate her husband for his hostility and lack of control. And she'd be right, of course. What she had never learned, or perhaps never cared about, was that with high-octane adrenaline flooding his system, Chase wasn't going to be particularly receptive to her criticism. Or perhaps she simply had as little control as he did. She, too, had to attack—never strangers, of course; just her husband.

The officer pursed his lips and squinted. He probably practiced that expression in front of a mirror every morning, just after kissing his Bible. "Have a real nice day, sir."

Thwack. Splat. He grunts, crumbles, begs forgiveness, offers his badge and a fistful of cash. "You can pee on me if you want." This with a childlike pout.

Aaron was just a little more than a year older than Chase, and yet he'd never, even in childhood, seemed quite comfortable with himself. Unlike his siblings, he was always a little chubby, his hands were big and fleshy and too often his new toys would break before he'd had an opportunity to enjoy them. More disturbing was the fact that he couldn't seem to get his mother's attention. She seemed deaf to his voice, blind to his presence and totally oblivious to his needs. Maybe that was why he'd chosen to become a high school teacher: he had a guaranteed audience. Still, a credible explanation for Aaron's self-involvement did not make the trait any easier to abide. Yes, Chase had sympathy for him, but that only made him more uncomfortable with his own anger. And whom else could he blame for his guilt for being angry with Aaron but Aaron? Perhaps not consciously, but certainly it played out that way at the time. Only later could Chase dissect his responses with a modicum of reluctant objectivity.

When he'd put the truck stop and the shit-brown Days Inn behind him and was only about three miles from his brother's house, Chase decided again that he wasn't ready for the drama, for the picking of old wounds, tearing at scabs and abrading of raw emotion—all that he'd hoped to discard when he, faithfully following in the footsteps of his sister and their mother before her, abandoned the sunken ship that was their home. He checked his mirror before signaling and slowing to make a right turn into the parking lot of the Tannersville Inn.

But for a recent coat of pale yellow paint, the exterior of the building was unchanged from his recollections. Inside it was like a recurring nightmare: the heavy wooden beams with diagonal braces supporting an unfinished ceiling; the rectangular bar, above which were suspended two shelves, the highest of which held a shoddy platoon of old mugs, trophies and kerosene lamps, an antique tricycle and a CD player that was coated with dust. On the lower shelf were the bar's glasses, glimmering and neatly arrayed. Hanging haphazardly from the wall to his left were beer posters, faded photographs of television actors and pop musicians and a few rust-encrusted farm implements. And suspended from the perforated far wall was a battle-scarred dartboard, probably the same one that had been there the last time he'd visited. The place was a graveyard for flea market rejects.

Chase grabbed a stool and sat down.

"Like to see a menu?" The bartender came from a kit: just under six feet, medium build, white shirt, black pants, black vest, dark hair with a few scattered streaks of premature gray, thirty-two hours' beard growth, dull eyes, practiced smile and his faithful companion, an invisible effluvium of stale cigarette smoke.

"No thanks. Just a bottle of Beck's."

Two men stepped through the doorway. Dress slacks and button-down shirts, sport jackets draped neatly over their arms. "It's unchartered territory," the taller of the two said. In unison they hung their jackets over the backs of two stools.

"Uncharted, I think you mean." They sat down.

"Yeah, it's uncharted territory."

"But nobody goes out to dinner in downtown East Stroudsburg."

The bartender placed a glass in front of Chase and poured his beer. Chase nodded and took a sip.

"That's what I'm saying," the tall one continued. "There's really no competition."

"There's no competition because nobody goes there."

"Well who do you think lives in all those buildings?"

"Sure, people live there, poor people, janitors and carwash attendants, but even they don't go out there, at least not if they're looking for good food, decent wine and a nice atmosphere."

"That's 'cause there's no place there to go."

"Do *you* ever go out to dinner in East Stroudsburg?"

"No. Of course not. There's no place to go."

"That's because nobody goes there."

"No. It's because there isn't any good place to go."

"Well if *you* wouldn't even go there, what makes you think other people would?"

"I *would* go there if there was a good place. I mean, I think I would." He rubbed his forehead. "I'm *sure* I would."

"Where would you go?"

"I'd go to a place like the one I want to open, like a nice wine bar with food and a good atmosphere."

"So you'd be, like, the only customer in your own fancy wine bar."

The tall one stared with his mouth hanging open. "No," he said after a rapid series of frowns and scowls. "What I'm saying is if there was a place like that I think people would go there. Plus the rents are really low."

"Sure they are. Of course they are. The rents are low because there's no business, no commerce. Nobody goes there."

"But if someone opened up a place like I'm talking about, and really did it right, like I've been *say*ing here, then people would come."

"If they did, the rents would just go up and you'd be in the exact same situation."

"The same as what?"

"With the high rents and all."

"Maybe they *would* go up, but they wouldn't get as high as they are where there's more foot traffic."

"Well, that's because people don't go there to have dinner or drinks or just about anything else."

These pickled Poconos minds made it so easy to feel superior.

The tall one sighed. "I'm saying they *would*, the place would *bring* them."

"Nope. Not in downtown East Stroudsburg. You don't go there, I don't go there. Nobody goes there."

"But they *would*."

"Well, if this is such a great idea, how come nobody's already done it?"

"I guess nobody's thought of it."

"So, like, you're such a better businessman than anybody else in the Poconos, even though you never owned a restaurant or a business of any kind."

"I just think it could be a really good idea if you did it right."

The shorter one shook his head. "No. It's a bad area."

"How is it a bad area? There's the college and the hospital. How is it such a bad area?"

"So, if you were lucky you'd maybe get a few poor college kids and the sick and injured on their way to or from the hospital."

Great to be home.

"No, you idiot! What about the professors and the doctors?"

"I'd bet anything they don't go out in East Stroudsburg."

"That is because there is *no place to go*."

"Right. You know why?"

"Yeah. Cause you're a fucking idiot."

"Huh?"

Too bad the cop wasn't here.

The tall one stood up and grabbed his coat.

"Where're you going?" the other one asked.

"I'm going to get a drink somewhere where you aren't." He turned and started toward the door.

"Yeah, well I bet anything you're not going to East Stroudsburg." He got up and followed his friend out.

Chase laughed and the bartender approached him. "Everything okay?"

"Is there an entertainment charge?"

"Today?" He shook his head. "No. Only on Friday and Saturday nights when certain bands are here."

Try again. "Are those two married?"

The bartender looked around the bar. "Those guys that just left?"

"Never mind."

"I'm pretty sure they're straight," the bartender said. "Sorry." He pulled a rag from under the bar and began rubbing away imaginary spots.

"Do you have a good single malt?"

"Sure." The bartender motioned to an array of bottles.

"I'll take a Glenlivet, neat."

The bartender took a glass from above the bar and poured a double. "Don't let it get you down," he said as he placed the glass on a napkin.

"Excuse me?"

"There's plenty of other guys."

Chase didn't realize until his collision with the afternoon heat that he'd left his land legs at the bar. The waves in the parking lot rolled gradually enough, but their rhythm was uneven and they came crashing from all sides. Advancing in a straight line required serious concentration. Halfway to his car he realized he'd adopted a sort of John Wayne stride and he laughed out loud. He looked around to see if anyone was near enough to notice. No, he was alone, although it didn't tax his imagination to envisage the born-again trooper crouching like a sniper behind a fence, peering at him through a high-power riflescope. *Thwack, splatter.*

Open the car door. Good. Get in. Okay. Put the key into the ignition. Okay, one more try. Good. Turn. Only a couple miles. Take it easy and pay attention and nobody will get hurt. Really, this was the only sensible way to approach a family reunion, inoculated by a healthy dose of alcohol. Anyway, this was as ready as he was likely to get.

Only as he approached Aaron's long gravel driveway did it occur to Chase that his brother might not appreciate his condition, mild and pleasant and downright comforting as it was from the inside. He might not appear grave enough under the circumstances. The trees spread to reveal the house. He feigned a grave expression and snorted. Then he noticed all the cars and something tightened in his abdomen. He parked behind the last car in the driveway, stepped out of his car and sprinted toward the house. The front door swung open as he approached it. Bradley, who'd become a little person since he'd last seen him, was gazing up at him.

"Grampa's dead."

Chase felt his face flush. "I'm sorry sweetheart." He knelt down and patted Bradley's head.

"Daddy says you don't care."

Chase took his nephew in his arms and held him close. Suddenly the child began to sob as though his own father had just died. Chase held him tighter, rocked him. He could feel the dampness of Bradley's tears on his own face.

The boy pulled back. "Don't cry, Uncle Chase," he said. "Daddy says you don't care." His clear young eyes were sympathetic and perfectly dry.

2

Alone in the foyer, Chase listened to the drone of somber voices emanating from the living room. He slipped quietly past the doorway and stepped into the kitchen. Aaron was leaning against the refrigerator with his hands in his pockets. His eyes were shut, his head leaning to one side.

"Aaron?"

He opened his eyes and folded his arms over his chest. "Thanks again for making sure I get stuck with all the shit."

"I'm sorry." Chase took a seat at the table.

"I'm sure you have a very good reason for missing Dad's death." He rubbed his eyes.

"Please sit down," Chase said.

Aaron eased himself into a chair across from his brother. He was pale, puffy, and, Chase realized, entirely justified in his anger.

"I'm really sorry. I just didn't think it would happen so . . . so fast."

"You mean you didn't believe me. Or you didn't give a shit. Either way, I'm always the one who has to deal with this stuff."

"A cop stopped me—"

"A cop stopped you."

"Yeah."

"Really? How long were you in jail?"

"And then I stopped at a bar."

"*There* you go."

"I'm sorry, Aaron. I just lost track of time. I had no idea—"

"So you're getting drunk while I'm watching Dad die. Does that seem fair to you?" He squinted at his younger brother. "Does it?"

"Fair?" All Aaron could see, even in his father's death, was how it affected him. The death itself was little more than an inconvenience. What was upsetting him was that he'd had to deal with it, whatever that meant.

"Yeah, I know your routine," Aaron said. "Nothing's fair. But if it isn't too inconvenient for everyone else, I would really like fair just once, just to see how it feels."

"What can I do, Aaron? What do you want me to do?"

"Nothing." Aaron looked down at his hands. "No, there is something." He stood up. "Be somebody else," he said, and stepped out of the room.

Now what? He wasn't wanted here, and he understood that, and yet he couldn't very well leave. Or could he? No. That would cause a permanent scar. It would take some time, but Aaron would eventually warm up to him. Even if he didn't forgive him, he'd realize he needed him, though what they provided one another wasn't clear. Perhaps it was something as elemental, and as nebulous, as their genetic link. That, at least, they had. And they shared a history, however dissimilar their versions of it might have been. On the other hand, it didn't matter what it was that they provided one another, or why.

Physical presence was the least either of them could offer. It also seemed to be the most they could give.

And yet there was a sensitive side to Aaron. The old movies they'd watched as children still touched him. By his own account, he'd wept one recent Christmas while watching *It's a Wonderful Life* on television with his kids. Yes, he was capable of genuine sadness, but it was somehow tainted. His sorrow wasn't really for the characters in the film; he'd only responded to their sadness with thoughts of his own. In fact, if asked he most likely wouldn't have been able to tell you what their troubles had been: *Uh, something about Christmas, I think*. Instead, he had seen their pain, and in seeing it had been reminded of what really mattered: his own eternal free-floating grief, grief that he would never acknowledge because to do so might cast aspersions on his parents and make him appear weak. Or perhaps he'd simply found a way to distance himself from emotion in all but the safest circumstances. With all of that, he saw himself as happy and well-adjusted. And in times of doubt, he always had the comforting illusion of God.

But in spite of what he knew, what he'd learned repeatedly, so powerful was Chase's eagerness for some meaningful connection that when he detected a hint of sensitivity in his brother, he was affected, deluded anew. *He loves me*. It wouldn't be long before he was faced again with that familiar disappointment and all the resentment it provoked.

Was their father's body in the house somewhere? Was there something Chase was expected to do now, some hideous ritual he'd be required to perform? And why had he reacted so strongly to the news of the death of a man who was little more than a grumpy stranger? Why did he have to fight to hold the tears back now? He'd known it would eventually come, and he'd thought about it more than once, but in anticipation of the event, when it was merely theoretical, there had been no sadness, no suffering, just a hint of regret that they'd never found a way to connect, that they were strangers who, perhaps, didn't need to be.

"Chase." Sarah's voice extinguished his thoughts.

He turned and looked up at her. "You look very tired."

"I am," she said. "Do you want to see your father?"

"To be honest—"

"I think it would be a good idea." In spite of her smile and her choice of words, Chase knew this was a command.

"I'd never argue with you."

She rolled her eyes. "Are you okay?"

"I'm always okay."

"No. You're always full of shit."

"That, too."

"Come say goodbye to your father before . . . before they come to take him."

He followed her to the end of the hall, where she opened a door and motioned for him to go in.

Chase stood at the foot of the bed staring down but trying not to see, not just because of who was lying there, but because of the greater message: we all die. He held his breath, as though the air were tainted, as though death were a contagious condition one could avoid by taking the proper precautions. With his head resting on the pillow, his arms flanking his body on either side and the bed sheets pulled up to his armpits, it was obvious that someone had taken the time to make him appear comfortable. But he looked chalky and poorly constructed, like a discarded wax mannequin. He seemed smaller, too, and his color was all wrong, as though he'd been drained, the substance excavated, leaving only this anemic husk.

Now he was nothing more than rotting meat, waste. It might already be too late for safe ingestion, though wild animals seemed quite happy to dine on decomposing carcasses. Perhaps the dogs in the neighborhood had already sensed his presence. More likely they were too addicted to Purina and Alpo to be interested in some wrinkly, old dead guy. But why was uncooked meat so toxic to humans? In the cartoons he'd watched as a child, cannibals always cooked their victims in giant cauldrons, but old cartoons probably weren't the most reliable source of information regarding the eating habits of different cultures. Cartoons. *I'm thinking about cartoons.* In any case, he was too stiff and pasty to be very appetizing. Where was his color? Where had it gone?

Breathe.

And where was the part of him that mattered? More to the point, where had it been when he was alive? Or was that just another part of the myth of humanity we were all so blindly eager to believe? These questions would never have occurred to the man whose remains lay before him.

Talk to me.
"*How are you feeling, Dad?*"
"*Grunt.*"
"*Are you getting out at all?*"
"*Well. . . .*"
"*Why don't you sell the house and move into an apartment?*"
"*Ngg.*"
"*Or at least a smaller house?*"
"*No.*"
"*Wouldn't you be more comfortable?*"
"*Oh, I don't think so.*"

"If you lived in an apartment you wouldn't have to worry about the yard or the rain gutters or the roof. You'd meet people. Don't you want to meet people? I hear they're nice."

"What do you want from me?"

"I'm just trying to help."

"I'm dead. I have absolutely nothing to say."

"You really didn't have much of anything to say when you were alive."

"Well. . . ."

"*But* why?"

"Because I'm just not interested."

"Not interested in what?"

"Anything."

"What goes on in your mind? What do you think about, or care about? Give me a clue, something to work with when the others are busy mourning."

"Please leave me alone."

"Okay. Okay, just one more thing."

"Sigh. What?"

"Did you ever try to find Mom?"

"Oh no."

"Why?"

"Well . . . grunt."

"I'm sorry."

"Sorry?"

"Sorry you . . . sorry that you died, I guess."

"Oh?"

"Sorry you found life so. . . ."

"Hmm?"

"I don't know. You tell me. You tell me."

"Well. . . ."

"It wasn't very good, was it?"

"What do you want from me?"

"I don't know. Something."
Anything.
He was more responsive now than when he was alive.
Next to the bed was a chair. Chase slid it a little farther from the bed and sat down. He looked at his father's face. Not much improvement. *My father is dead.*
Breathe.
Asshole. He shook his head and snickered. *Fucking asshole.* "You're a fucking asshole." He began to sob, his body shaking with grief, or one of its lesser subsidiaries.

The eruption had been swift and violent, but like a tropical cloudburst, in a minute it was over. Always he mistrusted tears, questioned the ostensible association. Who or what had really engendered them? From which historical offenses had they evolved? Or were they just a byproduct of some vestigial instinct? On the other hand there were a few clear, obvious reasons to be sad, and in that he found some consolation. The consciousness that for nearly seventy years had occupied this corpse had never seemed completely at home there. There had been no real human connection, little joy or enthusiasm, just a reluctant, perfunctory acceptance of the responsibilities with which he'd been charged, from all appearances without his prior consent. That was terribly sad. There was the grief of those who remained: Aaron, his wife and their children. However mystifying their reasons, they were mourning this passing. And then there was Chase, who in losing his father had lost nothing at all; reason enough, he supposed, for this stunted sorrow.

He rose, stepped toward bed and leaned over his father's body. Cautiously he reached out. He rested his hand lightly on the sheet next to his father's arm. Then he turned and stepped out of the room.
Breathe.

Sarah's parents sat on opposite ends of the couch, their pretty younger daughter between them, while Sarah and Aaron stood by the picture window talking with Kirk and a woman Chase didn't know, tall and slender with reddish brown hair and a pale, clear complexion. She didn't seem to be wearing any makeup, or to need any. Nor did the absence of a bra detract from her appeal. Peeking shyly from beneath the sheer fabric of a long beige dress that straddled the line between a formal gown and an Earth Day frock were two nipples, alert, proud, confident. Her parents had probably met at Woodstock. Now her mother was a professor and her father was a banker, no, an attorney, a corporate attorney and an alcoholic—one somehow compensated for the other. They had affairs and resentments. And they had a farm, one to look at and talk about rather than to actually farm on. A farm with horses viewed through a soft focus lens in slow motion. They still smoked pot, which might explain the soft focus and the slow motion. Her hair smelled like wheat and firewood and she read Kafka and Hesse. She was lovely. *Hi, nipples.* He smiled at her but she didn't seem to notice. *Over here.* What was wrong with him? He loved her so much.

Kirk glanced over and nodded. With other people around, Aaron would at least be cordial. Chase approached the group and reached for Kirk's hand. Kirk pulled him close and embraced him. "I'm sorry," he said and tightened his grip.

"Thanks." Chase backed away. "And thanks for being here." Where did that come from?

Everyone had gotten here so quickly. They were probably all on call, aware that if they failed Aaron in his time of need, they would suffer for eternity. Or maybe they simply cared enough not to let him down.

"How are you holding up?" Kirk assessed him.

"I'm okay." Chase turned toward his brother. "How are *you* doing?"

Aaron shrugged and Sarah put her arm around him.

"He's having a hard time right now, but he'll be fine." She reached out toward Chase. "And we're glad you're here, Chase."

"Thanks," he said. "I should have been here sooner." *Blah, blah, blah.*

"Well, you're here now," Kirk said. "That's what matters."

Wheat and Firewood was standing quite close to Kirk, but they weren't actually making physical contact, which was a comfort. Why didn't someone introduce them?

"Are you still at that little newspaper?"

Chase would have preferred almost any other topic, but Kirk was making an honest effort to involve him in the conversation. "Well, no. I decided it was time to move on."

"Wow. When did that happen?"

"I think it might have been the day they fired me."

Even Aaron let a chuckle escape. Wheat and Firewood was the only one who didn't laugh. She didn't even smile. *I hate her.*

"What about you," he said to Kirk.

"Still teaching and playing. Plus I've been doing some programming."

"Music programming?"

"No. Back-office stuff for banks and financial institutions."

"Oh." He felt his face scrunch up. A little impulse control would be nice, at least in social situations with people he was fond of. "I'm sorry."

"No problem. It can be a little tedious, but I enjoy it. We both enjoy it." He smiled at Wheat and Firewood and put his hand on her shoulder.

Fucking bastard shithole fuckhead.

"I'm sorry. This is Haley, a programming prodigy and music lover."

"Good to know I've offended friends and strangers alike."

"I'm not offended." Her expression didn't change.

"I guess I need to try harder." Chase offered his hand. "I'm Aaron's brother, Chase."

"Good to meet you."

He was smitten and she had absolutely no interest in him. Was it as obvious to everyone else as it was to him? Hopefully, rather than worrying about his inappropriate floundering, they were all reflecting on the death and those affected by it—like normal, emotionally balanced humans. It wasn't that he wasn't touched by his father's death. He was, despite himself. But the impact was sporadic: violent slaps of grief separated by periods of giddy desperation. All he wanted right now was to touch her breasts, kiss her thighs, bury his face in her and make subaqueous sounds. Bluh, bluh, bluh, bluh, bluh. And his head was beginning to ache, as it always did if he stopped drinking too early in the day. "Can I get anyone a drink?"

Kirk's eyes widened. "I'll take a beer if Aaron will have one."

"Sure." Aaron nodded. "But I'm going to need to eat something soon."

"Maybe I can find something to throw together," Sarah said. "I'll see what mom and dad want to do." She turned toward the couch and Chase excused himself.

He was rooting through drawers searching for a bottle opener when Sarah and her sister stepped into the kitchen.

"They're screw-offs," Sarah said.

"Shh." Chase put a finger to his lips. "They have feelings, too."

"Hi, Chase."

"Hi, Christine."

"How are you doing?"

"I'm okay. Just sort of stunned and a little woozy."

"Makes sense."

"Yeah, I guess."

"But never too stunned to notice an attractive woman."

"Excuse me?" Had it been that obvious?

"I think this is the first time we've been in the same room and you haven't come on to me." She tilted her head. "Well, except when we were dating."

Sarah planted a hand on her hip. "His father just died, Chris."

"I think it has a little more to do with his new friend."

Sarah's mouth dropped open. "Are you *jealous*?"

Christine laughed. "Actually I was going to thank her for taking the pressure off, but then she really didn't have any choice in the matter."

"Chris." Sarah scowled.

"It's alright. She's cute when she's being a nasty bitch."

"That's more like it," Christine said.

"How's the shop?"

"Shops. I've got a second one now."

"In Stroudsburg?"

"At the Stroud Mall."

"You've hit the big time."

She reached out and gripped his arm. "I'm sorry about your father. Really."

"Thanks." He drew her closer and kissed her cheek.

It had only lasted a couple months between them. The sex was frequent and action packed—more like an Olympic event than an intimate connection—and she was smart and funny. For a while it was fun, at least when they weren't arguing, but they were both stubborn and competitive and neither of them could stand to lose, so once an argument began it would continue until their tempers boiled over. He would become sarcastic and the contempt would bubble out of her like burning lava in search of a primitive village to devastate.

"You always think you're right," she would snarl, and her lovely face would rearrange itself into an expression appropriate to the accidental ingestion of fecal matter.

"Of course I think I'm right. Do you think you're wrong?"

"Don't be an ass."

"I just don't understand why anyone would have an argument if they thought they were wrong."

"You don't have to be so arrogant, so dismissive and trivializing of other people's views."

"I'm not dismissive. I just think you're wrong. Should I pretend to agree if I think you're wrong? That's ridiculous."

"Now I'm ridiculous."

"No! No, your *argument* is ridiculous."

"You are so fucking arrogant. You think everyone else is stupid."

"No. I sometimes think other people are wrong, as I'm sure you do."

"You smirk and shake your head and—"

"I'm animated. Why should my confidence or my way of expressing myself offend you?"

"You think you're smarter than everybody."

"You're wrong."

"Of course I am. I'm always wrong and you're always right, because you're so fucking smart."

Often it would take days for both of them to recover. And then, after a brief period of emotional peace followed by almost feral sex, it would happen again. Somehow, after all of that, he felt he'd never really gotten to know her. That still seemed vaguely unfortunate. And he wouldn't mind seeing her naked again, though he could do without the postcoital chafing.

Haley was standing by herself in the living room when Chase approached her.

"What happened to Kirk and Aaron?"

"They stepped outside." She raised an eyebrow.

There was probably some cryptic message there, but not one he was equipped to decode. Or maybe it was just a facial tick. In any case it was lovely. He really did love her. What he wanted was just to say it: "I think you're wonderful." Or he could ask her to have dinner with him; in fact that would make him very happy. The problem, the main problem, was that his father had just died and an advance right here, right now, might seem faintly indelicate. On the other hand, she might accede out of sympathy. And that would be okay, like a gift from dad, one that Chase really wanted for a change. That would be perfectly fine. Just to sit across from her sipping wine and discussing Kafka and Hesse would make him so very happy. It would solve all of his problems. Life would be good. He would live forever. Wheee.

"So you're a journalist?"

"Well, I was a couple weeks ago."

"What do you have to do to get fired from a job like that?"

But perhaps she was brought here to hurt him. "It's a little embarrassing."

"Good." She granted him about a third of a smile.

"I was caught stealing semicolons."

"I didn't realize people still used them."

"They don't. They're collector's items now. Very rare." He sipped his beer. At least she got it. Ready, aim, fuck it. "Would you like to have dinner with me?"

"Why?"

"I just think you're adorable."

"No," she said. Now she was smiling. Jesus.

"Please."

"No. I'm sorry. You're just a little too . . . balled up. And I—"

"Balled up?"

"You're a bit of a wreck."

He looked down and scrutinized his clothing.

She laughed. "Emotionally."

"Thanks for noticing."

The front door slammed shut and a minute later Aaron and Kirk strolled merrily into the room, the scent of pot clinging to them like an accusation. Chase handed them each a beer.

"I need to try to eat something." Aaron wiped the lip of his bottle.

Kirk took a sip. "I'd like to take everyone out for dinner."

"Somebody has to stay here for the. . . ." Aaron's eyes were red, from crying or from the pot. Probably both. He looked as though he was about to topple over. His God didn't seem to be offering much support. "I have to stay here."

"I'll stay," Chase said.

"Really?"

"Just tell me what has to be done and I'll deal with it."

"Can we leave the kids with you?"

"Are they still here?"

"Of course. They're upstairs swigging vodka."

"Yeah, sure. If it's okay with them. And if they've left some for me."

Aaron nodded. "They'll be thrilled," he said. "For some reason they like you."

Though he rarely saw them, Chase adored Bradley and Sophie. Still, this was not something he wished to do. Ever since he was a teenager, and probably long before that, he'd been terrified of death, particularly his own. Notwithstanding his recent preoccupation with suicide, thoughts of his own demise still nauseated him and made him gasp for air. But it wasn't only his own death that frightened him. Images of death, death in any form, natural and calm or painful and violent, could cause him to twitch and squirm like a burning snake. When an animal's carcass appeared on the road ahead he would avert his eyes. He was an expert at avoiding funerals. Even the most distant thought of death would set his mind racing in every direction for some diversion.

"Do I have to do anything with . . . ?"

"No. They'll take care of . . . they'll take care of him."

It wasn't enough, but it would have to be. He would stand there and watch out of the corner of his eye as soft-spoken strangers clad in white pulled off the sheets and lifted his father's body out of the bed, as they placed him on whatever conveyance they used for their grisly work. He would try to look away but he would catch a glimpse as an arm dropped down, or a leg, stiff and lifeless as a wooden plank. He'd concentrate on his own breathing but still he would hear the dull crunch as his father's head leaned to one side. He would gird himself against the dresser as his father's intestines shot out in a rancid spray and the room filled with roaches and bloodthirsty rats, flames shooting from their eyes.

"I'll handle it," he said, feigning confidence. Only the most oblivious, self-absorbed observer would have bought it.

Aaron seemed reassured.

3

*Ashton Stoller, Retired Banker and Grunter,
Deader at Age 73*

Mr. Stoller, who for twenty-three years served as vice president of the Stroudsburg branch of Northeastern Bank of PA, died early Saturday afternoon in his eldest son's home. The apparent cause of death was an unrelenting lack of interest. If not for a sudden drop in the number of sighs and grunts in the home, it might have taken his family weeks to realize he had succumbed.

Born in Easton, PA to Joseph and Helen Stoller, Ashton Stoller secured a position at NBP shortly after graduating from Muhlenberg College in Allentown. Two years later, out of boredom or desperation or because they'd both lost a bet, he married Helen Morgan of Scranton. Together, geographically speaking, the couple raised three profoundly unbalanced children, Aaron, Hannah and Chase.

Over the forty-seven uneventful years of his employment, Mr. Stoller gradually worked his way up to the position of vice president. He was a banker. Sometimes he played cards. But mostly he banked.

Mr. Stoller is survived with a minimum of enthusiasm by his three children and possibly his wife, who vanished or spontaneously combusted when the children were old enough to defend themselves.

It certainly hadn't been easy watching strangers cart his father off, but neither was it as difficult as he'd anticipated. With the children there he simply couldn't allow himself to wallow in weakness or submit to his fears. Their need, or his perception of it, was his motivation to get through it. Perhaps they were perfectly fine, but their vulnerability, real or imagined, provided him with a kind of temporary courage.

Unfortunately, he hadn't been prepared for their questions.

"When will he go to heaven?" Sophie scrutinized her uncle.

"I'm not exactly sure how . . . how the system works."

Bradley grabbed his hand and looked up. "Daddy said he was going to heaven."

"Well, I'm sure your father knows what he's talking about."

"Why don't *you* know?"

"Well, maybe he's smarter than me."

"Really?"

"No."

"Why did Grampa die?" Sophie again. They were double-teaming him.

"He was just old, and, you know, old people get sick sometimes." *I am an idiot.*

"Will I die?"

A horse kick to the sternum. "Don't say that." *Fuck.* "No. You aren't going to . . . to be old for a long time, Bradley."

"Are you sick, Uncle Chase?"

"No. No, I'm fine, sweetheart." He wiped the perspiration from his forehead and knelt down. "Do you two want some food? Would you like to play?"

Sophie scrunched up her face. "Play with *food?*"

They all laughed.

"When are Mommy and Daddy coming home?"

"I'm not sure. In a little while I guess."

"Are you going to make us dinner and put us in bed and everything?"

"I guess I am."

"Goody."

At least Aaron and Sarah had trusted him with their children. Perhaps they didn't think he was completely useless, though they were also comfortable with toys that looked like alien assassins, wielded huge bazooka-like weapons in both claws and had names like Deathray and Bloodgusher, which just seemed wrong and more than a little peculiar for two schoolteachers. But had they somehow forgotten that the children were also affected by their grandfather's death, that they might need or simply want their parents tonight? That sort of selfishness was typical of Aaron, but Chase had never seen that side of Sarah. Perhaps more curious was that Aaron had left the house knowing that his father's body would be gone when he returned. Maybe it really was all about the drama for him, or the need to be a martyr. It was possible that he truly needed to escape from the pain he was feeling, however inexplicable that pain was to Chase, but there was no point in attempting to understand someone else when he couldn't begin to decode his own emotions or the perplexing actions they provoked. At least he hadn't let them down. And in spite of his trepidation, the worst of it had been that unfamiliar twinge he'd felt as they drove off with the body, really nothing more than the recognition of the final loss of something he'd never truly possessed, like failing to win a lottery for which you'd purchased no tickets. If, buried in the deep, murky depths of his subconscious, there'd been even a hint of hope that he and his father might ever find a tiny patch of common ground, that hope had been finally and irrevocably obliterated by nature's ultimate act of mercy. Now he was free to feel what he'd always known. And it was little more than an emotional speed bump.

After feeding and bathing the children, Chase escorted them to Sophie's bedroom, where they'd been sharing a bed during their grandfather's brief occupation of Bradley's room. Chase squeezed between them on the narrow bed and read them several chapters of *Charlotte's Web*. He closed the book and reached over to dim the light. He was about to get out of bed and kiss them goodnight when Sophie asked if he could tell them a story.

"What story would you like?"

"You pick one."

"Well . . . okay." He leaned back. Although he hadn't thought about their story in years, without much effort he was able to summon it back.

"Once upon a time, not too long ago, in a place not very far away, there lived a little boy and a little girl, brother and sister."

"Like us," Sophie said.

"Yes, like you. Except their names were Blip and Snoodle." He could just as easily have used Chance and Hope, but they belonged to another time.

Sophie sat up and smiled. "Which one was Snoodle?"

"Snoodle was the girl."

"Good," she said.

"Good." Bradley sat up and nodded.

"Okay, now you two have to lie down and close your eyes."

They both flopped back down.

"Snoodle and Blip lived in a huge tree in the middle of a forest. They ate tree bark, worms and berries, and drank by sticking a long hollow reed into the clouds and sucking rainwater from it. Snoodle slept on a branch close to the ground because she liked to munch on daisies during the night, and Blip slept up higher because he always woke up thirsty and this way he was closer to the clouds."

Bradley shook Chase's arm. "What about if it wasn't cloudy?"

"If it wasn't cloudy?" Why had he never asked that question? Or had he simply forgotten?

"Yeah. What did he drink?"

"On clear nights he would lick the dew from the leaves."

"Oh."

"During the day they played with the squirrels, chipmunks, rabbits and birds. They played hide and seek with the squirrels and rabbits and played tag with the chipmunks. They loved all the animals, but the rabbits were their favorites. They were so soft, so sweet and gentle."

"What games did they play with the birds?"

"They sang songs. And sometimes a flock would lift the two children into the air on a mattress of branches and twigs. They would glide over the treetops observing their forest and the snowcapped mountains that surrounded it.

"One day they smelled something they'd never smelled before. They walked for a long time, following the scent. At the edge of a clearing they heard voices. Through the trees they saw a tent, and next to it were three people sitting around a campfire: a man, a woman and a young boy. Never before had they seen a tent or a fire. And they'd never seen or heard other people. Excited, but a little frightened, they climbed a tree not too far from the campsite and sat in the branches watching the three strangers. But they were tired and soon they fell asleep.

"They woke to the sound of a voice: 'Hey. Hey you?' The boy from the camp stood by the trunk of the tree staring up at them. 'What are you doing up there?'

"'Come on down,' he said. 'My name's Axelrod.'

"Axelrod was so excited to meet Blip and Snoodle that he had to know all about them. But when he asked about their parents they didn't understand.

"'What are parents,' Snoodle asked.

"The boy explained that parents teach you and love you and protect you. But soon his own parents called out and he had to run off.

"One day when the birds were carrying them particularly high, Blip and Snoodle noticed two figures moving along the river in the distance.

"Though they didn't talk about it both children hoped that the two figures were their parents. After that Blip and Snoodle were especially alert, watching and listening for any change.

"They were playing with the rabbits one day when they noticed a vine of berries climbing the base of a nearby tree. They were big and purple and covered with fuzz. The rabbits just sniffed them. Snoodle said they looked yucky but Blip ate three. A few minutes later his entire body swelled up and he became very ill. For two days he lay on his branch moaning and sweating. Snoodle dripped cool water on his forehead and sang him to sleep every night. The animals gathered around and brought him gifts: the red berries he'd always loved, some shiny rocks and twenty-three fat worms. On the fourth day he felt much better and soon he was back to normal.

"Then one day there was a noise, like something huge trudging through the underbrush. That evening Blip and Snoodle heard other strange sounds: grunts, snorts and hoots. Perhaps these were the sounds parents made.

"The next morning when Blip awoke it was quiet. Even the birds, who normally spent their mornings singing and squawking, were silent. When he looked down, he saw his sister still asleep, and below her, sniffing the air and reaching up toward her with their front claws, were two furry black creatures. They were massive and their eyes were black and shiny."

"Uh-oh," Bradley said in a sleepy whisper.

"What's going to happen?" Sophie asked. "Are they going to be okay?"

Chase turned toward her and petted her head. "Just keep quiet and be still and you'll see." Even after all these years he felt vaguely traitorous sharing Hannah's story, though he knew she would happily do the same.

"Okay."

"'Snoodle,' Blip called to his sister."

"When she didn't stir, he called a little louder. 'Wake up, Snoodle. Wake up!'

"Her eyes flashed opened. 'What's wrong, Blip?'

"'Don't look down, just climb up to me.'

"She did as her brother said and when she reached his branch, he motioned to the creatures. She looked down and gasped.

"The creatures were clawing at the tree, drooling and grunting. Blip and Snoodle felt safe until the larger one managed to dig his claws into the tree and lift himself up. Suddenly the forest filled with noise. Shrieking and pecking, the birds dove at the creatures, but the beasts just grunted louder, thick ropes of drool dangling from their jaws. A family of squirrels leapt at the bigger one, but it brushed them aside."

Sophie was squeezing Chase's hand now. Had he been afraid the first time he heard this story? Had Hannah comforted him? Those memories had evaporated.

"Don't worry, sweetheart. Snoodle and Blip are going to be okay."

"Are you sure?"

"I'm sure."

"Promise?" Bradley asked.

"I promise.

"Just as the larger creature reached the lowest branch Snoodle noticed all the rabbits huddled around the vine with the big purple berries.

"'What are they doing?' Snoodle asked her brother.

"'I don't know.'

"When the smaller creature turned toward the rabbits, they began a frantic dance. Then they huddled for a minute, and when the huddle broke up, several of the rabbits hopped toward the vine and attacked the berries.

"'No! Don't,' Snoodle cried.

"Blip screamed, 'Stop! They're poison.'

"But it was too late. Within seconds they'd devoured dozens of the berries.

"In less than a minute, the rabbits were three times their normal size, bloated balls of fur.

"Slowly the swollen rabbits waddled toward the children's tree, each of them dragging a branch of berries behind. The smaller creature noticed them first and let out a low grunt. Then the larger one looked down. Suddenly they charged. One by one, they grabbed the rabbits, forced them into their massive jaws and swallowed them whole.

"For a moment there was silence. The creatures were still licking their chops when they began to moan and groan. Then the swelling began. The larger creature leaned to one side, then toppled over. The smaller one let out a howl before collapsing. A minute later they were both completely still.

"Blip and Snoodle looked at one another, tears welling in their eyes. But then there was a strange sound, like something scratching the walls of a cave. They looked down at the creatures. The bigger one's jaws parted and a furry paw reached out. Then a head peaked out. One after another the rabbits stumbled out. A minute later the other creature's mouth opened and the rest of the rabbits climbed out. They all looked a little less swollen.

"The rabbits were still sick, and for a while there was no playing and very little singing in the forest. The children and the animals passed their days watching over the brave little rabbits. But within a few weeks they'd all recovered and there was a celebration. The forest returned to life.

"Then one breezy night as they were lying back in their branches, Blip called out to his sister.

"'Did you hear that?'

"'What, Blip?'

"'Listen. Listen real close.'

"At first she only heard the breeze and the rattling leaves.

"'What is it, Blip? What do you hear?'

"'Just keep listening.'

"She closed her eyes. *Weeeooooo*, said the breeze. *P'teck*, replied the leaves and the branches. *Hyoooo*, the breeze whispered. *Weeooo . . . p'tek hyooooo*, they repeated. *P'teck hyoooo . . . P'teck . . . hyooooo.*'

"Before long Snoodle began to drift off, and as the arms of the tree rocked her gently back and forth, she finally heard what her brother was hearing. The forest was whispering to its children. *We'll protect you, . . . protect you.* They were children of the forest, safe in its embrace."

Chase lay motionless, the children pressed against him, their breath slow and even. Unable to move for fear of disturbing them, he let his own eyes fall shut, his sister's loving voice still whispering sweetly in the distance.

4

It was still dark when Chase awoke. But for the distant ticking of a clock and the children's steady breathing, the house was silent. He tried to go back to sleep but it was hot and he couldn't find a comfortable position between the children, who seemed to have sprouted additional limbs while he slept. Cautiously he sat up, climbed out of bed and crept out into the hall. In the darkness he turned toward the room where his father had been. No. Still there in the room, in the bed, was whatever death left in its turbid wake: mysterious stains, dried perspiration, germs in search of a shiny new host, pubic hairs, foul, suffocating odors, his father's final exhalation, the noxious fumes of discouragement and regret. Was there a grunt in there waiting to emerge? He found the switch for the hall light, turned it on and made his way into the living room.

The couch was short and spongy and the carpet made him itch. He dropped down in the recliner and checked his watch. Only ten thirty. "Shit."

"Who are you talking to?" Aaron stood in the hallway buttoning his shirt.

"I thought it was the middle of the night."

"You were sound asleep when we came home."

"Where's Sarah?"

"She's sleeping. I was, too, for about twenty minutes."

"Meat tenderizer."

"What?"

"I feel like my brain's been marinated in meat tenderizer. And I must be hungry."

"We had a good dinner."

"That's very helpful."

"There's probably something to eat here, and there's plenty to drink."

"No. I need to do something." Chase stood. "I'm going out. Want to join me?"

"Yeah. Okay."

The percussive rumble of bass and drums percolated through the walls as they stepped on to the Deer Head Inn's broad wraparound porch, a flurry of piano notes pouring out like confetti when Chase wrestled open the old wooden door. The tables in the dining room were packed and a swarm of bodies hovered around the end of the bar closest to the stage listening to the music, talking and posing. Chase and Aaron snaked through the shifting crowd to the far end of the bar, where they found two unoccupied stools.

They sat down and Chase turned toward his brother. "You want something to eat?"

"I ate way too much already."

"I'm paying."

Aaron shook his head. "I'll just have a beer."

For a while they listened to the music, an assortment of re-harmonized jazz standards with an occasional Latin influence.

The musicians, none of whom could have been over twenty-five, were technically capable but uninspired. The music sounded stiff and mechanical, the correct notes played without passion, without interest. After about twenty minutes, a gray-haired man in an ill-fitting black suit stepped up onto the stage. Very slowly and methodically he freed a tenor sax from its case, hooked it to a neck strap and put it to his lips to wet the reed. His playing raised the level of discourse considerably and brought the entire room to life.

When he had finished his burger and fries and they were each well into their third beer, Chase motioned to a woman sitting at the opposite end of the bar. "I think I know her."

"That's Alice something."

"Oh yeah. She went out with Jim something. I used to. . . ." He grinned.

"I believe you had plenty of company."

"We didn't actually. . . . We just sort of fooled around. Whenever I found myself thinking seriously about sticking my penis in her I forced myself to consider what those before me might have left behind."

"*You* exercised re*straint*?" Aaron's mouth hung open.

"I was young and afraid of blindness and insanity. But she did have an incredible body. She still looks pretty good."

"From here, maybe. She's gained about eighty pounds."

"Really?"

"Below the neck she's a blimp."

"Oh well." He finished his beer. "By the way, in case you didn't realize it, your kids are great."

Aaron nodded. "Maybe you should have one."

"That's very generous, but I don't think it would be fair to separate them."

"I'm serious. I started late. Not that you care, but so did Dad."

"Well, according to tradition, a job and a woman should probably come first."

"Were you screwing around?"

The bartender wiped the bar. "Two more?"

"Sure."

"Were you fucking somebody else?"

"No."

During the first years of their marriage, Chase had indulged in only two dalliances, neither of them more significant than scratching an itch or enjoying alone a movie one's spouse had expressed a mild interest in seeing. It was the affair that began in their fourth year of marriage that for a time had threatened to tear them apart, not because Jennifer knew anything—in fact, she betrayed no suspicion either during the affair or later—but because as it became more serious his sense of confinement increased. By that time the marital dialogue had been reduced to routine nightly expressions of dissatisfaction and disgust, not with one another, but with life in general. Any joy he felt, he concealed from his wife. Somehow that was safer; it created a comfortable distance, an excuse to be absent and unavailable when he felt himself drifting away or losing interest. And it was fair warning: *I can't give you anything because I'm depressed and I don't have a clue what I want*. Behind those messages was the one even he hadn't allowed himself to consider: *I may not be with you forever*. Though she was ultimately the one to leave, in some ways he was already gone. The relationship had begun to demand far too much of him: his attention, a positive attitude, honesty. Life always seemed to ask too much and give too little. And he *was* unhappy, though certainly not as devastated as he attempted to appear. He wanted someone new, someone who didn't know him so well, someone he could fool for a while and, most importantly, someone who didn't demand anything. And the truth was that he and Jennifer had lost the capacity to see each other. All they could see by then was what they expected to see. Spending time together was like paging through a book you'd long ago committed to memory. There were no surprises and nothing was going to change, not because they weren't capable of change, but because they'd both lost the capacity to see any change in the other. But he loved her. When she was sick, he cared for her like a doting parent, and when she was sad, he did his best to comfort her. He must have cried for her dozens of times, and the tears were heartfelt. He was sensitive to the slightest atmospheric change in her and always eager to make her feel better, to help her address her problems at work, with her incompetent boss, to help her cope with her father's alcoholism and her mother's cancer, to help her understand and conquer her self-doubt and her increasing difficulty sleeping. He was always there for her, unless, of course, her issue was with him. Yes, he loved her. The problem was that in time he came to love Janice, too, probably because she seemed to love him and certainly because it was new. Cautious and wise, Janice didn't yet demand as much from him as did his wife. So for a while he resented Jennifer and shared everything he thought and felt with Janice, bringing them even closer, filling him with admiration for his new lover and creating even more distance between his wife and himself.

Of course Janice's comfort with the status quo couldn't last—he understood that. And just as he'd expected, after a couple months of sharing him, she began to express her own needs—for more commitment, to be the only one, to live together, to eventually get married and have children and a house and a dog and two cars and life insurance and matching cemetery plots under an ancient oak tree. *You first. No, you go ahead.* He'd already begun to lie to her about his intentions regarding his marriage and before long he resented them both. But he loved them, too. He did. And he felt guilty and weak for stringing them both along and deceiving them. He didn't want to hurt them, not in any way. Still, he reached a point where he would have been willing to do anything to relieve the strain engendered by this dual deception. But the pressure only continued to increase. He just wanted a break, but neither woman would relent. The walls were closing in, threatening to squeeze the life out of him. If one of them would just give up—by this time it didn't matter which one—he would be okay.

Soon he found himself fantasizing about a disappearance. The problem was that there were very few ways for people to actually disappear. Although he wouldn't allow the word entry into his thoughts, he knew that what he was hoping for was a swift, natural, painless death. He knew what this said about him, and he wasn't especially pleased about it, but there it was, like a facial wart. It certainly wasn't personal, and he would have no part in such a tragedy—he did love them—but it had become too much, and death—an undiagnosed heart condition or a tumble headfirst down the subway steps—seemed the only solution: silent, sudden, done. Janice was younger, successful, confident, and she was innocent. She'd really done nothing wrong. But Jennifer had remained with him through the worst. She certainly didn't deserve to die. Neither of them did. Of *course* they didn't. But this was too much. And yet when he thought about it, he realized that wouldn't be a solution anyway. Both women had been tainted by this mess. The only real solution was to start fresh with someone new. Terrible as it was, his emotional survival seemed dependent upon the elimination of the two women he loved. If they both died he'd be okay.

He'd miss them terribly, he'd mourn for them, for their friends and families and for himself. He'd never quite recover from the loss, but he'd move on. Cooperation was not forthcoming.

Eventually Janice, always patient and forgiving, recognized his weakness. She was bright enough and confident and independent enough to back away. But so great was his relief that his love for her grew like a teenager's erection. Devastated and smitten anew, he did everything he could to keep her hanging on. But she'd gotten the message. He cursed himself for letting her go. Only after an appropriate period of mourning did he decide to recommit himself to his marriage, to invest himself fully in that relationship and find some way to make it work. After all, he loved his wife.

It was at about that time that Jennifer began her long, unfaltering retreat, something that he knew he'd earned through his actions and his thoughts.

"It had nothing to do with anyone else. I did it all by myself."

"What are you so bitter about?"

"What I don't understand, Aaron, is why you *aren't* bitter."

"I haven't had a bad life. That's the difference between us. *My* childhood wasn't so bad. *My* parents did their best. You just saw. . . . I don't know what you saw."

"Maybe I saw something that you missed."

"Maybe you invented what you saw."

"Maybe *you* didn't want to see it."

"I'm not the one with a problem," he said, the glassy glow of a believer in his eyes. "I'm fine."

"There are at least two of us with problems, Aaron. Or have you forgotten Hannah?"

"I haven't forgotten her. But since you mentioned it, weren't *you* supposed to be her best friend? You're the one who stopped visiting as soon as it became a little too much trouble."

"She has no idea who I am. She's not even there."

"So it's inconvenient *and* uncomfortable."

"And pointless. She doesn't know or care."

"How do you know? How do you know what she feels?"

"You've seen her. And anyway, that's not the point."

"What is the point, Chase? That you need to blame somebody else for screwing up your life? You need to blame Mom and Dad because the alternative is to take responsibility and that might spoil your day." He shook his head. "They did the best they could, like we all do."

"Look, I can understand why you'd defend Dad. It's not as though he was evil. He was just incompetent . . . when he was there. Mostly he was absent. You can't hate a vacuum. It's like wrestling with air. But Mom was another story."

"You always misread her. No matter what she did, you saw the worst. That was what you wanted to see. You think she didn't feel that?"

"What are you saying? She left because of how *I* felt?"

"Who knows why she left?"

"That is truly hilarious."

"You always misread her. She didn't hate us."

"Maybe you're right. Maybe what I perceived as hatred was really just a sort of repulsed loathing."

"Your humor doesn't always play, Chase. She was not the monster you made her out to be."

"You're right. She wasn't a monster. She was a fucking heartless ghoul who probably left us to suck dicks in a whorehouse."

Aaron faced his brother and cocked his right arm.

"Go ahead." Chase stared back at him.

Aaron let his arm drop and shook his head. He looked as though he was about to cry.

"They're whatever you want them to be," Chase said. He felt deflated.

"They didn't do me any harm, Chase."

"Maybe not."

"I want to go."

"Go ahead."

"How are you going to get back to the house?"

"I'll be fine."

Aaron rose. "I'll leave the door unlocked."

5

Chase motioned to the bartender.

"Another beer?"

"No. A shot of Glenlivet."

The band stepped onto the stage and the late crowd began to filter in.

A woman of around thirty, tall, thin and well dressed, stumbled onto the stool to his left. She had an oval face, not unattractive but a bit swollen, and her light-brown hair was pulled neatly back. She smelled of alcohol, perfume and affluence.

"Are you okay?" He smiled.

"It's all good."

The bartender set Chase's drink on the counter and turned to her. "What can I get you?"

"Patrón?"

"A shot of Silver?"

"Yeah, I guess." She smirked. "Patrón, right?"

He nodded.

She planted a leather purse on the bar and tugged at the zipper. The purse fell to the side and several items slid out onto the bar.

A condom came to rest next to Chase's elbow and he chuckled.

"It's all good," she said.

He turned to face her. She wore a pearl necklace and matching earrings. Her makeup was perfect, but her eyes were bloodshot and about half shut.

"What does that mean?"

"What?" She squinted at him.

"It's all good. What does that mean?"

"It means it's all good, sweetheart." She lifted her right hand and waved it as though she was shooing a gnat. "Don't worry about it."

"I'm really not worried, I just can't figure out what the hell that's supposed to mean."

Her drink came and she raised it in his direction. "It's not a problem."

When the band took a break, the woman with the condom stumbled away and Chase ordered another Scotch.

He sipped his Scotch and set the glass down. He thought of Haley, her unassuming beauty, her presence, confident and calm. But so distant. And the rejection had stung. It still did. No matter what the circumstances, the ragged blade of rejection always tore at him, but with a woman that interesting and attractive, the pain was more acute, the sting that remained more lasting. Was he unattractive, offensive, hideous? Would she laugh when she told her friends? Just thinking about it now made his heart race. His face was on fire. Something was pressing against his back.

"If somebody would move over," a bass voice bellowed at the back of his head, "my fiancée and I could sit together."

He took another sip. *Slow down.*

Again the pressure on his back. "If somebody would move over my fiancée and I could sit together." The pressure increased and he turned.

Hovering too close, broad-shouldered and at least a couple inches taller than Chase, was a man in a dark suit and conservative tie, navy with standard-issue diagonal stripes. His hair was painted on and he was scowling down at Chase the way you might scowl at a dog that had just dropped a heavy load on your shoe.

Chase smirked. "Did you want something?"

"Yeah, I do." He puffed up his chest and slid between Chase and the stool to his right.

"Then why don't you just ask like a normal human?"

"I did ask."

"No you didn't." Getting hot. "You bleated like a fucking sheep."

Sudden acceleration, a jerky blur of actions and sensations. Pressure on his chest. A hand? The man mumbles something. Angry. Fuck him. A thump on his chest, or inside it. More pressure. Chase's left arm rushes up. He's gripping the man's tie. He yanks and the man's chin collides with the bar. Chase grits his teeth and brings his face close to the one at the business end of the silk noose. "I will fucking kill you," he snarls and pulls a little harder. The tie is wrapped around his left wrist. He doesn't breathe.

"Oh my God, he's strangling him!" She looks like the next victim in a horror movie, and the man's head is still dangling there in front of him like a helium balloon with painted hair. "He's killing him." It's the fiancée.

Chase, still holding on, was laughing now. He released his grip and the man rocked back against his fiancée.

Someone slid between them and the bartender was saying something. He heard his own name. The bartender was frowning.

"You're going to have to leave."

Inhale. "It wasn't my fault."

"Excuse me?"

"He grabbed me." Maybe he had. He must have.

"Not that *I* saw. What *I* saw was you attacking the man."

*Some*thing must have happened. "The asshole grabbed me."

"You're going to have to go."

A glass fell and shattered at the far end of the bar. "You can't blame me for that," Chase said and smiled.

Local Man Critically Embarrassed in Bar Fight

At around 11:30 last night, give or take an hour, Mr. Lance Sprayhair of Fine Street in the Attractive section of Stroudsburg was assaulted with his own conservative tie. Witnesses say Mr. Sprayhair and his fiancé, who had stopped into the Deer Head Inn in Delaware Water Gap for a nightcap after an evening of admiring each other in various attractive poses, were attempting to find a place to sit together and admire each other in various attractive poses when a wild-eyed, unemployed, soon-to-be divorced, drunken lunatic leapt at Mr. Sprayhair and grabbed his Italian-made necktie, mussing his painted-on hair. The perpetrator apparently pulled so hard on the fine silk neckpiece that Mr. Sprayhair's arrogant sneer literally dropped onto the floor and broke into hundreds of little sneers. Sprayhair's fiancée, who wishes to remain anonymous unless we promise to print a really attractive photograph of her in an attractive pose, refused to answer any questions. Her prepared statement, delivered to our office by her conservatively dressed, attractive attorney and brand new fiancé, read as follows: "I just couldn't marry a man whose arrogant sneer wasn't more firmly attached."

"Chase?" A woman's voice.

He turned. Alice something.

"Alice?"

"Hey, I thought it was you." Her face had migrated south, but she didn't appear to be overweight. Not at all.

"I thought it was me, too."

"What in the fuck are you doing here?" She was smiling, deep pleats shooting out like streamers around her mouth and eyes. But he remembered her firm breasts and tight stomach. She'd done hours of gymnastics every day just for the workout. She'd had a gorgeous body. Aaron had either lied or been very mistaken.

"Getting thrown out."

"Tom, sweetie." She reached out to the bartender. "He's not looking for any trouble."

"Well, he's found some, Alice."

"How about if me and him go sit at a table?" She leaned hard against Chase's thigh, rested her hand on his back. "I'll keep an eye on him."

The bartender shrugged and sighed.

My groin is a beehive.

6

If not for the vicious hangover, the nausea, the brutal, all-consuming headache and the exhaustion, he'd have to face his rage and disgust directly, without any filter. It was an idiotic, foolish, asinine, destructive, suicidal, vile night. Even while it was happening, even through the scumbled lens of inebriation, the images lurching and reeling, flashing on and off, it was hideous and difficult to bear. But it wasn't just the images; it was the knowledge of how far he'd plummeted. Had the man grabbed him or had he snapped without cause? Why had he gone home with a woman who, even with her clothes on, had had no more appeal than a moldy scrubbing sponge? And what the hell had actually happened?

He tried to rise, to get an almost sober look at the room. It was still too painful. He was still drunk. Slowly he turned his head to the right. Bolted to the end table between the two matching beds was an imitation woodgrain digital clock radio; its glowing green numerals read 9:48. He had no grounds for argument.

He recalled her talking about her ex-husband, or maybe it was an ex-boyfriend, an alcoholic or drug addict. Maybe both. She'd had enough. It was finally over. They were still in touch, of course, but she wasn't going to sleep with him any more. At least she didn't plan to, though she'd said that before. Blah blah blah. And there was Jim, the troubled, vaguely charming smalltime criminal Chase remembered from his youth. She'd eventually married the nasty little thug, had his child, a daughter, was still seeing him, perhaps. Or maybe it was all about Jim. She'd been on a diet for a couple months. It was great. Not working out like the old days, but eating right. Yippee. They continued drinking and she went on, something about a hysterectomy. A fleeting moment of visceral unease. How did that affect a woman? Did they still enjoy sex? Did they still produce moisture? Why not? She wasn't pretty any more, though he could still see the basic outline of the younger face if he squinted hard. She'd become an old Pocono gal, probably looked like her mother. He pictured her standing by the charcoal grill in a trailer park chain-smoking Camels, taking regular trips inside the singlewide to fetch ice-cold Buds for the old man and his buddies and adjust her dentures, talking about the bowling league and between cigarettes sucking on a formerly mint-flavored toothpick from the night before. Keep squinting. Remember the body, amazing, perfect, ready for action. She kept brushing against him and he kept drinking whatever was in front of him. They were sitting close, molesting one another, the feeble pretense of subtlety disintegrating rapidly. What the hell.

His erection. Did it have anything to do with her or was it just an unconscious reflex, a disembodied symptom of some pressing primal urge? It didn't matter. It had taken over, and he was just delighted as hell to yield his dubious authority to any force or entity willing to take responsibility for it. Let someone else take a turn. Couldn't do worse than him. Well. . . .

More alcohol, more groping. Are your eyes okay? She asked this several times. A short drive in a rattling Dodge, or maybe it was a Buick. The smell of exhaust and gasoline. Another bar, darker, another drink. Maybe two? Why are you squinting? Her house, no, a friend's house, something odd about it, the man, an uncle perhaps, wasn't around, was away or out for the night. A couch, photographs of someone's family, another drink, but he couldn't drink any more. *Just put it down. Just go home, or anywhere else.* She'd become even less attractive but the erection was still there, still pressing, leading this aimless march like a blind drill sergeant. Drill, sergeant. Too drunk, too weak to fight. Was that an excuse? Not good enough. Onward piston soldier. He wasn't interested, didn't like her, not even a little. She undid his belt, or he did. His button and zipper. Boing. She was still dressed, his hand inside her blouse, her bra. Those firm breasts had turned to rice pudding, had curdled and collapsed. Her voice, blabbering about nothing. Blah blah blah. *Be quiet. Take me home. I don't want to be here, with you. Anywhere with you. Don't even want this.* Her hand on him, caressing softly. Well. . . . His penis was no longer an appendage. It was a solo act without a hat and cane. It was the cane. It was invulnerable, uninterested in truth or reason, unconcerned with the elements—through rain, snow, sleet or hail or cellulite. *My penis is a postal worker, a working post.* He could have had a nail in his eye and it wouldn't have mattered now. Alcohol, anger, hurt, terror. Terror of death. How did her clothes come off? Touching him. Ah. Dark, but not dark enough. This was too clear, hazy but clear enough to see, to want to look away or gag. Hadn't Aaron said she'd gained a lot of weight? She'd been on a diet, a power diet, she'd said with pride. Oh. Yes. Naked she looked like an inflatable

Ways of Leaving

woman with half the air let out. If she fell off a building she could just spread her arms and with her flaps of extra flesh she'd glide to the ground like a flying squirrel. Plop. Pffft.

He sat up in bed because he knew how much it would hurt, shook his head, and gasped. The shades were drawn, a minor blessing. A repulsive room. These weren't real colors; they were shades of despair. Dry recycled air, a year's exhalations, a rotating television staring blankly back, a wide mirror over the dresser in case you forgot who you were pissed off at. He made a fist, punched himself in the forehead. Not helpful.

Finally, it had been quick, clumsy and entirely pointless. Drunken clowns. They'd set a gland speed record. And then . . . my sergeant is dead. A traitor. Return of will. Struggle to separate these unfamiliar bodies. Leave. Get out. Run. He'd dressed as quickly as his condition would allow, mumbled something meaningless and somehow made his way here on foot. Couldn't stand the thought of her knowing where he was. If he'd left something behind, his cell phone or wallet or keys, he would have stolen a gun and a box of bullets from the sporting goods shop on Main Street and pressed the barrel against his temple and squeezed the trigger over and over until his finger cramped. Then, if he had any energy left, he would have gone back and shot her. Not because he blamed her, but simply to destroy the evidence and because he was pissed off. No pleasure, none. Of course it must have been the same for her, flopping around with a bitter, angry drunk. So why? Desperation? Fear of irrelevance, of death? Well, it didn't help. His dick had ordered the drinks but he'd paid. Was he becoming an alcoholic, too? Motherfucker.

He pushed the sweat-drenched sheets aside. *How many people have slept on these, fucked, sucked, pissed, vomited, bled, died on these sheets? Grab the headboard, wobble, stand up, stumble into the bathroom.*

Don't look down. Don't face the traitor. Is it ashamed? No, that's my job. An entire wall of mirror under merciless fluorescent light. Naked, pale, drawn, unshaven, hunched over, a goddamned ghoul. His nose had grown. And he was beginning to gray. Great.

No memory of a condom. He punched the door. "Fuck." A feeble act, to prove what to whom? And he'd pulled the punch.

She must have fucked hundreds of guys: crooks, cowboys, and crybabies, bankers and bartenders, drug dealers and drummers, saxophonists and sexagenarians, him. *All my fault. God. No. No God. Karma? I got syphilis from Karma. Or did I get it from Aaron's God. Aaron, your God gave me syphilis. But no, syphilis would be good luck. Congratulations, you only have syphilis.*

Was it an act of violence or aggression? Didn't that require some sort of passion, some emotional involvement, a hint of awareness? He hadn't felt anything but a sort of muted, helpless, feral yearning, and that had dissolved before they'd reached the house. By then the sarge was fully in charge. He was just along for the ride. His mind was absent and his body had become an appendage, flaccid matter flopping around behind his undiscriminating, ravenous dick. Globba globba globba. Sir Richard. This is dedicated to the one-eye love. *Are you satisfied now?* He looked down. At least it wasn't covered with lesions. It wasn't spitting white foam and snarling up at him like a rabid dog. Not yet.

Fucking cocksucker.

He turned on the shower, stepped in and closed his eyes. With the water pouring over his back he leaned against the wall and tried to cry. He held his breath and squinted his eyes. He swallowed hard, gritted his teeth and clenched his fists. Nothing. *I have no mother and my father is dead.* Nothing at all. He yanked a few hairs out just above his left ear. Nope. *My brother hates me and I abandoned my darling lunatic sister. Fuck it.*

In the parking lot the sun was glaring down like a prison searchlight. *Don't shoot.* His head was growing, ready to pop open and cover the ground with outrage and animosity. *Shoot. Turn it off and get in the car.*

"You from out of town?"

"Yeah."

"Here on business?"

"No."

"Pleasure trip?"

"Apparently not."

Chase slid his sunglasses up his nose and sighed as loud as he could.

The cab driver stopped trying.

For a couple minutes Chase just stared at the grubby vinyl back of the front seat. When his stomach began to twist he glanced out the window. "Where the hell are you going?"

"Pardon?" The driver peered into his mirror.

"You're going the wrong way."

"You know a faster way?"

"Yeah. Why don't you try the same direct route you'd have taken if you'd been aware that I know my way around?"

"I guess I got a little turned around."

"Fuck you."

The driver stopped his car and pivoted to look at Chase. "I'm going to ask you to get out of my car."

"Just shut up and drive."

"Get out of my car."

"Shut up and drive or I'll puke all over you."

"I said get out of my car."

"*You* get out of your car."

"Excuse me?"

"I told you to get out of your car, *asshole*." He was trembling now, or shivering, angry, sick, cold and a little frightened.

The driver shook his head. "You're out of your mind."

There were bits of egg on the man's cheek and on his chin. Another speck of something beneath his nose, cheese perhaps. Cheddar? Monterey Jack? Chase tried to glare at him, to hold onto his advantage, theoretical though it was. Then he noticed bits of egg up higher, in the man's eyebrows, and he laughed.

"Did you forget to put a pillowcase on your omelet?"

"What?"

"Do you use egg shampoo?"

"Huh?" The man checked his face in the rearview mirror. "Oh, yeah," he said, and he began picking at the specks of food.

Chase opened the door, stepped out and let it fall shut.

"Hey," the driver called through the open window. "What about your fare?" He was still picking food scraps from his face.

"Don't worry about it," Chase said. "It's on me." He turned away.

He'd taken only a couple steps when his stomach clenched and heaved. He stopped, folded forward and threw up on his shoes.

I am quite a guy.

7

"Your name?"

"Chase."

"Chase. . . ." She was waiting.

"Stoller. I'm her brother."

"Oh, I haven't seen you before."

"I've been out of . . . I've been a lousy brother."

"Oh. Well. . . ." She seemed to be trying to smile. "Just take a seat and we'll bring her out here."

After his encounter with the taxi driver, he'd walked to a diner, where he'd used the restroom to clean up and then had a big, greasy breakfast. He was about to call another taxi service when he decided to take a chance on his brother. It had been awkward, Aaron had groaned and hesitated, but he'd finally agreed to pick him up. He could include this detour in a list of errands he'd planned without *too* much trouble. In spite of his initial grumbling, they had a good time together, almost like brothers.

"The kids wanted to come," Aaron said when Chase got into the car.

"Why didn't you bring them?"

"Because after about three minutes they would have started whining about being bored."

"I have that effect."

"It's not you. In fact they couldn't stop talking about how much fun they had with you last night. What story did you tell them?"

"It was just something. . . ." It had been their private story, his and Hannah's. "Something I made up."

"Well, they want to hear it again tonight."

He never asked where Chase had spent the night, never mentioned their argument, which was probably wise, and when Chase invited him to go along to see Hannah, he said he needed to spend the time with the family. Wasn't she family, too? Still, he'd come for him and they'd had a little time together without conflict. If they joked, if they tiptoed around the surface, avoiding even the most peripheral fringes of controversy, perhaps they could enjoy each other's company for entire minutes at a time. But what did that make them?

Now he was waiting for a sister who would have no idea who he was. In fact the Hannah he'd known was as dead as their father. Perhaps the person she was now had never had a father, a mother or a brother. In losing herself, she'd gained the advantage of having lost nothing at all.

An objective person observing Chase for the past couple days might suggest he had a future here, pacing these permanently stained linoleum floors in unmatched slippers and a threadbare gown, staring blankly at the institutional walls and seeing phantoms of his own devising, receiving clandestine orders, his old self lost and damaged beyond repair, another fading shadow among the forgotten forgetters. And there was something alluring in that, by golly. Unfortunately, it wasn't going to be that easy for him.

The lazy swoosh of slippers. He glanced up. Leaning against an immense black attendant was an old woman with short gray hair and sunken cheeks. Her left hand was opening and closing, her eyes, set deep in her head, were in frenzied motion. She looked like a neurotic cadaver. It couldn't have been that long. Two years, a little more? His heart thumped as he stood and approached her. Instinctively he offered his hand. She winced and grunted. Her mouth twitched. He retracted his hand. Their forest had failed to protect her.

"Hannah, dear. This is your friend."

"I'm her brother."

"You remember your brother, don't you?"

"Is there somewhere we can sit and . . . where we can sit together?"

"Sure." The attendant turned to Hannah. "Would you like to sit outside or would you maybe be more comfortable in the visiting room?" Without waiting for a response, she gripped Hannah's arm and steered her to a large sparsely furnished room with windows looking out on a small yard bordered by trees.

This was the same room where they'd sat the last time, the time he'd finally acknowledged that it didn't matter anymore, that they were nothing more than strangers. But even strangers could communicate. They were more like two different species. It had become excruciating to sit across from her and be so far away, and she seemed unaffected by his presence. But as difficult as it was to admit, Aaron was right. There was no way to be certain what Hannah knew, thought or felt. If there was even the remotest possibility that his presence somehow enhanced her existence, how could he deny her?

The attendant sat them across from each other at a table by the window. "I'll leave you two alone now." She smiled. "But I'll be close by if anybody needs me."

He felt such affection for this broad black woman whose name he didn't know that he could have wept. She was only doing her job and being kind, behaving the way a person should behave, but because of the situation, because of where they were, because of his sense of vulnerability in places like this, and perhaps because of what he'd come to expect, her kindness struck him like a body blow. He wanted to look deep into her eyes and tell her how wonderful she was. He wanted to hug her, to get her a promotion, to paint her house, buy her new shoes, really comfortable ones, or maybe a car. She probably stole drugs and tortured the patients when no one else was around. He shook his head.

"Thank you," he said, unable now to look at her.

He sat back in his chair. "Hannah."

The last few times he'd come she'd been unwilling even to make eye contact. She'd recoiled when he'd reached out to her and leaned away from him throughout the visits as though he were a leper. Perhaps lucidity *was* like a disease to someone who'd abandoned it. But then he had to remind himself again that her retreat from reality hadn't been voluntary.

"Hannah, it's Chase, your brother. It's me." Great start.

But was there a flicker of recognition in her eyes, or had that just been a flash of sunlight reflected from the leaves outside? More likely it was his own need he saw reflected there.

"Hannah, I'm sorry I haven't been around." He was talking to himself. He was the lunatic. She knew better. Just be quiet and the syphilitic idiot with puke-scented shoes will go away. "I just didn't think it mattered. You don't seem . . . you don't seem interested in me, in anything." Weren't those the words he'd put in his dead father's mouth? And even now he was playing with words, entertaining himself while his sister sat there wondering who he was, who she was, perhaps wondering when the voices would begin ordering her to rip out all her eyelashes.

That had been one of the first signs. They'd finished dinner and were waiting to be officially excused when Chase noticed that there was something different about her. When he finally figured it out he laughed. He knew enough not to mention it at the table. But at their nightly debriefing he asked her about it.

"I had to," she said.

"Why?"

"They told me to."

"Who? Karen and Cynthia?"

"Shh." Her lashless eyes widened. "They don't like me to talk about them." She was terrified.

He looked at her now. How had this happened? Had there been some trigger? "I wish you'd talk to me, or just show me that you can hear me or that you know who I am."

She stared at the floor.

"I'll just talk for a while. Okay? I'll just talk about me." His stomach rumbled.

"For some reason I can't seem to stop screwing up my life. I don't know what's wrong, but I don't have any impulse control. I get sad for no reason and then I get so angry I could . . . I act out all the time. It's a little scary. I just don't know what's happening to me."

Aside from the frantic eyes, the opening and closing of her hand and the uneven rhythm of her breathing, she could have been a statue sculpted there in the chair, some mad artist's homage to madness.

"I'm not sure you ever got really angry. But isn't it strange how much we forget? Maybe you've forgotten everything, and maybe that's not such a terrible thing. All I remember is the painful stuff . . . and you." He looked for a reaction. Nothing. "But there must have been more than that. We must have had some pleasant moments with Mom and Dad, and certainly with Aaron. We *did*. But the other crap is so oppressive, so predominant that. . . . And I think we . . . I think you and I were predisposed to focusing on the ugliness. We all saw the same things, but we responded differently. I turned into someone who drinks too much, acts out and whines, Aaron found God and denial and you just checked out. I don't blame you, Hannah, but I do miss you. I really do."

He wanted to touch her hand, to experience that brief moment of physical contact.

"I don't know if you can understand what I'm saying, but I feel like I should tell you. . . . " He had to force himself not to reach out toward her. "Our father. . . . "

"Who," she said, her voice raspy and unfamiliar, her expression unchanged. It might have been a question or a statement, or some impulse totally unconnected to his comment.

He leaned a little closer. "Our father," he said again.
"Who."
"Our father who?"
"Art."
He rubbed his forehead. "Art?"
"Art."
"No, Hannah. *Ashton*, our father."
"Who art?"
"Our father who art?"
"In heaven."
"Our. . . . " He sat back. Shit.
She frowned and picked at her ear. "Howard."

"Who's Howard?"

"Howard be thy name."

He laughed, a little uncomfortably.

She sat up straight, widened her eyes and folded her hands on her lap. "There was a young lady named Lil, who tried dynamite for a thrill. They found her vagina in North Carolina and bits of her tits in Brazil."

Chase chuckled and Hannah gasped. She hid her face in her hands and began to sob.

Just let me touch you.

"I'm sorry," she said. Then her shoulders shook and the sobs came.

8

"We were wondering if you'd mind babysitting for a couple hours tomorrow morning before the funeral."

"Sure." Chase and Aaron were standing out in the yard watching the children play while Sarah prepared dinner. "What time do you need me?"

"Just from around ten till noon or so. Are you going to stick around for a few more days?"

"I don't know. I don't really have to get back for anything, but—"

"That's what I figured. And don't forget we need to go through Dad's things."

"Okay."

"We should probably go right to the house after the funeral." Chase nodded. "What should I do with them?"

"With what?"

"The kids."

"Whatever you want. Take them to a playground or just hang around here if you feel like it. I assume you're coming tonight."

"I was planning to. Unless you need me to watch the kids."

"No. We booked a sitter weeks ago. I really want as many people there as possible."

He was nothing more than a seat filler, and Aaron had no interest at all in his visit with Hannah. Of course none of this was surprising, but even after all this time it had the power to disappoint. Although Chase understood that selfishness was a primary motivation, perhaps the sole motivation for human behavior (vanity, narcissism and the survival instinct were certainly the dominant forces in directing his own actions), his brother's absolute disregard for the needs and desires of others—a trait of which he seemed to want to appear innocently unaware—carried a payload of brutish aggression that ignited in Chase an overpowering urge to strike back, to scream that he mattered, too, and to smash his brother across the face with a wooden plank. Perhaps Aaron's selfishness and Chase's violent reaction to it were both responses to the same childhood stimuli, but really, it didn't matter. Cold logic did nothing to diminish his thirst for vengeance and deep bruising.

"Come on in," Sarah called from inside the house a minute later.

As the children sprinted, screaming and smiling, toward the front door, Chase's anger dropped swiftly, silently away. For the moment, at least, he felt like the perfect uncle in the perfect American family. And it was a surprisingly gratifying feeling.

In the dining room Sarah circled the table dishing the food onto the plates. When everyone else had been served, she filled her own plate and took a seat at the end of the table opposite her husband. Hands folded, they all sat quietly while Aaron said grace. "Let's eat," he finally said, but only after he'd raised his fork did the others reach for theirs. There was something unreal about their ritual. It was too orderly, almost mechanical, and Chase felt embarrassed having witnessed it. Recalling the forced formality, the atmosphere of oppression that pervaded their childhood dinners, he shuddered.

For a few minutes the only sounds were the clinking of silverware against plates, mouths chewing and throats swallowing. Then Aaron put down his fork, sat back in his chair and sighed. "You didn't give Sophie any brussels sprouts, honey." He wiped his mouth.

"You're right."

"Why not?"

She smiled. "She doesn't eat brussels sprouts."

"Well, she *can't* eat them if you don't give her any."

"That's true. But she *won't* eat them if I *do* give them to her."

"They smell like farts." Sophie wrinkled up her nose.

Sarah sighed. "Don't use that word."

"There are lots of things *I* don't like." Aaron frowned at his wife.

Was there another message there?

Bradley looked up at his mother. "What's wrong with fart, Mom?"

"Sometimes *I* don't like to go to work," Aaron continued.

"Why is fart bad?"

"Sometimes you *don't* go, Daddy," Sophie said.

"It's just not nice." Sarah rubbed her forehead.

"That's not the point, sweetheart."

Bradley set his fork down and looked at his father. "And you *never* eat peas."

"I'm not a seven-year-old who needs vegetables."

"Wow," Chase said. "You still don't eat peas?"

"Don't grown-ups need vegetables?" Bradley tilted his head.

"Yeah," Sophie said. "And peas don't even smell like farts."

"Sophie!"

"Yes, Sophie." Beads of perspiration had formed like an armada on Aaron's forehead. "Grown-ups *do* need vegetables. But I am your father and I'm in charge now."

As forceful as he was, there was a hint of uncertainty in his voice. Perhaps he, too, was hearing the echoes of their childhood.

"Mom, too," Bradley said.

"Yes. Mom and I are in charge, and if we tell you to eat your brussels sprouts then you need to eat your brussels sprouts. Your job is to listen to us, not to ask us about what we eat and what we don't eat. We are old enough to make our own decisions about what we are going to eat and what we are going to not eat. But you need to listen to us, because you are the child and we are the grown-ups, and what I'm telling you to do right now is to eat your brussels sprouts. Is that clear enough?"

"Sort of."

"What do you mean, sort of?" Teeth clenched.

"Well, I can't."

"Oh really?" The veins in his forehead were pulsing. "Why *can't* you?"

"Mom didn't give me any brussels sprouts."

Aaron closed his eyes. "I know."

Sarah scooped a couple brussels sprouts from the bowl and plopped them on her daughter's plate. "Is everybody happy now?"

"I'm not," Sophie said.

"Well?" Aaron stared at his daughter, his eyes narrow.

"They really, really smell like farts."

Aaron reached across the table, grabbed her fork and skewered a sprout. He held it in front of her mouth. "Open."

Lips clenched, she turned her head away.

"Open."

"Aaron." Chase knew he shouldn't get involved, but this was too painful to watch.

Aaron glared at him. "What?"

"Does she eat other vegetables?"

"Yes, Chase, she eats other vegetables."

"Will she eat the rest of her dinner?"

"Not if he keeps this up," Sarah said.

"*Please*."

"Does she generally listen to you?"

"We both do," Bradley said. "She just doesn't like brussels sprouts. But I do. I like peas, too."

"Is this really that important?"

Aaron's eyes narrowed. "Chase, if and when you have kids of your own you can decide who eats what and what's important. Okay?" He turned toward his daughter. "Open your mouth, *now*."

Tears flooded her eyes.

"It's just a vegetable, Aaron." Chase tried to control his voice.

"*Now*, damn it."

"Aaron!" Sarah folded her arms over her chest.

"Now!"

Sophie began to wail.

Chase reached out and grabbed the fork from his brother. He shoved the sprout into his own mouth. He let the fork drop and with his hand he grabbed the other sprout from her plate and stuffed it into his mouth and chewed. Everyone stared as he seized the vegetable bowl and crammed all the remaining sprouts into his mouth, chewing and swallowing them as quickly as he could. Before anyone could speak, he'd cleared the vegetables from every plate on the table. Then, still chewing, he wiped his mouth and said, "They *taste* like goddamned farts, too." He rose and left the kitchen.

9

Chase knocked on the study door. Apologizing to Sarah was easy, but now it was time to face his brother's wrath. No matter how right he believed he was, intervening in a private family dispute was an idiotic thing to do.

"Who is it?"

"Can I come in?" They were both wrong, but it wouldn't be particularly productive to mention that. Probably Aaron wouldn't let him get that far.

"Sure."

Aaron was sitting at his desk, his back to the door. "Would you mind closing that?"

Chase pulled the door shut and girded himself for a long, tedious diatribe.

Aaron turned toward his brother and smiled. "What's up?"

"I just wanted to apologize."

"Don't worry about it."

"I really shouldn't have gotten involved."

"It's okay. I probably got a little carried away."

Displayed toward the top of Aaron's computer screen was a glowing cross; underneath it an animated figure stood facing a series of doors with labels over them: *Bible Reading, Prayer, Worship, Children's Room, Sharing, Sing-Alongs, Counsel, Chat, Sanctuary.*

Aaron grinned. "Interactive Virtual Church."

"Is it a . . . a video game?"

He laughed. "It's a church, a virtual church."

"Okay." *Just shut up.*

"It's a place of worship." He pressed a key and the figure pivoted to the right. "And that," he pointed at the screen, "is my avatar."

Chase tightened his facial muscles. Pretend you're brain is being X-rayed. His stomach twisted, rolled.

"You know." Aaron swiveled his chair toward his brother and folded his hands on his lap. "I bet you'd be a lot more comfortable with religion if you didn't have to go into a church."

"Yeah, maybe." *No.*

"I'm serious. I'm not always crazy about that part either."

"How often do you do this?" At least they weren't fighting.

"I just found out about it a few days ago, but I think it's a great idea." He reached into his desk drawer and pulled out a bottle of Scotch and two shot glasses. "Can't do this in church."

"I guess not." Chase felt sick, bloated.

"I think more people would worship if they knew it was this easy." He poured two shots.

"Is it supposed to be easy? I mean—"

"Well, convenient." He handed Chase a glass and raised his own. "It's just more convenient."

"So what do you do with the character?"

"Avatar. That's what they call it. It's supposed to be me."

"I could tell." Chase sipped his scotch.

"Really?"

"No. What's with the beard?"

"I don't know, I just . . . " His face flushed. "I just liked the one with the beard."

"You look good with a beard. Older, but more distinguished."

"Do you always have to be a wise ass?"

"Mostly, I guess."

"Here." Aaron pulled another chair over. "Check it out."

Chase sat down and Aaron turned toward the desk. He pressed a couple keys and the avatar spun around and faced a wall between two massive doors. "Crap." He pressed another combination and it walked into the wall. The computer speakers emitted a dull grunt. Aaron shook his head and sipped his Scotch. "I'm still learning how to control this thing." He leaned over his keyboard and pressed some keys: nothing.

"What are you trying to do?"

"I want to get into the cathedral and pray."

"Isn't there a legend or a key somewhere?"

"A legend?"

"You know, the thing where they show you the keystrokes."

"I don't know. I think you're just supposed to know."

"Like faith?"

Aaron took another sip and leaned closer to the screen. He pressed some keys and the avatar turned left. His hands moved and the figure stepped forward, toward the door marked *Cathedral*. "See?" Another set of keys: the avatar raised its arms over its head and it's mouth opened: "Lord in heaven." The voice sounded like a bullfrog in an auditorium.

"Damn."

"Did you pick the voice?"

"Yeah. Most of them aren't that good. I'm trying to open the door." More keystrokes: the avatar put its hands over its face and grunted.

"Did you try knocking?"

"How?"

"I don't know." Chase grabbed his stomach. "I feel like I'm going to erupt."

"I don't think he'd knock on a cathedral door."

"Try typing 'Open.'"

"No. You have to use the other keys, too." He pressed 'Shift' and 'O' and the door opened. "Yes!"

With a few keystrokes he was able to maneuver his avatar into the cathedral. The ceilings were high and there were rows of pews. He steered his avatar forward and then to the right. He stopped it between two rows of pews and pressed some keys. The avatar turned around and croaked, "I have sinned."

"Shit."

Chase laughed.

"Shh." Aaron clicked some more keys but nothing happened. He tried another combination: nothing. Then a message appeared on the screen: "Kneel."

"I'm *try*ing, damn it." More clicking and cursing: a dove flew by, the screen faded. More furious clicking: the screen lit up and a bible appeared, opened then slammed shut, producing a cloud of dust. Angels sang.

"God damn it."

"Try 'Shift,' 'K.'"

"'Shift,' 'K'?"

"To *kneel*."

Aaron swigged his Scotch and poked at the keys. Some sort of translucent gray body started seeping out of the top of his character's head. "Don't die!" Aaron cried. The character moaned and wobbled. "No, no, no, *no!*" He stabbed at the escape key. The spirit vanished and his avatar grunted and buried its face in its hands. "Forgive me," it groaned. Then it began rocking back and forth, tearing strands of hair from its beard. "Fuck, fuck, fuck, fuck, fucking *fuck*." Aaron punched the keyboard and another character appeared to the left, a tall man in a black gown, perhaps a minister. His avatar turned toward the man. "Kneel, God damn it, kneel." Sweat dripped from Aaron's face. "All right, all right," he said. He pressed 'Shift,' 'K' and his avatar stepped back and kicked the man in the leg. The man gasped and Aaron's avatar kicked him again. The other man opened a Bible, but Aaron's avatar kicked the book out of his hands. Aaron cursed and banged the keys over and over while his avatar kicked the man back into the aisle, where he dropped down onto his knees and cried out, "My son!" Aaron's avatar kicked him in the head and he fell back. "Sinner, burn in Hell." Screams, a flash of fire and then the screen went black.

"God damned stupid fucking cunt bastard!"

"Kill, kill, kill," Chase roared. He laughed so hard he fell backward in his chair.

Aaron, his face swollen and red, turned and glared down at his brother.

Chase was lying on his back, giggling. "I'm pretty sure I've been saved."

Aaron was panting, his face glazed with perspiration.

"But I think it might be a little more fun in a real church." Chase burped and his mouth filled with a mealy mass of partially digested brussels sprouts.

10

The band was on stage connecting wires, assembling stands and adjusting amplifiers when Chase stepped through the doorway of the Deer Head Inn. Perched on a chair just to the right of the entrance was a young woman with skin so clear and white she could have been a paraffin sculpture. On the small table in front of her sat a metal cashbox.

"Is there a guest list?"

She pushed back her jet-black hair. "Sure is."

"My name is Chase Stoller."

"Aaron's brother?" Her smile revealed a mouthful of teeth that appeared to be jockeying for position.

"That's me." He stepped into the club.

"I'm sorry."

He turned back toward her. She was studying a wrinkled sheet of paper.

"I'm afraid you're not on the list."

He chuckled and handed her a ten.

"Chase," Kirk called out.

"Kirk." But where was she?

Kirk stepped off the stage and extended a hand. "Glad you could make it, man."

"Thanks. I can't wait to hear you guys."

"Well, I don't know if we're quite ready for prime time."

"Aaron seems pretty excited."

"Yeah, he thinks we're ready to record a CD and do a European tour."

"Delusions of adequacy."

"Ouch." He winced.

"I'm sorry."

"Hey, I'm just having fun."

"I really shouldn't have said that, and I certainly didn't mean you."

"Don't worry about it."

"Where's your girlfriend?"

"My girlfriend?"

"Haley?"

"Oh no." He shook his head. "Don't let my wife hear you say that."

"I didn't realize you were married."

"Yep." He held up his left hand.

"I've really been out of touch."

"It'll be eight years in December."

"Well, then it's time for a girlfriend anyway."

"Not if I plan to age."

"Is your wife here?"

"She'll be here later. Haley will, too." He smiled and looked toward the stage. "Why don't you find a table? Maybe you can all sit together."

Listening to his brother's bands had been a frequent feature of Chase's teen years. At first he'd attempted to ignore his ears' harsh assessment, but he was never able to develop any enthusiasm regarding Aaron's dreams of fame, fortune and creative genius. Some of his songs had interesting moments, a few were mildly touching, but too many of them were tinkling and nebulous, the musical equivalent of Miller Lite on the rocks. There was no substance, no relevance or gravity, not a hint of passion. Or could envy have tainted his opinion? Chase was convinced he had a good ear for music, but perhaps with his brother he wasn't as objective as he liked to think he was. Perhaps he was simply wrong. That, too, was possible. And the fact was that this was one setting wherein Aaron's awkwardness seemed to drop away. He was confident of his abilities here, and even if that confidence was unwarranted, it gave him pleasure and provided him with a kind of temporary strength. What difference did it make if he was deluded as long as he never felt the merciless slap of reality? And he wasn't likely to accept a dissenting opinion, regardless of its source. *You are free to shut the fuck up.*

"What can I get you?"

Her smile glowed as though she really meant it, which, of course, was impossible. Still, it was almost gratifying. And even her standard issue black skirt and white button-down blouse couldn't conceal a lovely figure, pneumatic breasts to the north, a waist that gradually tapered before flaring out to hips that were just broad enough for purchase from fore or aft.

"Do you have a decent dry red wine?"

"No."

He laughed.

Eyes narrowed. "You wouldn't want me to lie to you, would you?"

"Well," he smiled. "Not about that."

She planted her free hand on her hip. "What would you like me to lie about?"

Be charming. Twinkle your eyes or something. "Your irrepressible attraction to me?"

"I find you extremely unattractive."

"I love you very much."

She laughed. "I'm supposed to be the one telling the lies."

"I guess I'll have a darkish beer of your choice, followed by frequent visits."

She turned. Very callipygian.

A minute later she reappeared and poured his beer. "I'll be back."

The band started and Chase sat back and tried to relax. It was silly, idiotic—she probably got hit on fifty times a night by younger, more attractive men than he, and she probably already had a boyfriend, or a girlfriend—but he wanted her to come back, to smile and talk and flirt and promise him her heart, or at least a night of gratification, one that wouldn't make suicide even more appealing. He'd decided earlier to control his drinking tonight, but the more he drank the more often she'd have to return to his table. On the other hand he didn't want her to think he was an alcoholic. That wouldn't be a good start, not unless her father was a drunk, which wasn't at all unlikely given the local demographic. The idea that she would give him that much thought made him laugh. He looked around to make sure no one had seen him. Maybe some food. No, the brussels sprouts were still down there stirring things up.

He tried to focus on the music, on Aaron's familiar, pleasant, infinitely bland voice. It was the same as it had always been, maybe a little more controlled. Kirk sounded good, as he always did, but even his playing was uninspired. The guitar player, a young guy Chase hadn't met, had a good sound, but when he took a solo, he played far too many notes, some of them simply wrong, exceeding both his own abilities and the constraints of the song. The sonic bullets just shot out of his amplifier in a blinding, chaotic stream of irrelevance. The other guys were just the canvas for his enfilades of brilliance.

Another song and they were wallowing deep in the land of the trite. The rhythms, the melody, the lyrics were all pale clichés wrapped in plain white vapor.

"Another?" She leaned close.

"Please."

She straightened up. "Was that frequent enough?"

"No."

"No?" Hand on hip.

What was she trying to show him? "I missed you."

"I'll try to do better."

Hard to tell.

He sat back and let his eyes fall shut. *Here I am, doing this, and my father's funeral is tomorrow. Well. . . .*

The band had just taken a break when Haley appeared, luminous, iridescent and, if her expression was any indication, terminally indifferent to the world. Still, she wore her insouciance like a Gucci gown. Another woman was with her. *Don't wave, don't signal or make eye contact. Let her come.* Of course he had an advantage. The club was crowded and there were three free chairs at his table.

Kirk approached them and directed them to his table. "Chase, this is my wife Jillian."

She extended a hand. "You're Aaron's brother, the journalist."

"Yes and no."

She frowned, then smiled. "Oh yeah. I heard."

"Aaron talked about me?"

"No. Kirk mentioned something about it."

"Sorry," Kirk said.

"No problem," he said. "My life's an open sore."

"You remember Haley."

He nodded. "Have a seat."

When they were all seated the waitress came over. "I see how it is." She pursed her lips.

"No you don't."

She grinned. "Can I get anyone a drink?"

They ordered and the banter began. A few people stopped by the table to talk to Kirk about the music or just to say hello. Haley added little to the conversation. Her contribution was her presence. When the band went on again Chase ordered another beer for himself and another martini for Haley. Jillian was still working on her first glass of wine.

Chase turned to Haley. "Tell me something," he said over the music.

Haley leaned a little closer but said nothing.

"Anything. Just tell me something about something."

"We don't have any choice."

"Who? You and me?"

"All of us." She looked around the room.

"About what?"

"Anything."

"So, our lives are all laid out for us?"

"No, not really."

"Okay."

"They're not laid out. We just can't do anything else but what we do."

"Because. . . ."

She sighed. "We're preprogrammed."

"By?"

She shook her head.

The waitress brought their drinks and smiled at him before walking away.

These two very dissimilar women were each lovely in a different way. Haley was at least a few years older than the waitress, and she certainly seemed more serious, more grave—she was probably better educated, maybe better read—but the waitress had a playful quality, a sense of humor and some fine equipment. He could have fun with the waitress. They could laugh and fuck and suck and it wouldn't matter much, though he'd enjoy it and her. He could fall in love with Haley. And that was a problem. Unless he was also having recreational sex with the waitress. *Hey guys, how about it?* They'd probably fall in love with each other and dump him. They probably had no interest in him in the first place.

"By our experience, or chemistry, or aliens or what?"

"Experience," she said. *"And* chemistry."

"And you don't think we can circumvent the programming."

"What I think is that the desire to circumvent the programming, if we have it, is programmed in, too. I mean if you want to circumvent it, that's just what you're programmed to want to do."

"You're cheering me right up."

She shrugged. "You asked."

"Okay, what if you have two options, and you feel yourself drawn to one of them, and then you decide to fight the urge because you just don't think it's good for you—it's part of a self-destructive pattern you're trying to break—and you force yourself to do the other thing? Can't you consciously choose what you aren't naturally drawn to?"

"Sure, if you're programmed that way."

"What about when more than one option fits your programming?"

She shrugged and sipped her drink.

"I think you might be wrong," he said. "I mean, I agree up to a point, but I'm not convinced that we can't conquer some of what we're programmed for, or override it, without it just being a result of the programming. We're animals and we have instincts, but we, at least some of us, fight those instincts, tribal instincts, things like racism and territorial stuff. We don't piss on our carpets."

"We have leases."

"But we sometimes overcome our instincts."

She looked away.

What was he programmed to do? To obsess about a woman that he might not even like if he knew her better? To fill his mind with thoughts of sex in order to obscure the endless list of issues he'd rather not confront? Did it matter? He still wanted to bury his head between her legs.

These new songs were interchangeable, dotted eighth notes always in groups of three followed by tinkly riffs, derivative lyrics, slightly reprocessed, themes of lost love and missed connections. But Aaron was in his element now. Here and with his God he was comfortable and self-assured. Shouldn't that make him happy?

The set ended and Kirk sat down next to his wife. Aaron was hopping from table to table, beaming with pride, probably unaware that his brother was here. More drinks. The waitress brushed Chase's shoulder when she passed. Thank you.

He turned. "Thank you."

It took her a moment. Big smile. "You're welcome." She strolled off.

Why do I want to marry the dead one?

He turned to Haley. "I enjoy talking with you." *So, you like beverages?*

"Why?"

"Your favorite question."

Nothing. Maybe she has that disease where your face gets stuck in one unchanging expression.

"Because you're bright and interesting."

"And you want to get laid."

"Getting laid isn't so hard."

"But you want to fuck me."

"I, uh. . . ." Shit. "The thought may have occurred to me. But that's not what I'm. . . . You aren't making this easy."

"I wasn't aware that I was supposed to."

"Would you like another drink?"

"No."

Just give up.

"Not here."

When the waitress came over he asked for the check. Jillian and Haley were talking when she came back and dropped the check on the table.

"Are you going to miss me?"

"I don't know." She pursed her lips. "You're kind of fickle."

"How often are you here?"

"Every night."

"Really?"

"Yep."

"Thanks for being so much fun."

"Hmm." She narrowed her eyes and walked away.

11

She set two Scotches on the table in front of the couch and sat down next to him.

He turned and leaned toward her. Her eyes revealed nothing. Did anything affect her? He kissed her and she put her arms around him.

After a minute he leaned back and scrutinized her. "I like you," he said.

She unbuttoned her blouse and let it fall open. "This is what you wanted."

"Part of it." Chase reached out and slid her blouse over her shoulders. "Don't you want anything?"

She took his hand and stood up, led him into her bedroom. She turned to face him. He saw nothing but her. He unbuttoned her jeans and pulled the zipper down, then knelt in front of her and drew the jeans down around her ankles. She stepped out of them and he lowered her down onto the bed, leaned her back on the bedspread and kissed her. She reached down and unbuckled his belt and struggled with the button. "Sorry," she said. He rose and undressed and she slid up toward the head of the bed and waited there. He eased himself down and kissed the downy skin of her stomach, ran his tongue over to one hip, then to the other, then down beneath the elastic band of her panties. She moaned and reached down for his hand and brought it up to one breast. He slid up toward her and put his lips around her nipple. It was stiff and she was shuddering. *This is where I want to be.* He sat up and slid her panties down. Just a tiny patch of soft gentle curls, a reminder that she was real. He lifted her legs and slid his shoulders under them and moved up toward her, licking and kissing one thigh, then the other, sliding up until his shoulders pressed against her butt. Very lightly he brushed his lips over her. She gasped and he did it again, his warm breath washing over her. Then he put his right hand under her, his thumb resting in the moist intersection of her legs. Slowly he moved it up and inside her. So warm and wet. *Do you want anything?* He pressed his lips against her and searched with his tongue, licking circles, darting. I do not exist. Free. Only this. Breathe her in. Taste her. Nothing else. Nothing. God. She bucked, tensed, bucked again. "Oh. Oh." Pressing his mouth hard against her he pushed his thumb deep inside her and she shuddered, moaned, tensed and let go. "Oh yes." Yes. A wonderful soft moist gentle fist clutching, squeezing, wringing his thumb again, again as her body twitched and writhed to some internal rhythm. When the eruption was over she clutched a handful of hair, pulled him toward her. He moved on top of her and she took him in her hand and led him to her, stroked herself with him. He moved slightly forward and she opened up. Sinking. Bliss. He stopped when just the head was inside her. Oh fuck. Fuck. This. Her hands on his butt, pulling, harder, raising herself to him. Inside, all the way in until he felt that mysterious little nub. Everything buzzing, sliding, moving, every inch another heaven. Every movement god.

God. Bliss, euphoria, utopia, exaltation, rapture. Rapture. Stop thinking. Look at her. Look. Beautiful where is she does she feel oh god or care in deeper out slowly back inside not too fast eyes closed then her back arching arching pushing free nothing else because I'm here I am here no control give up nothing else nothing else this is god breathe oh who is she so unhappy and coming again wait not me not yet hold on make it last forever more more please never end roll over oh yes straddling me in deep look up beautiful sad face small perfect wonderful breasts skin pale silk everywhere there is no me god too much not yet on my lips in my head her scent is this it the love no is it does it matter and bucking now no not yet oh fuck bucking now look up at her who is she beautiful milkweed skin sad blue eyes full raspberry lips just a tiny swizzle stick o between them please smile am I here slides off moves down to take me in her mouth more warm wet soft lips tongue dancing aaaaaaaah what are you doing how oh hair brushing over me over my stomach straight auburn smoldering oh oh god make it last not yet touch her face are you there oh oh god n pl pl jes I lo climbing me holding me close rolling me over I look down is that a smile sinking in again sink in farther in farther filling you everything I want that's it oh please I can't can am oh pl pl hav plea not yes uh bu I oh god oh g oh

"God, oh God. Oh God. Fuck. Jesus." He collapsed on top of her, embraced her. Catch your breath. "Um." He kissed her cheek, her neck. "I'm," he laughed. "I'm panting." He rolled off of her and gently turned her face toward him. *Don't talk. Don't.*

She let her eyes meet his, said nothing. Was she sad, serious, thinking, waiting for something? It was unknowable. *Are you there?* She moved closer to him and rested her head against his chest. Minutes passed. Silence. Just breathing.

Then: "You're leaking out of me."

"Sorry."

She shook her head.

What are you thinking? Why did you do this? Why are you here with me? Tell me something.

Tell me something.

He was alone. He looked around, examining the room he'd barely noticed, hardly seen the night before. Even with the morning light struggling to nudge through the curtains it felt like dusk. Muted colors, nothing floral or bright, genderless furniture, dark wood, a room hiding in its own shadow, like its enigmatic inhabitant. Funeral today. Yippee. Where is she? Now what?

He got up and found his clothes folded over the back of a chair. When he was dressed he pushed the door open and cleared his throat. Fair warning. She sat at a small wooden dining room table reading the paper, a cup of something in front of her. *Please be nice to me.*

"Good morning," he said. He didn't know what to do with his hands.

"Can I get you some coffee?"

"No thanks." He smiled, but it took effort.

"Tea?"

"Sure. If it's no trouble."

She rose and handed him the newspaper. "Tea is no trouble."

Was there a message there? Tea, as opposed to—

She called out from the kitchen, "Peppermint, green, Earl Grey, dandelion?"

"Anything with caffeine."

"It's hot." She set the cup in front of him.

The scent of shampoo. He wanted to reach out and touch her—"Do you have the day off?"—to grope her. What he wanted was everything.

"I'm going in late."

"I'm sorry. You could have gotten me up."

"It's fine." She shook her head.

"How are you feeling?"

She let her eyes meet his. "A little uncomfortable."

"I could leave." He gave a shrug.

"Is the tea that bad?"

"Was that a joke?"

"I guess my jokes are worse than my tea."

They were both staring down at the table.

"Nice table," he said.

12

"What can I help you with?"

Aaron sat on the couch with a rag in his hand, his electric bass resting across his lap. "There's really nothing to do at the moment, but I will need you to go with me to his house afterwards." He ran the rag up and down each string.

"You mean you're not going to bring people back here to eat microwaved finger food and drink cheap wine from paper cups and make bad jokes and feel awkward until they think they've suffered long enough to leave without offending anyone?"

"Am I supposed to?"

"I think so."

"I guess they'll just have to feel awkward on their own."

"Good. That's great."

"He didn't even want a funeral."

"Then why the hell are we doing it?"

Aaron shrugged. "Cause everybody expects one." He picked up his bass and threw the strap over his shoulder.

Chase nodded. There was no point in arguing. "I really do appreciate your organizing things."

"Well, he did most of it."

"Excuse me?"

"He didn't want it but I told him we didn't have any choice, that people would expect it, so he arranged almost everything."

"Okay." Chase was giddy from his night with Haley, on the verge of arousal, but filled with apprehension about what, if anything, would come next. She hadn't seemed disgusted by his presence this morning. That was something. And she'd come at least twice. *Buzz. Where am I? Oh yeah.* "You guys sounded good last night."

"Yeah, it went pretty well." He played a few notes. "We just need to do one or two more gigs and we'll be ready to go into the studio."

"That's great." *No you won't.* "I'm going to take the kids out."

"Uh huh." Plunk, plunk. "They're upstairs playing video games." Plunk, plunk, plunk.

"I'll go get them."

Aaron was lost in his instrument. Chase could have whipped his dick out and pissed on the carpet without disturbing him. It didn't matter. He couldn't stop thinking about Haley, their wonderful night, the odd morning.

After finishing his tea he'd risen and asked if he could help with the dishes. No, she had to get going, she'd do them later. She rose and walked him to the door.

"I'd like. . . ." He was nervous and as vulnerable as an upended cockroach. A word could crush him. "Would you be willing to give me your number? Or to take mine?"

"Okay."

"Okay?"

"I'll give you mine."

He pulled out his cell phone and programmed the number she gave him. "I'll call you."

"Okay."

He was attracted to her in a way he didn't understand, but he had no idea what she might be thinking and he'd learned from experience that it was generally best not to push too hard. She might not want to divulge anything, to be forced to say out loud whatever she was thinking or feeling. Of course the uncertainly left him off balance, and perhaps that was the point, though her attitude didn't seem contrived.

He stepped toward her and draped his arms around her, gave her a gentle hug, drew back to study her face for a second, then kissed her cheek. "I like you." He was ten again.

"It was . . . nice." She looked at her feet. "I had a nice time." She looked up at him, "Really," looked away.

"Okay. I believe you." *What are you hiding from?* He smiled and turned, tried not to walk like he knew he was being watched.

Gallump, gallump.

Fuck.

When he finally looked back the door was closing.

"Are you going to play with us?"

They held his hands and dragged him along, turning to look up at him, smiling, excited, as they made their way down the hill toward the sprawling playground. It was so simple to make them happy. Their world was full of nice, friendly, decent people and fun, interesting things. Everything was new for them, every minute full of promise. Of course that was an exaggeration, but it was close enough. Any damage they sustained now wouldn't be truly felt for years. If he waited long enough to become a parent he could be dead before his children were in therapy. Probably Aaron's kids' lives were better than most. Like all parents, theirs were flawed, but they loved them, and, aside from the Megadeath Planetblaster toys and the fascination with violence that too often made its way into their banter, these two seemed well-adjusted and happy. Perhaps successful parenting relied more on what you avoided than what you did. He was smiling, too. It was contagious.

"Are you," Bradley asked. "Are you going to play with us?"

"Of course."

"Yay," they screamed in unison and tugged him forward.

Suddenly he was a hero.

Summer in the suburbs: sibilant sprinklers, children's cries and slapping footfalls, women's voices, praising, reprimanding or frantic. The playground was like a movie set.

And there were women everywhere, young mothers and babysitters of varying shades, shapes and sizes. Most of them were sitting on the benches, but a few, particularly the ones with younger kids, were playing with their children. Some looked bored, uninterested, or both; some appeared exhausted and a few seemed confident and calm in their roles, their faces jubilant. A smorgasbord of femininity in its multifarious manifestations. Raw power in its most appealing container.

The children, too, came in a variety of sizes, shapes and colors, and their behavior, he noticed as they roamed around in search of a bench to use as home base, ranged from near perfect to borderline criminal.

But Bradley and Sophie seemed completely at home. They screamed with joy when they saw someone they knew, and children they'd apparently never seen before soon became their friends. They were far more confident and comfortable than Chase had ever been.

He played tag with them and followed them down the sliding board; he pushed them on the swings and the three of them ran back and forth through the sprinkler, soaking their clothing. When Bradley found some other kids to play with Chase stayed with Sophie. After a few minutes of running around she tried to climb down into one of the sandboxes, but a bigger child with streaks of dirt on his face stood in her way. "It's just for boys," he said. His expression would have deterred a rabid badger.

Before Chase could intervene Sophie was sobbing. He knelt down and put his hands on her shoulders. "You can go in if you want." He glared at the boy and his friend. "I'll go in with you." She shook her head.

"No girls allowed!"

"*Every*body's allowed," Chase snarled. He picked Sophie up and stepped past the boy. Then he lowered her and said, "Go ahead sweetie, go ahead and play."

"Hey." The boy stamped his foot. "No grown-ups either." He hurled a handful of sand over his head, showering the four of them.

Chase brought his face close to the boy's. "Listen, you little shit." He wanted to grab him and shake him. How did kids get so mean? And why was he always on the edge of rage?

The boy turned toward his friend. "Let's go. This guy's a jerk."

Suppressing his urge to wrestle the boy to the ground and make him cry out for his mother, Chase turned back to Sophie. "What do you feel like doing?" He managed a weak smile.

"Can you help me make a sand castle?"

"Sure." It was so easy to feel for them, to be overcome by something like love. Or maybe it was just a safer, more distant way of feeling for himself.

Working together, with no tools but their hands, they dug down to find the moist sand, scooping it up and gathering it in a pile, then starting on the base of the structure. She had a clear sense of what she wanted but seemed more interested in the process and the collaboration than the quality of the results.

When he thought they had a passable finished product, Chase said, "How do you like it?"

"I love it." Her smile was radiant: fireworks in her eyes, flowers in her hair. Miss mousey, will you marry me? His heart was on a trampoline.

"Great."

She wrinkled her brow and tilted her head. "What about the mote?"

"How in heaven's name could I forget the mote?"

He'd just begun to dig a trench when three boys, probably four or five years old, climbed down and began to dig three holes. "We can connect them," one of them said.

"Wow," another one said. "That's a cool castle, Mister."

"Thanks," Chase said. "She did most of it."

Sophie stood up. "I want to go on the swings again."

"Alright." Chase rose and brushed himself off. "Be careful not to dig too deep, guys."

One of them looked up. "Why?"

"Crocodiles."

"There aren't any crocodiles," he said.

"Just two or three."

"No." They stopped digging and looked at each other.

"They aren't that big."

They stared.

"And only one of them bites."

The tallest one stood and shook his head. "There's no crocodiles." His voice faltered.

"I wouldn't worry too much," Chase said. "He only bites on Tuesdays." He started to walk away, then stopped and turned back. "Wait. This *is* Tuesday."

They stared up at him, then scrambled up out of the sandbox.

He was about to apologize when one of the boys ran up to a woman who was sitting on a bench reading a book. "Mom," he said. "Is it *really* Tuesday?"

Chase laughed.

"You're silly," Sophie said.

"Me?"

"Yes."

He grabbed her hand and they headed toward the swings.

When should he call? And what should he say? Just start with a standard-issue dinner invitation and go from there. *If* she agrees to dinner. He was pulsing with sexual energy. His stomach was fluttering and there was a warm tingle in his pants. The inguinal bees were back. *I'm walking on the playground with a four-year-old girl and there's a hungry lump swelling in my jeans. Great. Where's the cop? If I were alone in the woods I'd fuck a tree.* There really was an aphrodisiac quality to nature, a lesson learned on a camping trip with Jennifer. They couldn't keep their hands off of each other. They fucked as soon as the tent went up, again before going to sleep and once more in the morning. He wanted to fuck her again in the rowboat after they left the island—she was sitting across from him in her shorts and he was salivating—but the river was crowded and when they stopped the ground was rocky and uneven, covered with twigs, stones and branches and swarming with insects. He'd had to row three miles with an erection. And here he was on a public playground walking funny. He could take the kids home now, drive out into the country and jerk off to the scents and sounds of nature. The kids. Shit. Where was Bradley? Chase stopped and scanned the area.

"Do you see your brother?"

"I want to go to the swings."

"In a minute. Let's find Bradley first." He tried to sound calm though his throat was suddenly dry and he could almost feel the individual beads of perspiration sprouting from the pores on his forehead.

Hand in hand, they paced the perimeter of the playground, stopping to survey each new area and call out for Bradley. Chase was trying hard to tamp down the panic that was bubbling inside him, and to conceal from Sophie his increasing sense of urgency. Runaway brain. A flash of Bradley sprawled on the ground, his face resting in a spreading pond of blood. Chase shook his head to dislodge the image. The child was fine. It was silly to worry. But he might have been abducted; those things happened. A smiling man with the promise of ice cream or a horseback ride. Or a threat: if you don't come with me I'll kill your parents. Fuck. "Bradley." His voice was louder now and his shirt was soaked. People were staring. He probably looked as frantic as he felt. While he was screwing innocent saplings somebody was kidnapping his nephew.

"What was he wearing, sweetie?" He looked down at Sophie. "Do you remember what he was . . . what he's wearing?"

"A T-shirt and some pants?"

"Here. Let me put you up on my shoulders and you can look around."

"Yay."

He stood behind her and put his hands in her armpits, lifted her over his head and then back onto his shoulders. "Look real carefully."

"I'm taller than anybody," she said.

"Yes, sweetheart. Now help me look for your brother."

"I don't see him. But I see Calvin. Is that good?"

"That's very good. Is Calvin your friend or his?"

"He's not really either one. He's mean."

"Alright."

"It's *not* alright. He says bad things and sometimes he even hits."

He twisted his neck around to look up at her. "I'm sorry. You're right."

"I know," she said, and patted his head.

"I'm going to keep walking and you keep looking. Just keep looking until you find him."

"Okay, Uncle Chase."

He'd taken a few more steps when Sophie grabbed a handful of hair. "I think I see him."

"Where?"

With both hands she twisted his head to the left. "Over there."

Sitting alone on the grass by a large tree was Bradley. He was very still, facing away from them, from the playground.

Chase eased Sophie over his head and set her down. "Let's race."

When they were close he ran ahead. "Bradley?"

He put his hand on Bradley's shoulder, moved around in front of him and knelt down. "Hey, what's wrong, buddy?"

"Nothing."

"What are you doing over here?"

"Nothing." He averted his eyes, shrugged.

Chase cupped the boy's cheek in his hand. "Bradley, I'm not angry. I just want to know what's wrong."

"Nothing. I'm just hiding."

"Are you playing hide-and-seek?"

"No." His face flushed. "I was hiding from you."

"From us?"

"No. From *you*."

"Why?"

"I don't know."

"You don't know why?"

"No."

"He does it a lot," Sophie said.

"Hides?"

"Sits by himself."

"What do your mom and dad say?"

"They don't mind," she said.

Chase checked his watch. "Do you guys want to go home?"

"I don't care," Bradley said. His expression had gone blank, as though the sweet little boy who resided behind it had slipped away.

They were far more complex than they appeared and Chase possessed absolutely no relevant skills. Something odd was going on in there, a switch had been turned, a door closed. Suddenly he had no access and it was distressing. He only wanted them to be okay.

"Come on," Sophie said, and took her brother by the hand.

How can anyone do this?

13

"His was a quiet life, a life lived outside the spotlight." *He was asleep."* A life devoted to a set of beliefs and values that not too long ago God-fearing men and women took for granted: to be of value to his community, to contribute to society more than he withdrew, to keep his accounts in the black . . ." *oh my,* ". . . support and protect the family he loved, to be a solid citizen and a devout Christian."

And a grunter.

Chase surveyed the room: rows of heads, mostly gray, balding, or both, slightly bowed between slumped shoulders; white men in dark jackets and matching women clothed in black. What were they thinking? Did they, too, have angry, irreverent voices in their heads? Or were they so eager, so desperate to believe that they never dared to doubt? Had they really liked him? Had they even known him? Who the hell were they? *Mom?* Was she here? Should he look for the twitch? What about the mysterious twin uncles? Of course Aaron and Sarah and the kids were there, and sitting next to them Sarah's parents and Christine, who looked slim and fit and exceedingly fuckable. There were a few familiar faces from the bank, too, though the only one he could have identified by name was Millie, the mousy little woman who'd been his father's secretary or assistant or something at the bank when Chase was still in grade school and for hundreds of years after. Most of the others could have just drifted in from a movie set, dressed for the funeral of an elderly, Caucasian, small-town banker.

"Ashton Stoller had no interest in wealth or power."

Or anything else.

"A big, fancy car would have been an embarrassment to him. He would have felt awkward and uncomfortable in an expensive handmade suit. Better than most, he understood the meaning, the importance of responsibility, and he never flinched from his duties as a citizen, a husband, a father or a man. In his quiet, confident way, he enriched the lives of those fortunate enough to get to know him." *Examples?* "I have no doubt that when Ashton Nathaniel Stoller steps forward for his final judgment, the . . ."

He'll grunt.

". . . that truly matters, his will be a warm, enthusiastic reception.

"Yes, there is always sorrow and regret in the loss of a loved one. But let us not mourn too long or too deeply the passing of this humble soul. Let us celebrate his life." *That'll be a hoot.* ". . . be an inspiration to those who remain behind while he moves on to a better world, bringing with him the tranquility . . ." *Apathy?* ". . . demonstrated every single day of his life here on Earth. When you reflect on the life of Ashton Stoller, think not of his illness or his death, but of his generosity of spirit, his courage, his unflinching faith and the wellspring of goodwill that was his benefaction to those he loved."

This was an opportunity to rewrite history, to transform a dreary life into something noble and sublime. And it was the perfect time and place to assure the living that if they continued to believe and to abide by the dictates of The Church, someone would stand before a room full of friends and acquaintances too terrified to doubt, spouting comforting lies while their lifeless remains were putrefying, being consumed by ravenous insects and bacteria.

". . . in this room have all been touched by . . . "

Another spin-doctor, spinning for the dead, for his version of God and for Church Almighty.

". . . isn't that why we are assembled here?"

The air was thick with righteousness. Someone was sniffling. *Turn the voice off. Let them be. They want this, they need it and I'd probably be far happier if I could embrace the deception. Let them have this childish bullshit if it helps. Where is the harm? Who's the injured party? Or do I just need to sneer, to find some way to feel superior because in my dark, cold heart or my overactive brain or wherever such painful truths fester, I know I'm pitifully deficient?*

". . . more than any mortal can see. For only God is qualified to fathom the intricate workings of the human heart. He is the one who makes the final judgment. But if you aspire to a life of piety and virtue, you'll not find a finer example to follow than that of Ashton Stoller." *Help.*

"Now I'd like to read from. . . ."

But there *was* harm. Their belief made them smaller somehow; it relieved them of personal responsibility, mitigated their misdemeanors and forgave their felonies, validated the wars they smugly waged in the name of Their Holy version of Right. They bent and twisted it to fit their needs and their greeds, adjusted it like a thermostat to keep their sweating to a minimum when some distant, all-but-forgotten voice whispered that *they* were the transgressors. With Faith and God to sanction their acts anything was possible; they were free to commit atrocities without the minor inconvenience of guilt.

Even if all that was true, why was he so deeply offended? He'd lied and cheated, adjusted his morals to suit dozens of situations. Why was he so invested in debunking these particular myths? Perhaps it was something as basic and unseemly as unalloyed envy. *In spite of my merciless condemnation, I'd give anything to overcome this suffocating terror of death. This is my face; the truth is a pillow.*

"Let us pray."

Who am I? A skeleton wrapped in skin. What do I want?

"A lovely service."

"Yes," Chase said and extended his hand. "Yes."

"I'm so sorry."

He smiled. "Thanks."

He'd agreed to stand outside with Aaron, to thank those who'd come, but Aaron had cornered the first couple out and was now huddled with them on the sidewalk blathering about how his father's death affected him, about his band, their plans for the future, everything but his anal itch. Given time, he'd get to it.

"You're Chase, aren't you?" It was Millie.

He nodded. "Yes."

"You probably don't remember me, but I was with your father for. . . ." She closed her eyes, shook her head.

"Hi, Millie. Are you still with the bank?"

"Oh, no. Not for years now."

"Thanks for coming."

"Yes, well. We worked together for quite a long time."

"I'm . . . I'm sure this is hard for you . . ." What was he supposed to say? ". . . hard for you, too."

"Oh yes." She did look a little sad.

"I'm sorry."

"It is difficult. We weren't really close, but. . . ."

There was nothing to say. "Do you remember Aaron?" He motioned to his brother.

"Oh yes. I remember all you kids."

"Hey, Aaron." *You thoughtless fuck.* "Remember Millie?"

Aaron turned and frowned.

"She remembers *you*."

"Yeah," Aaron said. He stared for a moment before turning back to the couple.

"Still as shy as ever," Chase said.

"Uh-huh."

An elderly couple stepped out and Chase excused himself and approached them. "Thanks for stopping by." He was grinning like an idiot.

"You must be one of Ash's boys." The man wielded a pale, swollen hand that looked as though it was upholstered with elephant hide.

"I must be."

"I knew it!" He eyed Chase. "I know your dad from the Lions Club." He grabbed his lapel and pulled it closer so Chase could see the pin. His wife just stood there like a dog waiting for its master. "You a Lion, are you?"

"Uh, no."

"*No?*"

"No."

"Well why on Earth not?"

"I, uh—"

"Great organization. You ought to join up *and fast*. Oughtn't he?" he glanced at his wife but didn't wait for a response. "Do you some good and so forth."

"Mm."

"Now I've been a member for forty-five years." He turned toward his wife. "Isn't that right?" Again, he turned back to Chase without waiting for his wife to answer. "Forty-five years."

"Well, that's a long time." Chase nodded. "That's great." *Keep nodding.*

"You said it. Great organization." He narrowed his eyes and tightened his lips. He was serious now. "*Great* organization."

"Well, okay. Thanks for being—"

"Not just a social club, you know. Lions help the blind and so on." He glanced at his wife. "Am I right?"

"All right—"

"Great way to meet like-minded businessmen, make contacts and so forth. You married? Doesn't matter. Do you a world of good, a *world* of good. Have dinners and so forth. Did a lot of good for your old man with the contacts and so on. I truly cannot see one reason on God's green Earth why an ambitious young fellow like yourself wouldn't just rush on out and join an organization that . . . now we don't just help the blind, you know, there's more to it than that, we raise money for all sorts of, you know, and you won't find a better group of—"

"Aren't there some . . . bizarre . . . ," Chase shrugged, "bizarre rituals . . . like, you know, with candles and cloaks and chanting?"

"What?" The man grimaced. "What?"

"And, well, you know, animal blood?"

"*No.*" The man drew his head back and wrinkled his brow. "No. No, no, no, no, no. That isn't so, is it?" Turned to wife, ignored her. "Now where on God's green Earth did you get such an idea?"

"I don't know." Chase shrugged. "Maybe that was one of his other clubs. He was into all kinds of weird shit and so forth." Chase excused himself.

Aaron was still babbling about his band when Chase approached him. "I'm sorry to interrupt."

"Yeah, what?"

"I need to take a break?"

"A break?"

"Potty." Chase shrugged and smiled at the couple. They looked as though they were in a trance. "Sorry."

"Oh no," the man said with enthusiasm. "We really have to run anyway."

His wife waved. "Good luck with your record album," she called out as they sprinted down the sidewalk.

"Can't you hold it?"

Chase looked up at small crowd forming at the top of the steps. He really didn't have to go, though it would be gratifying to walk away and let Aaron deal with the creeping crush of senility that was oozing out of the church. On the other hand, the consequences would be unpleasant and lasting. How could he be so fucking oblivious? "It's okay," he said. "I'm wearing my rubber pants."

"Why do you—"

"Thanks so much for coming," Chase extended a hand toward Christine and grinned. "Your support at our time of need means more than you know."

She clutched his hand and pulled him close. "Why are you being a jerk?"

"Tradition."

She sighed and shook her head. "I'm sorry about your father."

"Lovely service, wasn't it?"

"No. I could almost hear your thoughts."

"Listen to this one," he said and eyed her.

She put a cupped hand to her ear and closed her eyes. "Nope. Nothing." She shrugged. "Better check your equipment."

"Thanks so much for coming," Chase reached out toward an old man who was clinging to the railing as he struggled to negotiate the steps. "Your support at our time of need means more than you know."

"Pardon?"

"Your support means more than you know."

"What?"

"Thank you." Chase gripped his arm to help him down.

"Watch it, sonny." He jerked his arm away and continued down the steps. "That's my bad arm."

"Idiot."

"Pardon?"

"Jerk."

"Asshole." The man dug a heel into Chase's foot.

"Fucker." Chase leaned down to brush off his shoe. After taking a quick look around, he reached out and yanked one of the man's shoelaces. The man shoved him but Chase kept his grip on the shoelace as he fell. In slow motion, the old man began to lean, one leg leaving the ground, arms flailing, a windmill collapsing in a hurricane. In a vain effort to right himself, he managed to grab a passing woman's skirt, pulling it down to her knees. The woman screamed. Her schnauzer produced a high-pitched yelp as the man came to rest on top of it.

Chase was standing up looking for an escape route when someone squeezed his arm. He swung around, ready to throw a punch. Alice. "Oh. Oh." *Fuck me.* "Well—"

"I thought you'd be here."

A woman's voice. "You pulled my skirt down and squashed my Muffy."

He gripped Alice's arm and dragged her a few yards away. "Hi." *Please go away.*

She hugged him tightly. He stood there, arms dangling at his sides like a pair of dead chickens. He could hear the old man's voice: "Where is that son of a bitch?"

She pulled back and gazed up at him. "You must be upset." The sunlight was not flattering.

"Oh yes. I am." He coaxed her a little farther down the block. "I am very, very upset. This is horrible."

"I'm sorry. What were you doing on the sidewalk?"

"Looking for a contact lens." He brushed off his pants. "So, um . . . did you come here just . . . because you thought I'd be here?"

"I sure did." She smiled. More pleats than a Catholic schoolgirl's skirt.

"Is there something I can do?" A tentacle slithered around his waist.

Disembowel me. He sniffed and blinked. "I just . . . I just need some time alone."

"Aw. Are you sure?"

He stole a glance over his shoulder. The man was standing now, glowering, pointing at Chase and saying something to the woman. "I can hardly speak." He pushed his fingers hard into his eyes, twisted. "I don't want you to see me cry."

"I don't mind."

"I do. I really, really do."

She frowned. "Poor baby."

His face buried in his hands. "I'm hurting bad," he said and jogged to the end of the block and around the corner.

14

"What the heck was Alice doing there?" Aaron pulled a set of keys from his pocket.

"I don't know. She said she was just in the neighborhood."

"You didn't. . . ." Aaron looked as though he was sucking a lemon.

Chase shook his head. "I hope you don't think I'm *that* desperate."

"Kind of weird that she showed up," Aaron said. He slipped a key into the lock, turned it.

"Yeah, I guess. It was a nice service, wasn't it?"

"You liked it?" Aaron pushed the door open and turned on the light.

"Yeah. You know."

"When I saw you running I realized you really had to go."

"Yeah."

"You missed a very strange scene with some old drunk and a woman."

"Huh."

"Where did you go?"

"Oh, the um . . . the store there."

"The shoe store?"

"Yeah."

"Why didn't you just use the church bathroom?"

"I don't know. It just didn't seem right."

"You've gotten stranger."

"I prefer to think of myself as unique."

They stood side by side in the vestibule, white with eggshell trim. After a minute of silence Aaron said, "Seems a shame to sell it."

"The house?"

"He lived here for a long time."

They stepped into the living room, white with eggshell. "It's just a house. I mean, I don't think it had any other meaning to him."

"Why don't *you* move in?"

"What?" Chase turned to his brother. "Are you serious?"

"Why not? It's a nice house. You could do something interesting with it, make it more . . . whatever." The tan leather couch creaked as Aaron eased himself down. "It would be nice to have you living so close. You already own a third of it anyway, and I'm sure we could work out the rest of the financial details between us."

"I can't believe it."

"What?"

"He left a third to Hannah."

"Well. . . ." Aaron winced and looked at the floor.

"What?"

"He didn't."

Chase rubbed his forehead.

"A third for you and . . . well, because of Bradley and Sophie. . . ."

"I guess he thought it was safe to assume I'd never have kids."

"I have no idea what he assumed."

"He never discussed it with you?"

"He . . . he didn't think you were. . . ." Aaron sighed. "He thought you weren't there for him. He thought you hated him."

"I didn't hate him."

"I'm just telling you what he thought."

"Look, I don't care what he left me, and I'm glad he wanted to take care of Sophie and Bradley, but what about Hannah? She's still his daughter."

"She's taken care of."

"Taken care of? What does that mean?"

"It means there's money put aside, a separate account to take care of her."

"To keep her in there."

"It's not cheap."

"Lucky her."

"It's not like she could move in here."

"No," Chase said. "Not now anyway." Exhaustion was sucking him down like quicksand. "I suppose he did the right thing, at least from his perspective."

"What about *your* perspective?"

He shook his head. "Not available at this time."

"Excuse me?"

"None of it makes sense to me."

"None of what?"

"Death, family, life in general. None of it makes any sense."

"I know you don't want to hear this, but a little faith might help."

"I'm glad it helps you, Aaron. I really am. But I'm afraid I'm just not susceptible."

Even as a child he'd been a skeptic. Logic and reason had always obstructed the path to belief. But he'd been listening when God was mentioned, had heard the harsh warnings about doubt—the faithless were subject to God's awful wrath; there were plagues, there was death, blindness and terrible suffering for generations to come; even your animals were targeted, which was so unjust. So for a time he struggled to find a way around the impediments to his faith, to find anything to hold on to, just in case. But if God knew his mind, wouldn't God know that his efforts were no more than a desperate act of deception, that some part of him could never believe? Still, his faithlessness brought him little satisfaction.

"Okay. I'm not going to preach at you."

"Thanks. It wouldn't be much fun for either of us."

"But I will play big brother long enough to suggest that there isn't much of a future in married women."

"What are you talking about?"

"It was kind of obvious that you were taken with Haley."

Something cold and sharp in his gut. "Oh, that." He swallowed hard, closed off his throat to force back a scream. "Just practicing."

"I'm no expert, but wouldn't it be more practical to practice on someone who's available. At least Christine's not married."

"Yeah," he said, his voice even, his insides in icy knots. "I'm really not looking for a relationship right now."

"Didn't you used to have a sense of humor?"

"I guess it's gone underground."

"I miss it."

"I pretty much keep it to myself these days . . . out of respect for those around me."

"That's a shame."

"Well, it's not always fit for public consumption."

Aaron scrutinized him. "I really wish you'd think about moving in. I miss having you around."

"Really? Even without my sense of humor?"

"Yeah. I miss you."

"Why?"

"Well. . . ." He didn't seem to have an answer.

Anyone else would have noticed his absence as they worked together emptying drawers and stacking papers. But Aaron was so deep inside himself that he failed to sense the scraping of desire against newfound knowledge, failed to feel the heat of his brother's mushrooming rage, detonable now by the faintest spark.

"All the big stuff is inventoried, the furniture and appliances and all that, so all we need to do is collect the personal things. It's really not much, but there are a few things I want and I imagine you'll want some of it."

"I don't know."

"At least he didn't collect a bunch of crap. I've got stuff from when I was ten years old. I know I'll never do anything with it and the kids aren't interested in it, but I don't want to throw it out. It just sits there in boxes. He hardly kept anything."

"Of course not."

"Let's not get into that."

"All I'm saying is he wasn't big on attachments."

"He didn't get caught up in his emotions and wasn't especially demonstrative, but that doesn't mean he didn't feel."

"I'd feel a lot better about him, and *for* him, if we found evidence of some secret affair, some kind of passion, a woman or a dog he loved, or an old sled. Even Millie the bank squirrel would be better than nothing."

"He had his work and his family."

"Maybe he had his work. I'm not so sure he was passionate about that either. It was just the thing he did, and because there wasn't anything else in his life, we all assumed he cared about it."

"Most people don't love their work. They do it because . . . well, because that's what you do."

"Most of the world has other interests. If all you have is your work, and your work means nothing, what do you have?"

"Maybe you want too much. Life isn't here for your enjoyment. You know, the idea that life should be fun and satisfying is relatively new; it's a modern construct. Anyway, we're here for another purpose."

Chase pulled a drawer out of the desk they were emptying and held it to his chest. "Maybe. Maybe I do want too much. But what's wrong with that? Why should I ignore my desires? I can't help what I want. I don't want to be one of them."

"One of who?"

He set the drawer down. "Did you ever notice those huge apartment complexes on Route 80, on the left a few miles before you get to the George Washington Bridge?"

"Maybe. I don't know."

"They make me sick, I mean physically ill. I see them and I can taste the bile in the back of my throat. My stomach starts to tighten before they're even in sight. They could suck the personality, the passion, the life out of anyone. I look at them and I think . . . I think, what do they do, what do the people in there do? How can they stand it? You'd have more relevance as an individual in an ant farm. How can they live there without killing each other or blowing their own fucking brains out? How can they care about anything? Cardboard cutouts fucking the neighbor's cutout wife with a little cutout dick between identical yawns. Let's all watch some TV while we suck down some cardboard cookies. Then let's kill ourselves. God, just thinking about them nauseates me. Who the fuck are they? Look at me. I'm sweating."

"Why do they have to be so awful? You're so judgmental. How do you know there aren't bright, talented, even passionate people living there?"

"Because their brains would catch fire."

"You'd rather spend your life being pissed off than—"

Chase laughed. "You think I like feeling this way? You think it makes me feel good about myself? It's fucking horrible, but I can't help it. I didn't ask for this, and really, at this point, despite what you think, I don't give a shit whose fault it is. I don't care if it's Mom's or Dad's or my lesbian Sunday School teacher's fault or because I jerked off too much when I was ten and I always thought someone was watching. I'm just fucking sick of it and no, I don't want your God and he wouldn't take me if I did, and I can't adopt your attitude and it wouldn't fit if I tried it on, and I can't just fall in love with Christine because she happens to possibly be available, and you don't want to hear any of this because it's too personal and it's not about you and your imaginary life as an aging pop failure."

Aaron glared at his brother. "You've always been an asshole."

"Can't argue with that."

They stood facing each other in their dead father's study.

"I have to make a call, Aaron. When I come back in, it would be great if you just gave me a job that I can do alone so I don't offend you with my hostility and, more importantly, so we don't end up punching each other and bloodying the deep pile wall-to-wall or scuffing the white paint or eggshell trim."

"You really don't have to come back. I can do it myself."

"No, you can't."

The phone trembled against his ear. "Haley, this is Chase, the guy you cheated on your husband with. It would be really swell if you would call me back. I'd like to have a little discussion about honesty and integrity."

The sun was low and swollen, a few silver ribbons hovering just above it, their crimson veins glowing in the darkening sky.

Chase turned and surveyed his father's house, white with white trim. What happens when people like that are alone? Do they sit and stare? Everyone's a stranger. Everyone will always be a stranger. There is no closeness, no connection. It's all illusion, delusion. All the houses here had secrets no one would ever know. Worse, few would care. And nothing shocked anymore. Everything was possible and the worst wasn't unlikely. We all cheat and lie and fuck and get all caught up in our suffering and self-importance and it's all shit. Aaron's music is perfect. They are nothing coated in sugar. *Cunt.*

Maybe their father was the exception. Probably he had no dirty secrets, but that wasn't because he was better; it was because he lacked the interest, the will to act. He had no desire. Maybe that was even worse. Maybe not. Chase was leaning back against his car gazing at nothing when his phone rang. Her number flashed.

"Well hi there."

"I'm at work. I can't really talk."

"Excellent."

"I wasn't hiding anything."

"You weren't revealing anything."

"I wear a ring, Chase. Didn't you notice?"

"No. I don't look for rings."

"You really should."

"That's helpful."

Silence.

"So where is your hubby?"

"Away. On business."

"Where was all his man-stuff?"

"His things are there, in the house. If you'd looked around a little you would have noticed. There are two toothbrushes and a razor in the bathroom cabinet and his clothing hangs in the closet. I keep the house neat, but I don't hide anything."

"Did you tidy up before going out last night?"

She sighed.

"Okay, I have another question. Why, when I asked you out at my brother's house, did you give my being all messed up as a reason not to?"

"It was the truth. That was the reason."

"Then why the hell did you . . . did you invite me home?"

"Partly for the same reason I guess."

"What does that mean?"

"Maybe I'm attracted to messes."

"Well gee, I feel better now. Is there a club?"

"What would you like me to say?"

"Not a fucking thing." He pressed disconnect.

He turned and looked down at his car, bit his lower lip. *Breathe. Can you cry now? I don't even know her. Calm down. Drive somewhere; look at the scenery. Breathe.* He opened his car door and stepped in, grabbed the steering wheel and pulled, felt it give. "Fucking cunt." He got out. A flash of white. Someone screaming, hammering on something. Craters appear, silver blue with creases. The pounding of drums. *My hands.*

15

"Someone was trying to call you. I wasn't going to pick it up but it just kept ringing and I thought it might be important. Anyway, it was a woman. It sounded like Haley. I hope you don't mind, but I told her you were here."

Chase looked down at his hands. They were both wrapped in bandages and the middle finger on his right hand was in a cast. "Can you please make this bed go up?"

"Yeah." Aaron pressed a button and Chase's feet rose. Another and the entire bed began to sink.

"Please don't make me kick the priest."

Aaron laughed. "*There* it is."

"What?"

"Your sense of humor."

"Just a little psychotic break and I'm Mr. Hilarity." He remembered reviving next to his car, Aaron standing over him, the ride in the ambulance, the pain in his hands, the swelling, but it was all viewed through a fog.

"It works for me."

"Well that's all I care about."

"Me, too."

"Good one."

"It's in the genes."

"Lucky us. So how much damage did I do?" The admitting process was a shadowy blur of dull-eyed faces, mumbled questions and steadily increasing pain. After some debate they'd anesthetized him. Nothing else remained.

"The roof of your car looks like you got caught in the mother of all hailstorms."

"Fuck. What about my hands?"

"You broke the middle finger on your right hand and mashed up your left."

"That was the plan."

"By the way, the doctor who took care of you said to say hello. Remember Richard Best?"

"Dicky?"

"Yup."

"I screwed his girlfriend in twelfth grade."

"Carla?"

"Yeah. He hated me after that."

"Well, they're married now. Anyway, he set the finger and they did what he could for the bruising. He doesn't know why you were unconscious, but didn't seem terribly concerned."

"Great. I finally have an excuse for giving everyone the finger. When did you talk to her?"

"About ten minutes ago."

"I'm sorry."

"About what."

"Doing this."

"It's okay." He shrugged. "I hardly ever get to stay out late."

"I'd like to go before she gets here."

"You'll have to ask the nurse about that."

"No, I won't." He took a corner of the sheet in his mouth and leaned forward to rest it on his bicep above the IV. With his teeth he tore off the tape.

"Stop it!"

"I'm fine." He blew the tape off of his lip. "I don't want to see her."

Aaron frowned.

"I'm not having a breakdown. In fact I'm calm as can be. I just don't want to be in a hospital. It's not like I can drive anywhere." He took the IV in his mouth and yanked it out and folded his arm over the sheet to absorb the blood. "Will you please help me get dressed?"

"I don't know."

"Please? I'll go sleep at dad's house tonight and tomorrow I'll see a doctor. We can even stop for a beer on the way."

Aaron checked his watch.

"I'll buy."

She was sitting on the hood of her dusty blue Passat drinking a beer when they pulled up.

"You don't have to talk to her if you don't feel like it."

"It's all right. You go ahead home. Tomorrow we'll finish whatever it is we're doing here."

Aaron stepped out and opened the car door for his brother. "I'll walk you in and get you settled."

"No. Thanks."

When Aaron's lights had faded Haley slid off her hood. "How are your hands?"

"They'll be okay, I think."

"Who the hell are you?"

"Excuse me?"

"You don't even know me. You wanted to fuck and we fucked."

"You're pissed at me?"

"You act like I owe you something."

"You don't owe me anything."

"*I* know that, but I don't think *you* do."

"Consider me among the newly educated."

"How are you going to . . . to do anything?"

"I'm not going to do much."

"Good."

"What are you so pissed off about?"

She came closer. "You call me at work and give me all this attitude and make me feel like a bitch and all we did was sleep together."

"Yeah, that's definitely all we did."

"I thought I was giving you what you wanted."

"Very generous."

"It wasn't generous."

"Then what was it?"

"It was . . . nothing."

"Mm. I feel better now."

"It was what I had."

"I feel sorry for your husband."

"So do I."

He shook his head and began to walk toward the house.

"May I please come in?"

"Why?"

"Because. . . ."

"Yes?"

"Because I want to."

"I guess it's up to you."

They hadn't spoken, not another word, and now, again, she was gone, off to work or to another liaison or to her cuckold or to shoot up and write poetry or to slit her lovely wrists and watch the ice seep out. Now you see it; now you wish you hadn't. He'd eased himself down onto his father's recliner and she'd taken a seat on the couch. For a while he just sat there avoiding her eyes as though he'd done something wrong. Then he looked up at her, challenging her with his gaze, or trying to. Glasscutter eyes. Ten or fifteen minutes passed before she moved. Silent and expressionless, she rose. She reached out toward him just as she had the night before. Had it only been one day? His hands ached and there was a new pain in his right knee. He was tired and uncomfortable, disgusted and on the verge of tears. Sex couldn't do him any harm, assuming that was what she had in mind. It would take his mind off the pain, and sex without emotion was not unfamiliar territory. She took his wrists in her hands and helped him to his feet and he led her to his father's bedroom, just to add an element of surreptitious hostility to whatever they were doing. She helped him out of his clothes and onto the bed, where she passed her body softly over his, moving up until she was astride him.

Afterwards she slumped down onto him, resting her head on his chest. He was sure he'd seen tears in her eyes and he wanted to say or do something, to touch her. He was glad for the bandages.

He sat up now and surveyed the room, white with eggshell trim. He was eager to get to work, to take his mind off of Haley, but the bandages were big and bulky and his knee was sore.

In the bathroom cabinet he found a pair of scissors. With his left hand he nudged them into the sink and then maneuvered them up toward the brim. Kneeling down, he placed the cool metal handle into his mouth. He stood up and with one end of the handle in his mouth he wedged the other between his bandaged hands and pulled the scissors open. Then he held his left hand out and slid one blade as far under the bandage as it would go. After a few failed attempts he was able to cut through the gauze. He dropped his arm and watched as the bandage unraveled onto the floor.

The hand looked like a lion's chew toy.

Naked in his father's study, he opened drawers and rooted through papers, his purpose nearly forgotten in the activity. There had to be something more to the man, something he loved or hated or cared about or wanted. Did he grieve when Mom left? There were financial statements, some photos from his service in the Army and a few yellowed articles about his own father. Did he care at all, about her, about them? Where were the wedding photographs, the family albums, the love letters and precious childhood treasures? Was he really that empty? *Did you kill her? I might understand.*

In the bedroom Chase continued his search, digging through the dresser drawers, sweeping onto the floor dress shirts, sweaters and cufflinks, monogrammed handkerchiefs and dozens of blue-and-gold Lions Club pins. Maybe he'd find a vial of animal blood. He smiled. The closet was neat and tidy and there were no surprises. He'd dressed like a Republican, looked like a Midwestern Senator on a budget, if such a creature existed. He'd been clean and proper and careful and as empty and meaningless as a hooker's moans of ecstasy.

Chase stepped over to the window. A neat green lawn with neat green hedges. A neat, orderly life, colorless, routine and inconsequential, like a 1950s sit-com without the laugh track. Maybe that was it. It was a revelation: his father was Fred MacMurray, minus the heart, the wisdom, the charm and the humor. He'd been searching desperately for some proof of his father's humanity. The problem was that what he thought he wanted to find didn't exist. The man was what he appeared to be, nothing more. So what? His mother had disappeared and he would never know how or why and his father probably hadn't felt anything more than a minor twinge of confusion, and possibly relief. Oh well. If there was any message at all, it was this: it doesn't matter. People are weak, flawed, sometimes ignorant or cruel or both, and always disposable. Ashton Stoller spent his life running on automatic and that worked for him, by golly. Probably, it never occurred to him that there might be something beneath the surface, and he certainly lacked the curiosity and imagination to look for anything he couldn't touch. A worker ant, he did what was required of him. Okay. It was time to put it behind him now, time to stop using it as a crutch or an excuse and move on. *Visit your sister, find a purpose or whatever it is that will make this life sentence bearable.*

 Chase raised his eyes. Bulky clouds curled and crashed against each other like windswept waves, swirling gray shapes merging and dispersing. Let it go ahead and pour. And give me some thunder, some violence. Make me feel. Turn this into noise. Out of the corner of his eye Chase saw a flash of red. Another flash. It was moving up the driveway, peeking between the trees. A police car skidded to a halt at the end of the driveway. The doors flew open and two officers emerged. It was like watching a movie. Guns drawn, they surveyed the area, creeping like TV thieves toward the house. One of the officers looked up at the window and Chase shrugged and shook his head. What were they doing? The officer was holding his gun in both hands now, aiming up at the window, and he was yelling something as the other one rushed the house. "What's your problem?" Chase mouthed.

"Put your hands above your head." Through the windowpane the policeman's voice sounded shrill and remote, like a radio blaring in another room. A thud from downstairs, footsteps. A voice from behind him. "Don't move."

Chase froze. "Could you two please agree on what you want me to do?"

"Put your hands over your head and get down on the floor."

"I don't think so," Chase said.

"What?"

His heart drumming some accelerating primitive rhythm, Chase turned around. "This is ridiculous."

"Don't do anything stupid."

"You're the professionals." He grinned.

"I'm going to ask you again to raise your hands."

"You think I'm going to shoot you with my dick or beat you to death with my broken hand?"

The officer pulled a walkie-talkie from his belt and told his partner to come up. Then he unhooked his handcuffs from his belt. "Put your hands behind your back."

"I'm not doing your dance."

The other cop stepped into the room, his gun drawn. "Looks like we caught him with his pants down, Frank."

"Caught me doing what?"

"I'd say it's pretty obvious."

"Standing naked at my father's window?"

"That's a good one," Frank said. "Don't you usually do this on the day of the funeral?"

"I have no idea what you think I'm doing."

Frank scanned the room. "You're stealing from dead folks and their grieving families." He nodded grimly.

"Let's just cuff him and take him in, Frank."

"You're not going to cuff me."

"Oh really?" Frank took a step toward him. His hands were quivering and his uniform was spotted with perspiration, his broad, pale face a fertile garden of grog blossoms.

"Do you know whose house this is?" Chase said.

"I read the obits, too." Frank was apparently the spokesman.

"Do you remember his name?"

He just glared.

"Well, see, his last name was Stoller. Now, if one of you overpaid underachievers would just grab the pants over there on the floor and take my wallet out of the back pocket you'll find my identification, on which it shows my last name, which is also Stoller. Would either of you care to guess why that is?"

"Guy's a real clown, isn't he," the other one said. His teeth were at odds with one another, a row of faded yellow shacks knocked from their foundations in an earthquake.

"Just take a look."

"Shut up." Frank again.

The heat was increasing. "You're trespassing in my father's house."

"I said shut up."

"Just take a look at my wallet. I want to see if apes really blush."

"If you're his son, why were you in such a hurry to go through his drawers," the other one asked, motioning to the mess on the floor.

"That's none of your fucking business. Now I'm going to get my pants . . ." Chase started toward the bed.

Frank raised his weapon higher. "Stop right there."

". . . and put them on." He sat down on the bed. "And you're going to ask your partner to read the name on my license and then you're going to get the fuck out of this house."

"You reach for those pants and—"

"Despite evidence to the contrary," Chase said, waiting for his life to pass before him in a series of depressing slapstick vignettes, "I don't think you're dumb enough to risk shooting a grieving son in his dead father's home." He reached down for his pants, slid his feet in and rose. With his injured hands it was difficult, but he finally worked the pants up to his hips. "My wallet is in here." He turned his back to them. "Leave the cash."

The cold barrel of the gun prodded his back as the wallet slid from his pocket. He turned and watched Frank open it. His jaws hurt from clenching his teeth and he was shaking, with anger, with fear. He wanted to scream. You ignorant motherfuckers.

"Could be you. I'm just not entirely sure."

Chase swallowed hard. He tasted blood. "Arrest me or get the fuck out." He turned to face them.

The other cop looked at the walls. "There's been a lot of burglaries around here. Some creep breaking in during funerals. We was out here this time, but nobody showed. Then today we got a call someone was here. You can see why we thought—"

"Fuck you and your little sister Frank."

"You know," Frank said, his eyes dull slits of rage. "I'd be willing to bet we could find a thing or two to arrest you for."

"Maybe, but then all the other Girl Scouts would see what fucking assholes you are." Please *shut up before they kill you.*

"Come on Frank." The other officer reached for Frank's arm and Frank jerked it away.

"I'll be looking for you, slick." He turned toward the doorway.

"My ass turn you on?"

"That's it." Frank spun around, his jaw so tight the muscles rippled.

"No!" His partner's voice was firm. He turned toward Chase. "Don't push it, buddy." He slapped Frank on the shoulder. "Come on. Let's get out of here."

Chase sat on the bed, closed his eyes and breathed deeply. Assholes. Fucking assholes.

Yes, they were assholes. But at how many points could he have stopped the escalation? And when was he going to push someone too far? It was an entertaining story, one that might be fun to tell after a few beers, but only because they hadn't beaten him to death or shot his dick off. If he'd listened, waited and explained when he had the opportunity, they'd be embarrassed now, apologizing for their error, politely asking him to forget the whole thing. Instead, they were probably plotting his murder and dismemberment. What was he trying to prove?

Naked Funeral Burglar Gunned Down
Robbing Dead Father's Home

Armed with nothing more than their official police firearms and their wits, courageous Stroudsburg officers Quarrel and Lardy brought down the man responsible for the recent string of burglaries. The perpetrator, whose arsenal included a fully loaded, medium-size penis, a fresh mouth and a broken hand, resisted arrest when approached by the officers, who had no alternative but to blow his fucking brains out the back of his head. "We had no alternative but to blow his fucking brains out the back of his head," said officer Quarrel. "Plus which, we'd seen his privates."

Downstairs he opened the refrigerator: Kraft American cheese and Miracle Whip. Where was the Wonder Bread? He let the door fall shut. In a cupboard was a box of Cheerios. Trying to ignore the pain in his hands, he poured some in a bowl and took a carton of milk from the refrigerator. He opened the spout and sniffed. Rotting gym socks stuffed with old bleu cheese. He was hungry and the incident with the police was gnawing at his gut. The hostility built inside him until he felt capable of murder and a minute later it was replaced by overwhelming shame and regret. No matter how right he might have been, his behavior was irrational and self-destructive. Was he trying to get beaten or killed? No. It wasn't that. At least he didn't think it was. It was undiluted rage. But at what? Anything would have set him off. Apparently beating his car up wasn't enough. Then he thought of Haley. Do I call her or let it go? How much worse can it get? The ringing of his father's telephone startled him. He stepped over and pressed the button for speakerphone.

"Hello?"

"I guess they haven't cut the phone off yet."

"They'll probably do it while we're talking."

"You sleep okay?"

"I think so."

"I figured you'd want to sleep in."

"Thanks."

"Plus I had some things to do this morning."

A crack of thunder. "The police stopped by this morning."

"What did they want?"

"Just checking in, I guess."

"You think we can finish up if I come over now?"

"Sure."

He held the bowl of Cheerios under the faucet and turned on the water.

16

Raindrops pelted the windows, pebbles hurled by an irate mob. The wind buffeted the house and thunder snapped and growled in the distance, someone whipping a lion. Aaron had brought cardboard boxes and they'd spent the morning emptying closets and drawers, deciding what to throw away, what to give to charity, what to sell and what to keep. Now Aaron was marking the boxes and Chase was going through the bills.

"I still think you should move in."

"What the hell would I do here?"

"For a living?"

"For anything."

"Well, there's plenty of married women."

Chase leaned back in the dining room chair. "Between affairs I guess I could beat up cars."

"You fuck her?"

"No."

"Really?"

"She fucked me."

"What does that mean?"

Chase shrugged.

When the rain subsided they went out to the garage. A big Buick dominated the space.

"White," Chase said.

"He always bought white cars."

"White Buicks." Chase peered at the interior. "What would you call those colors?"

"I don't know," Aaron said. "Chocolate, I guess, and beige."

Chase smiled.

Aaron rolled his eyes. "Why?"

"No reason."

"Please don't punch it."

On the far wall hung a rake and two shovels, next to them on the floor was an unopened bag of salt. Two green plaid lawn chairs leaned against the wall, their aluminum frames dull with age and dust. On the floor next to them were a mower and a gasoline can. Bolted to the back wall of the garage was a small wooden workbench, spotless and uncluttered, over which hung a shelf that held three cardboard boxes.

"Did he ever use that?"

"The workbench?"

"Yeah. I just can't see him . . . fixing stuff."

"I don't know. Probably not."

"Did he ever play any sports, golf or tennis?"

Aaron frowned. "Now what are you trying to say?"

"I'm not trying to say anything. I'm just wondering what he did with all his spare time."

"Don't you feel just a little guilty for not knowing this stuff?"

"A little." He shrugged. "Not much I can do about it now."

"Well, he read the paper," Aaron said. "He went to Lions Club. He liked to go to the Laundromat."

"The Laundromat? Why didn't he just buy a washer and dryer?"

"I don't know. Maybe he just wanted to be around people."

"Since when did he like people?"

Aaron exhaled noisily, his traditional huff of exasperation.

"I'm not trying to start a fight. I'm actually wondering if he wasn't just terribly depressed."

"I don't think—"

"I know he never would have called it that, or thought there was anything special or unusual about him. If he gave it any thought he would have assumed that was just the way life was, that no one really enjoyed anything, that everyone sleepwalked through their lives."

"We really didn't talk in much detail about religion, but it's possible that he just thought of this life as a stopover. If you know there's something else all of this becomes far less important."

"I'm sorry, but to discard an entire life because of a fantasy just scares the shit out of me. What a horrible waste."

Aaron smiled his glassy-eyed, knowing smile.

"Even if you do believe there's something else, why not at least try to enjoy this?"

"Maybe he was fulfilled."

"By the Lions Club and laundry?"

"I'm not saying it's necessarily the right choice. I'm not qualified to make that judgment."

"I could see it if that made him happy. I have nothing against illusions if they actually make you feel better." Chase stepped over to the workbench. "Never mind." He smiled. "I'm sorry. Let's get this done."

"You want to hop up there and pull those boxes down?"

"I wish I could," Chase said. He held up his hands and grinned. "I really do."

"I can wait."

"You go ahead." Chase nodded. "I'll watch."

"Really. I'm in no hurry."

"Did you bring a pillow?"

"I've got all the time in the world."

"Remember the Ping-Pong tournament?"

Aaron laughed.

Chase was ten or eleven when they got the Ping-Pong table. Up to that point neither of them had had much interest in sports of any kind. When the two of them played together it was mostly board games, squirt guns, spies or battles in the woods, but within weeks they were both obsessed and, despite the age difference, the competitions were fierce. Sometimes they'd play for hours without a break. One day late in autumn they decided to have a tournament; they would play one hundred games and whoever won the most games would be crowned Ping-Pong champion of the universe. It was a long day and they were always within a couple games of each other; by the time they got past ninety games they were both exhausted, their feet were sore and blisters oozed on their hands. They were tied at forty-seven games each when Chase slammed a ball that bounced off the wall behind Aaron and rolled under the table, where it stopped. For a minute neither of them moved.

"Get the ball," Aaron finally said.

"You get it."

"You hit it."

"Yeah, but it's your serve."

"It's closer to you."

"You're older. Your arms are longer."

"So?"

"It's easier for you to reach."
"You don't have to bend down as far."
"Huh?"
"You're shorter."
Chase set his paddle on the table and folded his arms.
"Are you going to get it," Aaron said.
"No."
"I'm not getting it."
"I'm not getting it."
"Me either."
"I mean it."
"Me, too."

They stared at each other, both trying to look casual and unconcerned. After about ten minutes of silence Chase said, "Want to quit?"
"Do you?"
"Sure."
"Okay."

They shrugged and walked away from the table. That was the end of the tournament.

Aaron climbed up onto the workbench.
"Any reason you didn't use the ladder," Chase said.
"What ladder?"
Chase motioned to a rope that hung over the workbench. The free end was knotted and the other end was tied to a spring-loaded metal ladder.

Aaron stared up at the contraption. "Where did that come from?" He pulled a box out and placed it on the workbench. "At least they're light."

With his left hand Chase pushed open the top of the box. "Rags," he said.

Aaron set another box beside it and Chase pulled up the flaps. "More rags." With his left hand he pulled out a blue one. "Very fancy." A pair of women's panties dangled from his finger.

"Think he had enough rags?"

"He probably washed his car three times a day." Chase tugged at a swatch of pink. It was another pair of panties. "Aaron?"

Aaron glanced down. "No thanks. You can have them."

Chase shook his head. "This kind always gets stuck in my crack." He put them down and reached deep into the box. Nothing but panties. "Aaron?"

Aaron placed a third box on the workbench and leaned down to open it.

"I don't think we need to go through these now," Chase said.

"That's what we're here for." Aaron pulled back the flaps on the third box. "What the hell?" He adopted the expression of someone who'd awakened next to a dead moose.

Chase reached in and withdrew a yet another pair, white with vertical stripes of pale blue. Next he extracted a thong, pale green and big enough to fit a pregnant buffalo. He reached his hand deep into the box and brought out a handful of panties, assorted styles, sizes and colors. He dropped them onto the workbench and stood back to scrutinize them. It began as a tremor. He looked up at Aaron and held his breath to keep it in, then he looked down at the boxes, turned away. A snicker escaped, then another. He held his breath and thought about death. The first burst of laughter shot out like shrapnel. He wheezed and cackled until his stomach began to cramp. He looked up. Even through his tears he could see the contempt on Aaron's face. He forced himself to stop. "I'm sorry." He chuckled, swallowed and choked it back. "Maybe he just used them as rags."

"Right."

"I mean, you know, to clean up after he whacked off." He laughed.

"Shut up."

"Sorry."

Aaron climbed down. "At least they aren't all one size."

"What?"

"Well, he didn't . . . he didn't wear them." He grimaced. "Did he?"

Chase held up a pair that would have fit an anorexic cheerleader. "No, I don't think he did. Not around his waist."

"Where did he get them? What do you . . . what do you think he . . . ?"

"Who knows?"

"Is that a joke?"

"What?"

"Who *nose*?" He pointed to his nose.

Chase giggled. "It wasn't supposed to be."

"What the hell did he do with them?"

Chase rubbed his chin. "There are just so many possibilities."

"Are they new?"

"New?"

"I mean, have they been worn?"

Chase assumed a grave expression, forced a serious tone, a newscaster aspect. "I'd say they've seen some use, Aaron." *Don't laugh.* "There are some signs of . . . ," he pursed his lips, picked up a pair, stretched the waistband, ". . . of wear and tear."

"Don't."

"What?"

"Put them down." Aaron rubbed his head and frowned. He shook his head. "I can't deal with this."

"Okay, let's just put them back and I'll get rid of them later."

"He . . . he sniffed them, didn't he?"

"Yes." Chase let out a laugh, stopped himself. "Yes, Aaron, I believe he did."

"Why?" Aaron waved his hands in the air. "And where did he *get* them all?"

Chase shrugged.

"I mean, can you get stuff like this on eBay?"

"Maybe poonie bay."

Aaron glared.

"Maybe he snatched them, or got them from Victoria's secretion?"

"Stop!"

"Sorry."

"I can't believe you're enjoying this."

"He just became human."

"No." Aaron shook his head frantically. "No. He just became a . . . a panty sniffer."

"Well, I think that's uniquely human. I mean, can you think of another animal that does that?"

"Yeah. Dogs. Dogs do it."

"Oh . . . yeah."

Aaron just stood there shaking his head. "You're happy because we found something . . . something negative about him."

"That's not true, Aaron. It really isn't. It may not mean much to you right now, but . . . well, at least he had something that gave him pleasure."

"Why couldn't he have been a . . . a rooftop sniper?"

"There could be other boxes."

Aaron leaned back against the workbench and stared down at the floor. "God damn it."

"Hey, just because he. . . . Just because—"

"Go on. Just because his wife disappeared and he sniffed and collected—how many pairs of panties would you say we've got here?" He emptied a box on the floor. "Maybe a hundred, two hundred?" He dumped the second box, then pulled his leg back and gave the pile a vigorous kick. Panties flew into the air. A couple pairs landed on the hood of the car, one landed on Chase's shoulder and a black pair clung to Aaron's shoe. He tried to shake it off. It just fluttered like a pennant as he kicked and jiggled his leg. "Fucking fuck." He gave one final kick and fell back against the workbench. The panties shot into the air.

"Enemy fire," Chase screamed as they whizzed past his head. They landed on the car's roof. "Black frock down."

"Don't." Aaron tried to choke back a laugh.

Chase grabbed a pair from the hood of the car. "Gland grenade," he yelled, and tossed it across the garage.

17

"Shit." Aaron sighed and set his glass down on the table. "How the hell am I going to tell Sarah?" They were sitting at their father's kitchen table eating stale pretzels and sipping Four Roses.

"Why would you want to tell her?"

"I tell her everything."

"Why?" Chase leaned back. "Why would you do such a thing?"

"Relationships, ones that last, are built on honesty and trust."

"Are you serious? Who fed you that crap?"

"Well . . . ," Aaron wrinkled up his face, "Dad, for one."

They stared at each other.

"I'm a moron." Aaron took a sip.

"Well, no, but even without this latest discovery, he's about the last person I would have gone to for relationship advice."

Aaron shrugged. "It was just something he said at our wedding, but he's not the only one."

"Remember the other thing he used to say, the thing he always said when we talked about other people?"

"No. What?"

"You'll be happier and you'll probably live a lot longer if you keep your nose out of other people's business."

"So."

"Maybe if it hadn't been for those panties...."

Aaron chuckled. "I guess that's funny, but I can't stop thinking about Sarah."

"Well, I'm obviously not an expert on the subject of lasting relationships either, but I've got to tell you, I think total honesty is grossly overrated. If you feel you absolutely must tell her, which seems mildly pathological to me, you might want to first ask her if she's had any underwear mysteriously disappear since you two have been together."

Aaron's mouth dropped open.

"He had to get them somewhere."

"No." Aaron shook his head frantically. "I refuse to believe that."

"I'm sorry. You're right. He wouldn't have done that."

Aaron sighed. "Who knows what he would have done."

"Well, it turns out he was human. I'm as surprised as you are, but there are worse things in the world than a little fetish. He probably just needed—"

"How could he do this to me?" Aaron squeezed the bridge of his nose.

"Hold on," Chase said. He rested his hand on his brother's arm. "Now, can you tell me what's wrong with that question?"

"Well, I know what *you* think is wrong with it, but I would be willing to bet Hannah isn't bothered by it, and you're actually enjoying it. So, who else does it affect?"

"I don't know. Maybe no one, but I'm sure you were the farthest thing from his mind when he was doing whatever he did with those . . . things."

"That's pretty selfish if you ask me."

"Would you feel better if he'd been thinking about you while he was playing truffle pig with some purloined butt floss?"

"You're fucked up. You really are."

"I'm serious. This had absolutely nothing to do with you."

"I can't believe you're defending him. You didn't even like him."

"Not very much. No. And I'm really not thrilled about this either. I'd prefer to have found pictures of a girlfriend, but this does make him seem less . . . mechanical and uninterested."

"And more disgusting."

"I just don't see any reason for you to change the way you felt . . . the way you feel about him. Nothing else has changed. Remember, you're the one who had a good childhood, good parents. If that was true yesterday, it's true today. There's no reason to give that up for a few . . . a few hundred pairs of panties." He swigged his drink. "The truth is that we have no idea what he did with them. If you're going to make assumptions about someone you love, make them good ones."

Aaron rubbed his forehead. "Who are you?"

"I have no idea." That seemed pretty close to the truth.

But that wasn't quite it. It was more a question of whether he could do this any longer, and why he should try. Of course none of it made sense—that he'd recognized and reluctantly accepted long ago—but there were others who understood that, who saw what he saw, but somehow found or fabricated a reason to continue. Was motivation all he was lacking or did he also lack the tools, the emotional equipment? Did he owe someone something? Sarah was done with him, Aaron would find some way to make his death work for him and Hannah would most likely never know. His few friends would have a drink in his honor, and then another just for fun. By the end of the evening they would have moved on, the discourse turned to other matters, work, sex, sports or politics. No serious damage would be done, no lasting scars.

And yet his wasn't an entirely joyless life. Laughter was a reliable if temporary salve, and there was the warm, whimsical feeling that two glasses of wine could at times produce. Frequently he relished his work, and sex could be intoxicating, even rapturous. And then there was that elusive thing he felt when he believed, for perhaps an hour or a day, that he was in love. It tugged and twisted at something inside him, and it could cause enormous pain, albeit a warm, cuddly pain; it could bruise and cripple, but there was some affirmation in that, and a sense of validation. You are real. Tell me again. Tell me over and over again. Prove it. Make me believe. To have an impact, to make things move, change, break or grow, to create or build or destroy on a large scale, to influence and transform and to touch: these were the only proofs there were, the only proofs there would ever be. And even if he somehow achieved something great, something that provided more than a fleeting confirmation of his significance, even if he came to believe that it all mattered, that *he* mattered, that his was a good, valuable life, presiding over all of it was the promise of death, a constant, omnipresent reminder of the impermanence that ultimately guaranteed absolute irrelevance. When all traces of his life had faded or been expunged, which wouldn't be long after his death, what would have been its value? Without awareness, without consciousness, all his efforts, all his accomplishments would be utterly meaningless.

He simply lacked the internal filters required to forget or ignore what to him was as explicit as hunger, pain or fear. It was as clear and indisputable as is gravity to a man plummeting fifty stories toward the concrete.

There was something to be said for narrowing the focus. The big picture was simply too overwhelming and far too discouraging to be manageable. What about right now, today? What did he need or want? What would make him feel better? Love, sex, comfort, friendship, two good hands? What else? Hadn't there been other sources of joy before this vertiginous descent began?

Music and literature had once been a part of his life, an important part, but somehow he'd abandoned both without realizing it. For years prior to his marriage and well into the first year he'd spent hours every week on his bike; long, hard rides were exhilarating, liberating. Why had he given that up? He abhorred the gym, the air, the intimate odors. He didn't want to know that much about strange men with reams of fat and hair where hair should have the courtesy not to grow. On a bicycle there were few distractions. No matter how hard he was pushing or how swiftly the switchbacks approached, riding took him away from everything else and transported him to a state of exhausted tranquility. And there was the endorphin rush afterwards. The world was a glorious, delightful place, anything was possible—no, not just possible, likely. Wheee. So there it was. If he could work when he felt like it, listen to music and read in his leisure time, drink a couple glasses of wine with dinner every night, ride six hours a day, have sex before and after his rides and fall in love with someone new every week or two, he'd be happy, fulfilled. That might just be enough to enable him to forget for hours at a time that it was all just a hollow, fleeting joy.

Aaron was sitting back in his chair staring down at his hands. He looked as though someone had cut his power. Chase wanted to reach out, to put his hand on his brother's and tell him everything would be okay, and to mean it. Instead he poured two more glasses of bourbon.

Doctor Newman spread the file out on his desk and squinted down at it, his caterpillic eyebrows traveling up and down his forehead as he studied Hannah's history. Finally he folded his hands and sat back. "Yes, well, there's nothing out of the ordinary here."

Chase's head throbbed and he was still a little dizzy, but his thoughts were clear, or clear enough. "I just wonder if she wouldn't be more coherent, more aware, if she weren't so full of drugs."

The doctor pursed his lips, his eyebrows bobbed and he cleared his throat. "I suppose that's possible."

"Wouldn't it be better for her to know who's here, to be able to talk to her family, to communicate on some level?"

Eyebrows up, lips tight.

"She's just so . . . inaccessible."

"Hmm. Well, yes, these drugs," he scanned the file, "these drugs, at these levels, can . . . they can certainly numb a person. But your sister is, she's not equipped, the way you and I are, to deal with—"

"I know she's sick. I understand that. But wouldn't it be good for her to . . . to have the possibility of some contact with reality? I mean, how long has she been like this?"

"Like this?"

"Yeah, so out of it."

"Out of it?"

"Have you met her?"

The doctor drew a deep breath, sighed, rested his chin on his fists.

"She doesn't seem to have any idea where she is, or what's going on around her. Couldn't the medications have something to do with that?"

"There's nothing out of the ordinary about her treatment."

"I'm sorry, but do you think you could answer one of my questions? Just pick one."

"I'm just not sure I can do anything about your concerns." The doctor looked at his watch and rose.

"Sit down."

"I really—"

"Sit down. I'm not going to leave until you give me some clear answers."

The doctor rubbed his chin, sighed. "It may be that your sister would be more cogent if her meds were adjusted. But the meds keep her from acting out, and from becoming a danger to others and to herself."

"Is there any record of her ever hurting or threatening another patient or a member of your staff?"

"Well," he sat and moved the papers around, "there doesn't seem to be."

"Doesn't seem to be?"

"No. There's nothing here."

"It would be there if it happened. I mean, you do keep records of that sort of thing, don't you?"

"Well, yes."

"Why do I have to drag information out of you?"

"I don't—"

"Never mind."

"She *has* attempted to hurt herself."

"I assume that's not that unusual in a place like this."

"It happens, but we try to do what we can do diminish the likelihood of a recurrence. Your sister was disruptive for a time."

"Disruptive."

"Some of the residents are very sensitive, and when a patient acts out it creates other problems."

"You mean it's no fun?"

"You seem a little hostile, Mr. Stoller."

"I hope that wasn't your most difficult diagnosis." He grinned.

"Well. . . ."

"Listen, all I want is for my sister to have the best life she can have in her condition. Maybe it's inconvenient, maybe it's even risky to experiment with a patient who's under control. You give her her meds, pat her on the head and walk away. Maybe it's a little extra work for your staff, but if you aren't willing to make an effort I'd be perfectly happy to find myself an outside expert and, if necessary, move her somewhere else. I'm a journalist, Dr. Newman, and I know how to do the research, and people love to read about this stuff. I'd rather not make your life difficult, and moving her to another place would be inconvenient, and I realize I might find myself in the same situation, but I'm going to do whatever I have to for her. I'd just like a little cooperation. It would be best for both of us if I didn't have to prove to you that I can be more of a nuisance than an unruly lunatic."

The doctor plucked a pen from his desk and scribbled some notes on her chart. "Regardless of what you might think, Mr. Stoller, we're here to help the residents. I'll reassess her case and make some changes, as I deem appropriate. Just be aware, what you're suggesting may cause more discomfort for your sister than you anticipate."

"I don't know what to expect, but I don't think her life is likely to get much worse, and I'm sure you'll be monitoring her."

"Well, yes."

"One more thing. I want all her records and I want to be kept informed."

Doctor Newman frowned and shook his head.

"You're just too goddamned used to saying no. And I just don't want to hear it."

18

Somehow the house seemed emptier now that most of the work was done. This was a feeling beyond loneliness, as though it was he, rather than the house, that lacked any hint of human life. Even after another discouraging visit with Hannah, driving here he'd felt energized, proud of his actions on her behalf and ready to tackle the next problem, whatever it was. He would talk with his brother, *really* talk with him, make him understand that they needed each other, that if they wanted to they could still be brothers, if not in the traditional sense, then at least in a way that mattered. After that he'd deal with Haley, his wife, the economy and that horrific mess in Darfur. Then he'd get a job and think about his future, a wife, children. But by the time his headlights flashed across his father's house his confidence had crumbled. It was a physical feeling, as though his body's framework has dissolved, and with it all his hope. Had he just been temporarily intoxicated by venting his ire on the doctor, or was this descent triggered by the gradual realization that regardless of his efforts, and his own vague questions about what was motivating him—guilt for his absence, the need for closeness, the exhilaration of battle and his desire to feel potent—Hannah's life was unlikely to change.

He was hungry, weary, restless and in pain. And he was lonely. He had to do something but the thought of going out to one of the local bars was almost unbearable and driving with one damaged hand was awkward. Aaron was home with his family and the only other person he had any desire to see was a married woman who was either unwilling or unable to reveal anything beyond her corporeal self. He was reluctant to call, to make a wrong move, afraid he might frighten her away, but of course that was ridiculous. And his doubts about the wisdom of pursuing this were irrelevant. Wisdom as a driving force was feeble at best. He stepped outside and looked up at the sky. A celebration had ended and all the beautiful young women, clad in ornate gowns, had leapt, laughing, into the great black lake and drifted to the bottom, only their sequins floating to the now-undisturbed surface. No more difficult to believe than the existence of God.

"Thanks for coming." He'd been waiting outside.

"I brought pizza."

"Thanks."

"And wine."

"Perfect."

She took a box of pizza and two paper bags from her passenger's seat. With her hip she nudged her car door shut.

When he made no move toward the house she said, "Want to go inside?"

"No."

"Okay. What about a corkscrew?"

"I'll get it. And I'll get a blanket to sit on and some glasses."

They said little as they ate, and when they'd finished Haley poured them each a second glass of wine. "I haven't had a picnic in years."

"I think that's the most you've revealed about yourself since we met."

"It was an accident."

"I'd really like to know more about you."

"I'm not very interesting," she said, and turned her head away, no more than a faint shadow in the starlight.

"Is that just part of the persona you want to project, or do you really believe it."

"It's not a question of belief."

"Isn't it possible that I would find it interesting?"

"You don't have to work so hard. You're already getting what you want."

"Fuck you."

"Exactly."

He wanted to shriek, to break something. Tears threatened and now he was the one who turned away.

A chaos of news, gossip and greetings in a dozen avian dialects, shrill and urgent, sweet and dissonant. Musical. Eyes open. A pale blush filtering through silhouetted trees. Pastel morning. The comforting warmth of a sleeping body, an arm and a leg draped loosely over him, her head resting heavily on his chest, the steady rhythm of her breathing. Home. Let this be home. The grass was cool and wet with dew. Why not? What else matters? We are alive and this is all. Perhaps we can be better. He held her close, petted her head, closed his eyes tightly to keep the tears away, to stanch the flow. Stay.

"What time is it?" She raised herself up onto one elbow and squinted down at him.

"I didn't want to wake you." He glanced at his watch. "It's only 6:45."

"I have to go."

"It's early."

"I need to shower and change. I can't believe I fell asleep. Sorry." She stood up and brushed off her clothes.

"You're sorry you fell asleep?"

She shrugged.

"Please don't be." He sat up. "Can I . . . ? Is it okay with you if I like . . . if I care about you?"

"Why?"

"I don't know," he said. "Don't you feel anything?"

She winced as though she was in pain. "I feel things."

"Things." He rose.

"I'm just not foolish enough to trust."

"What happened to you?" He scrutinized her.

"Nothing very special."

"Something."

"Parents aren't to blame for everything."

"That's an interesting answer. Would you care to take a look at my father's panty collection?"

"Maybe next time."

"Next time?"

"Did I say that?"

"I couldn't swear to it."

"Phew." She allowed a playful smile.

19

Visit Hannah
Talk with her doctor or give him a break?
Learn to write better with left hand
Call Jennifer
Call David C about divorce settlement
Take kids out somewhere
Get clothing, supplies for an extended stay (how long? Is this wise? What difference could that possibly make?)
See doc about hands? Fuck me
See Haley! Please? Find out about husband and whatever it is that makes her so . . . whatever it is. Sure
Talk with Aaron re length of stay, plan for house (and panties – I get pink, he gets extra large)
~~Talk with him about Hannah?~~
What do panties really mean?
Buy a bike? Really?
Think about work (or just pry your eyes out with a butter knife)
Waitress for possible backup if needed?
Is this how you act when you feel good? Probably.

Burn list!!!

He lifted his elbow from the paper and released the pen. His hand was throbbing and he could barely read his own left-handed scrawl, but that wouldn't be an issue. It wasn't the list, but the process of writing it that seemed to fortify his memory. And the important issues would stalk him until he dealt with them or croaked.

They sat in the same seats as the last time, facing the same windows, the same restricted view. Her hands were calmer today, but her eyes remained dull, dormant, like the windows of an abandoned home. Probably Dr. Newman hadn't yet made any adjustments in her medication. Even if he had, any noticeable change this soon seemed unlikely. Chase recognized the desperation in his scrutiny, the unrealistic hopes, the yearning for some encouragement, but for years she'd been his only refuge. Now she was helpless and entirely inaccessible. Even if there was eventual improvement, any expectations of a real reunion were irrational, but perhaps her life could be a little less dreary; perhaps she didn't have to be quite so distant from everyone and everything she'd known. However flawed a lucidly perceived life was, her world looked from the outside like a neglected graveyard. He only wanted to give her something.

"Hannah." Cautiously he leaned a couple inches closer. "It's me again."

Today the place smelled of ammonia, rotting vegetables and urine, and he was restless, eager to be somewhere else. *Relax. Maybe she'll get used to you.* He wanted to make eye contact but he didn't want to make her more uncomfortable than she already was. His thoughts raced blindly. *What are you thinking?*

What are you feeling? Am I a stranger? Am I even here? Are you? Is there still a you?

After a few more minutes of silence he said, "I hope it's not too cold in there." He might have been alone in the room. *Just sit here. Just let it alone.*

When the nurse came in, he rose.

"Thanks," he said.

He looked down at his sister. Why was he trembling? "I love you," he said, and hurried out of the room.

"Nice job." Dr. Kim chuckled. "You do good work."

"I try."

"At least nothing's broken."

"What?"

"Just some nasty bruises and abrasions."

"But the doctor at the hospital. . . ." He laughed. He felt a reluctant fondness for Dicky.

Dr. Kim shook his head and gave a wave of dismissal. "Your left hand will heal quickly if you decide to treat it like part of your body. And you don't need that big bandage on your right hand. I don't know why the heck they did that. Anyway, we'll fix it up so it doesn't look so much like an obscene boxing glove."

"Are you always this much fun?"

"Depends on the day."

"So, is there anything I should do?"

"Buy a softer car maybe. Or get a bat."

"You're a hoot."

"My nurse will come in and abuse you in a minute."

"Thanks for seeing me so quickly."

"My pleasure. I can't wait to tell my wife about you."

*

Two down and it was still relatively early. He wasn't ready to call his wife or his attorney. Too depressing. Too real. He could check his e-mail and call his home answering machine, but there might be something that would require a response and he wasn't prepared to respond to anything of substance. A nap would be good except that he'd feel like a mugging victim when he woke up. He called Aaron, who seemed not to have recovered yet from the discovery of the panty arsenal. The kids would be available after three o'clock. Maybe he should just do the easy stuff.

The entire mall had apparently been airlifted stocked and fully populated from Long Island and dropped unaltered in a parking lot in Stroudsburg. Well, not quite unaltered. Based on the hairstyles and clothing it must have spent a few years in a holding pattern, during which time the inhabitants had done nothing but eat bacon cheeseburgers, curly fries and cake with extra gravy.

Sears, Penney's, Waldenbooks, prematurely aged somnambulists waddling alone or in pairs; Spencer Gifts, RadioShack, Foot Locker, stale cigarette smoke drifting like radioactive fog from the hair and clothes of blank-eyed passersby; Kay Jewelers, Pearl Vision, GNC, seven little shoebox movie theaters playing six worst-run movies; Hallmark, a half dozen wireless stores and a food court where, based on the odors, the only possible verdict was guilty of crimes against humanity. Dull-eyed, gum-chewing teenagers loitering in the halls emitting the sour, musty scent of apathy, the girls, too-seductive, dressed like apprentice whores, the boys, too-forbidding, practicing the minatory poses and attitudes they'd learned in thug school or at home, nearly all of them exhibiting the early symptoms of the obesity that, like chocolate-covered quicksand, had engulfed their parents, their aunts and uncles and teachers and parole officers. Gawd awlmighty, I'm in Uhmerrika. "Fuck." Holding his breath, he sprinted toward the exit.

In his car he dialed Haley's number. She answered after the second ring. No, I'm sorry. Not tonight. Maybe tomorrow. Sorry. Bye. It happened so fast and he was so stunned he hadn't thought to ask her why. Idiot. He began to dial again. No. He sat back, swallowed. I am at her mercy, subject to her whims, a willing victim to her moods. Willing? No, just powerless. Did she sound sorry? Was she dismissing him or was she upset? Why didn't she say she'd really like to? What was the message? How was he supposed to read her clipped responses? He wasn't.

He started his car and backed out of the space. Think about something else. Do the list. Simplify. Jeans, socks, underwear, a couple shirts. There had to be a Gap store nearby. And a drugstore for soap and shampoo, deodorant and toothpaste. He'd also need to find a grocery store for milk, eggs, coffee, orange juice, maybe bread and butter. Shit. Or he could just go back to New York and forget the entire ridiculous mess.

No. Hannah.

"Do you think I could keep the perishable things in your fridge until I bring the wonder-bunnies home?"

"I guess so." Aaron led him to the kitchen. "They're really excited. You're like a celebrity to them."

"Well, they've heard so much great stuff about me day after day."

"Yeah."

"Are you okay?"

Aaron shook his head.

"Did you say anything?"
"Not yet."
"Just forget it."
"Right."
"By the way, my hand isn't broken."
Aaron stared.
"Doctor Best finally got his vengeance."
"Uncle Chase." Sophie ran into the kitchen and wrapped her arms around his legs. She released him and darted out of the room. "Brad-ley," she sang out. "He's heeeere."

From the beginning Bradley seemed distant. Was he going to be the next heir to the family's legacy of despair? The thought that they were already doomed just because of who their parents and grandparents were was demoralizing, nauseating—innocent little victims of chemistry and poor parenting. He imagined a crowd of faceless children marching blindly forward, struggling against an invisible force that seemed always to be pushing against them but which was really inside them, slowing with each year, finally brought to a silent halt, mired down by the drear and daunting impossibility of life. At times while they were playing, Bradley's affect seemed to collapse and all that remained was an expression that simply did not belong on the face of a child of eight. Once he asked how many people you could kill with a tank. *Come back. Somebody do something. I'm afraid my nephew has been poisoned.*

Of course there were reasonable explanations for this and for all that had come before, for Ashton Stoller's emotional paralysis and his wife's simmering hostility. Even her disappearance could be explained without looking beyond her family history. Her parents had died when she was a child, both consumed in their sleep by a fire—poof—while she was spending the weekend with her grandmother, who had little choice but to accept the responsibility for her granddaughter's upbringing. Further details were not forthcoming. Young Ashton, too, had been orphaned. And although his experience emerged only in random fragments, any picture assembled from them would be witheringly gloomy. His parents had had little money, and his mother had suffered from some unnamed chronic ailment, but they'd had children. Alexander was the first, then Ashton and finally, just eighteen months later, and apparently unplanned, the twins. With their limited financial resources and Mrs. Stoller's illness, they weren't equipped to raise four children. Some sort of compromise was required. A couple living down the block had tried for years to have children but hadn't been successful. They were too old now to have a baby but still young enough to care for a child. It would be good for everyone involved, or nearly everyone. Alexander was special because he was their firstborn and the twins were too young, and they were believed to belong together. Ashton was the obvious choice; the sacrifice, it was decided, would be his. His new parents treated him as though he were their own, and although he still spent some time with his birth family, he soon sensed through silent signals that he was in a different category from his siblings, that he was only a visitor in their home. That would never change.

Even murkier than the early history was what occurred in the aftermath of Alexander's death. Perhaps with his older brother gone Ashton had expected to return to his home and move into the primary position. But Alexander's early death magnified his importance and calcified his dominance. His life ended before he had the opportunity to disappoint. Now the perfect son would always be perfect.

Certainly no one had ever volunteered a lucid, cohesive account of any of this. And Chase couldn't recall ever having met his uncles. These stories had been pasted together from information that had emerged over time, coded innuendo filtered through inhibition and habitual reticence. How much could his parents have known about each other? Images of awkward, silent matings, faces turned away. Muted sighs of relief when it was over.

Bradley was on a swing now and Sophie was waiting. A little boy jumped off the swing next to Bradley's and another boy grabbed it. "Hey," Chase called out. The child hoisted himself onto the swing. "Hey, you with the blue shirt. Wait your turn." The boy scowled, slid off the swing and gave the chain a violent jerk. How do they get that way? Though they didn't need his help, he pushed both the children for a while, running between their swings, popping up, first on one side, then the other. Bradley seemed more present when Chase was actively engaging him, but Sophie was always happy. To her, life was a series of hugs and adventures. But when would the constant pull of the family gravity begin to drag her down?

The three of them were walking toward the sandbox when a woman approached them. She planted herself in front of Chase and said, "I know you're going to do the right thing and apologize to my son."

"What?"

She wore glasses and her hair was a volcanic plume of blonde-and-gray cotton candy. She was pale and as shapeless as an insinuation and she blinked with astonishing rapidity. "I know you're going to do the right thing. You made my son cry."

"How did I do that?"

"The way you yelled at him. You made him cry."

"You mean the boy who was trying to take her swing? I didn't yell at him."

"I saw the whole thing. I just know you're going to do the right thing." Haughty smile. "My son is very upset and it's your fault."

"No. It's your fault."

"You made my son cry and—"

"No. You made your son cry by not teaching him how to wait his turn."

"Oh no."

"Oh yes. If you'd taught him to wait his turn I wouldn't have had to say anything."

"You yelled at my son."

"No. I told him it wasn't his turn, which you should have done."

"You're going to apologize."

"Get away from me."

"I'm just going to stand right here until you go over there and—"

"You can stand here until your son's third bail hearing if you want." Chase grabbed the children's hands and began to walk away. A second later she was next to him again, breathing in his face, blinking like a strobe and demanding an apology. He stopped, looked into her eyes and quietly said, "Get the fuck away from me."

"You don't scare me."

He glanced at the children. They still didn't appear interested. He brought his face closer to hers. "Fuck you, you stupid fucking cunt."

Still she pursued him, and now she was louder, repeating over and over that he'd made her son cry, that he had to apologize. He walked faster, pulling the children along, but they were watching now. Bradley looked fascinated but Sophie's expression revealed her distress. Chase increased their pace and the woman followed. She continued to chant and stalk. Finally Sophie broke into tears. Chase glared at the woman. He wanted to jam his heel into her foot or grab her wiry mane and knock her to the asphalt.

She threw back her shoulders, raised her pitted chin and said, "*That's* what you get."

He picked Sophie up and held her, comforted her. "I want to go home," she said through her sobs. He kissed her and petted her. He wanted nothing more than to wound this woman, to cripple her, physically, emotionally, in any way at all. There would be no hesitation, no guilt. It would feel good.

"Come on, Bradley," he said through his teeth. "Let's go get some ice cream."

Bradley seemed to have forgotten the incident by the time they reached the car, but Sophie wasn't able to recover enough to stop for ice cream. She was still upset and wanted to go home. During the drive Chase was so focused on Sophie that it didn't occur to him to interact with Bradley, and when he opened the car door to let them out his nephew's face had gone blank again. When Chase spoke to him Bradley ignored him and walked away.

Aaron was sitting on the couch wearing headphones when Chase walked in, Sophie still clinging to him.

"That was short."

"Yeah. I'm afraid she's a little upset."

"Huh?"

"She's a little upset."

Aaron nodded.

"We had a sort of run in with a crazy woman."

"Huh?"

"I detonated a nuclear device."

Aaron lifted one earpiece back. "What?"

"Your daughter got a little upset."

"I was scared."

"Of what?" Aaron asked, still holding the earpiece away from his ear. His head was bobbing slightly.

"That lady."

"There was a woman there who . . . I don't know. I probably should have handled it differently." He pulled his head back to look at her. "I'm sorry if I upset you, sweetie."

"It was that lady. Why did she do that?"

"I really don't know."

"Where do you think she is now?"

"I don't know."

"Does she know where we live?"

He squeezed her. "No. No, of course not."

"Yay," she said, and wriggled away.

Aaron was gazing into space, his eyes focused on some distant point.

"Aaron, can I just ask you something?"

He looked up.

"Could you maybe just pause that for a minute?"

He pressed a button on a small black box. "What's up?"

"I was wondering about Bradley."

"What about him?"

"Have you ever noticed . . . ? I don't know what to call it."

"Give me a hint."

"I don't know. Sometimes he sort of tunes out."

Aaron shrugged. "He's eight."

"Is he okay?"

"He's eight."

"Mm." He scratched his chin. "What about all those toys?"

"What toys?"
"All the weapons and warriors and stuff."
"That's what kids play with."
"They're so violent."
Aaron laughed. "You wouldn't believe the video games."

"Welcome back." She remembered him, and she was smiling. "Where are all your friends?"

"They abandoned me."

"I doubt that." Hand on her hip. "You here for dinner or just drinks?"

"I thought I'd just drink and annoy you."

"Unfortunately it's pretty quiet tonight, so I should have loads of time to be annoyed. What can I get for you?"

He drank slowly while she waited on the few other tables, stopping by to chat with him every few minutes.

The bar cleared out early and before long she was sitting with him, drinking shots while he sipped his beer. Zoë was from a small town in Maryland. She was studying psychology and environmental science, which Chase interpreted to mean she had issues and wanted to contribute something to society, which probably amounted to the same thing. I'm society, he thought. I have issues. She was fun and smart and great to look at, and she laughed easily. She didn't seem put off by his slightly altered explanation of how he damaged his hands, and she found his account of the police raid hilarious. For last call she bought him another beer and a shot of Jack Daniels. After that she bought them both another round.

"Now what," he said when the lights went on.

"I'm not ready to go home."

He'd dusted off the lawn chairs and brought them out to the yard. The bottle sat between them on the ground and they each held a glass. They'd gotten this far and yet something was holding him back. It wasn't a lack of interest and it certainly wasn't Haley. She was probably humping her hubby. The night was cool, faintly lit by a sickle moon, but, well, the signals weren't completely clear, and he wasn't sure he had the strength to handle a rejection.

"It must be hard losing your father."

"We didn't have an . . . ideal relationship."

"Does that really make it easier?"

"I have no idea."

"I guess there'd be things you wish you'd said to each other." She seemed to be talking more to herself now than to him.

"You never know anybody."

"Oh, I think you can if you try."

"Really?"

"Yeah, I do."

He rose, holding the bottle in one hand. "Let me show you something." He reached out for her hand, realizing only now how absolutely inebriated he was, and led her toward the garage.

He turned on the light and motioned to the underwear. "Ta da."

She looked confused.

"My father's private collection. My brother and I found it."

"This is so sad." She picked up a pair of panties and held them out in front of her.

"That's the problem."

She leaned back against the car. "What is?"

"I thought it was funny at first—I mean, it *is* funny—and I thought it made him more human, but the truth is he was still the same absent, empty guy, except that he had this urge that he couldn't talk about. It's like someone who's brain-dead compulsively jerking off. It's just ugly."

"It's more sad than anything." Her eyelids were droopy from drinking.

"I just wanted to find something he cared about."

"You mean you wanted him to care the way you care?"

"I don't know. Yeah, I guess."

"He didn't love anybody?" She was swaying. Or maybe it was him.

"I don't think so. No."

"Maybe he got some pleasure from . . . from whatever he did with these."

"Probably not."

"But maybe."

"Maybe." He swigged from the bottle and handed it to her.

She held the bottle to her lips and chugged. "You could still do something for him."

"Like what?"

"I don't know. Paint a picture, write a poem. You'll think of something."

"A poem?" Chase laughed, took the bottle back and drank. "Shit."

"Honor him in some way. Do something for *him*, not for yourself."

He reached into a box of panties. "I guess I could continue his collection."

She laughed. "I don't think he'd want you to have them."

"Maybe put them on display somewhere." He handed her the bottle.

"No!" She said this with unexpected intensity. "They're his." She took a long, bubbling gulp and wiped her mouth. "It sounds like they were all he had. Let him have them."

"Let him have them?"

"Yes."

After another minute he said, "Are you coming with me or do I have to do this alone?"

"Where we going?"

20

Giggling like juvenile delinquents, they made their way through the maze of gravestones, amorphous silhouettes lurking in the darkness like hunchbacked prowlers. Chase was lugging two clanking shovels in his left hand and a garbage bag full of panties in his right, but he no longer felt encumbered and his hands had long ago ceased to trouble him. The bottle was in her care, though there couldn't be more than a few inches of liquor left. Clouds had set up camp above and he'd forgotten a flashlight, so navigation was driven more by memory and instinct than by actual sensory information.

"I'm pretty sure I remember that tree," he said, and stopped to try to get his bearings. The air tasted of lilacs and alcohol.

"Yes, but does that tree remember you?"

"What tree?"

"Want a drink?"

"Am I really drunk?"

"I hope so. If not, you're just another grave-robbing lunatic with incredibly bad balance."

"Hey, I'm not robbing. I'm giving back."

"Tell it to the judge."
"Is he buried here?"
"Shit."
"What?"
"I bit my tongue." She laughed.
"Can I kiss it and make it better?"
"I'm okay."
"Have you ever done this with anyone else?"
"You're the only one."
"When this is done, are we . . . are you and I . . . ?"
"No."
"We have something special."
"Very special."
"If there's anything here that you'd like for yourself."
"For myself?"
"I don't think he'd miss one or two pairs."
"Oh, gosh no. I really couldn't."
"Well. . . ."
"Very generous."
"I think it might be over there."
"It would probably help if I had some clue where there was."
"It would help if I could read the fucking gravestones."
"Do you know Braille?"
"Is he buried here?"
"One of us is pretty funny."
"Or the other one is really stewed."
"Is that an old guy word?"
"Fuck you."
"*Well* then."

    After a few more minutes in the darkness he located what he believed might possibly be his father's gravestone.

    He released the bag of panties. "Okay. I need a drink."

She held the bottle out and he grabbed it, took a swig and handed it back to her.

"Maybe you could keep an eye out for ghouls while I dig."

"There's just the two of us," she said. "Anyway, I'm planning to do my part."

"No. I think I should do this myself."

"When's the last time you dug a hole, I mean, like, you know, in the ground and stuff?"

"Well, give or take a year, I'd say it's been about . . . never."

"I want to help. At least I think I do. At least I think I think I do."

"No. Like it or not, he was my father. I really think I should be the one who ends up in prison when we get caught."

"Don't you mean if?"

"If he was my father? What do you know?"

"Not much. How's tricks?"

"What?"

Pfft. A spark, then another, a sudden flash and her face lit up, lunar, her gaze stuck on pause. Now a faint orange glow, squinting eyes and the hiss of inhalation. "Want some?" The ovoid ash traveled a circuitous path in his general direction, hovered there.

"I haven't smoked . . . anything since I was . . . hoo boy. Okay." He reached out, snatched it. "Okay." A long draw, burning. Hold it in.

He dropped one shovel and got a firm grip on the other. Okay. "We're coming in."

The gritty thud of the iron blade as he thrust it into the soil above his father's grave was deeply gratifying. He lifted the shovel again, and again he plunged it into the earth. Again and again he drove the blade in, lifted it and deposited the soil behind him. Even through the odd, echoing drone of inebriation, he could hear the rhythm, feel it bump against the labored counter-rhythm of his breathing as he widened the area into something vaguely rectangular. His clothing stuck to him and his hands were numb and he had no idea how deep he'd gone, though he sensed at some point that he was raising the shovel higher to deposit the soil, that the world around him was moving up, the horizon slowly ascending. Don't stop. Stomach cramps, vertigo, the earth keeps moving, trying to dodge the blows. You can't get away. Soil and perspiration and still the taste of alcohol, dark and sweet and flammable and stop thinking. Thrust, push, lift, dump, more, don't stop, more, dig now, force it down, in, lift raise and hurl and down in lift raise hurl down in lift and don't give up it's so easy to give up and hurl and down in raise hurl down harder push stab stab tear heave more harder don't stop don't let go jab hurl here I come down stab lift can you hear me hurl down stab raise hurl count two three four five six one two three four five six one two four six eight ten twelve one thousand-seven one thousand-eight diglifthurldiglifthurlagainagainagaincomeonecomeoutassholefuc kingpantysniffingcocksuckerI'mcomingforyouhere'sagiftfromme toyouIloveyoustabwherewereharderwherewereyouwhodidyoulo vewantneedstabdidyoucrywhenwhywherestabgivemenothingIha venothingdigIwantsomethingmorethanwhatwereyouwherewhyf uckyoulifthurlpleasesomebodyhelpmeyouloseyou'redeadjustlike whenyouwerealivegoodbyegoodbyeImisswhatyoumighthavebee nImissnomorecomebackandholdmesomebodyholdmeholdmeso darkinheredarkinh—

"Okay. Okay, you're okay." Zoë was kneeling, leaning down, holding his sopping face in her hands. "Come on. Come on now. You're okay."

"Oh fuck."

"It's okay."

"Is it?"
"Yes."
"I'm panting, he panted."
"You are, she concurred."
"Can I stop now? Do I have to do anymore?"
"You can stop."
"Can I stop?"
"You hit the coffin."
"Really?"
"Well, it sounded like wood, or something other than dirt."
"His head's made of wood. The dirt's all inside."
She extended her hand. "Come on up. Please."
"I can do it." Grabbing fistfuls of soil, he wrestled his way out. He rubbed his hands on his pants, squinted and surveyed the area. "Where are the . . . where the hell are they?"

She rotated, took a couple steps, first one way, then another. Then she laughed.

"What?"
"You must have buried them."
"Shit. They're going to be filthy now."
She laughed. "I really don't think he'll mind."
He disinterred the bag and poured its contents into the hole he'd dug. "There you go," he said. "Have a party." He leaned down for the shovel.

"Wait."
"What for?"
"Maybe this'll mean something to him."

A dull snap and the quick rasp of a zipper. Just a wobbling shadow in the blackness, she slid her jeans down and stepped out of them, the pale skin of her legs phosphorescent in the darkness. Bending over, she eased the tiny triangle down. He wanted to lick her like a popsicle. "Not too fancy but they're pretty fresh," she said, and tossed them in.

"Oh my." Drowning in a sea of desire.

She put on her jeans and grabbed a shovel.

When the trench was filled and relatively uniform he turned to her. "You're pretty fucking amazing."

"That's a very fucking nice thing to say."

"I mean it."

"My mouth tastes like the bottom of a flowerpot."

He leaned closer. "I won't complain."

"No." She gripped his shoulder. "That's not what this is about."

"It could be."

"No. This would all be tainted. What we did here is . . . well, it's weird, but it's also special. I *think* it is."

"Everything's tainted. Nothing's pure."

"I hope you're wrong." She stepped back. "Let's have a drink to your father."

She found the bottle, opened it and said, "Rest in peace." Then she tilted her head back and drank. She handed the bottle to Chase and he drank.

In front of her apartment he shut off the ignition. "I'd like to see you again, maybe without the shovels and dirt."

"Stop by the bar any time. I'd love to see you."

"I was hoping maybe we could go out."

"I had a great time, and you are a fantastic guy. You really are. You're interesting and fun and a little crazy. But—"

"But. . . ." He winced.

"I'm just not interested in you that way."

An abdominal detonation. *Breathe.* "You're not attracted to me."

"As a friend, as a person, a drinking buddy."

He could find no reasonable response.

"You're just not . . . *that guy*."

"I want you to know how amazing you are. I'm pretty drunk, very tired and a little wired from our gravedigging panty-planting adventure. But you are really beautiful and amazing in every way." He wanted to cry or hit someone or both.

"Thanks." She reached out and touched his face. "You're pretty special, too."

"Yeah."

"Don't do that. There's no one I'd rather dig up dead people with than you. Now go home and take a shower. You're unsanitary." She opened the car door and stepped out.

"Okay," he said to her legs. "But first I'm going back to dig up your panties."

The scorching spray pierced his back like flaming darts. With all the steam in the room, breathing was like trying to inhale a hot pillow. Rivers of sludge streamed down his body, swirling down the drain in a grimy vortex. He was so ready, almost eager to be destroyed, his insecurities fully charged, primed for detonation. The fuse was short, tightly braded of shame and tethered to a lethal payload of vile, murderous rage. "God damn it."

Why couldn't he just let it go?

But her rejection made him small, pathetic, an object of ridicule. Silly little man. Silly little nothing man. Clown-boy. "Fuck." He pulled his fist back, tightened it, then let it fall, limp, to his side. If only that would help. Why did it matter so much? Why did it matter at all? Why do relative strangers have such power? Why do they get to decide who I am? He probed his left ear. Enough soil to plant begonias. He shampooed three times, scratching his scalp like a chronic case of pruritis ani. If he scrubbed his skin any harder his organs would pour out into a pile at his feet. After rinsing he coaxed the remaining ring of sediment down the drain and shut the water off.

He stepped out of the shower and began to laugh. Whatever else had happened tonight, he had done something that felt right and important in a way he didn't understand, might never understand. He'd risked shame and undoubtedly broken all sorts of laws: laws of the state, moral and religious laws, laws of society. He didn't know what his reasons were, or what it meant or why it mattered, but it felt good, almost good enough to wash away the pain Zoë's rejection had inflicted. He pulled a towel from the rack and wiped the mirror. Staring back with a forlorn expression was a weary red version of himself. He moved closer. Whoever he was, he was trembling and there were tears in his eyes. Now he swam. Swim hard. Follow the light. Swim to the surface now. Before you've gone too deep. Before you drown.

21

It didn't seem at all unreasonable to impute to the Christian Science phase some percentage of his emotional instability. Their mother had introduced the religion—brought it home like a stray mutt—but their father adopted it with something as close to enthusiasm as he'd ever been able to muster. It was a perfect excuse to avoid the prodding, the pain and all the unsavory reminders of mortality that doctors seemed to take such pleasure in emphasizing. And so they were taught that they were God's perfect children and that illness was an illusion they could banish with faith and proper thought. When they felt pain or discomfort they could only conclude that either they were totally oblivious to their own most basic sensations, or they were imperfect, unworthy, that perhaps God had abandoned them, disgusted and unwilling to take the responsibility for what He had wrought. "I'm sick." "No, you're not. You only think you're sick." Not terribly far from there to a total loss of identity.

Chase turned off his cell phone and stayed indoors, mostly pacing around the kitchen or lying in his father's bed staring at the white ceiling. He went out only when it was necessary and he called no one. Aaron telephoned the house a couple times, but he was too caught up in himself to notice that his brother was receding. After a few days of alcohol-free solitude, Chase decided it was time for another visit to Hannah.

She didn't seem quite as comatose this time as before, and most of the tics were attenuated, if not entirely absent. Still there was no hint of recognition, no sense of connection. The doctor was noncommittal regarding expectations, but willing to continue the experiment for a while and "see where it takes us." On the way back to his father's house, Chase took a detour toward Haley's house, but when he was a couple blocks away he changed his mind. It was ridiculous, but he felt too weak to face her or to react rationally to any sign of a husband or, for that matter, a postman. Ten minutes later he found himself in front of his old grade school.

The two-story brick building looked much the same as it had when he'd been a student there, although the playground had expanded, supplanting the wooded area that had once surrounded it, a natural bulwark against the still-theoretical terrors of the real world. He'd run and laughed and played and fallen and bled and cried on this grassy rectangle. Short, skinny and a year younger than his youngest classmates, he'd been a convenient target for the bullies. He wasn't difficult to catch and possessed neither the skill nor the confidence to defend himself in a fight. There was little bloodshed in these playground encounters, but the humiliation was searing. And enduring.

A little dark-haired boy files out with the other children, one of the last to emerge from the massive white doors. For a while the boy walks around, his eyes to the ground, trying to decide what to do. He could use the swings or try to find someone to run around with, maybe use the seesaw, though he'd have to sit far forward with even the smallest of his classmates on the other side. A child running past him taps his arm. "You're it," he calls out, his blond hair blowing in the breeze as he continues toward the far corner of the playground. Smiling, his eyes flashing with joy, he chases the blond boy, tries to remember his name. The boy slows and turns around. Something about his expression. Slowly the dark-haired boy turns away. Always he is on his guard. Even the ones who are nice at first can change in a second. There is no one here he can trust, and an attack can come from anywhere.

So what? Didn't all children grow up this way, or close to it? And didn't they eventually move on? If they hadn't the world would be populated by adults sitting alone feeling stupid for feeling sorry for themselves for being weak and pathetic and lacking the skills to survive what by any reasonable measure was a fairly normal life.

But by sixth grade things had begun to change. Like vegetation taking root and sprouting from a block of cement, his innate will to flourish had given birth to an arsenal of tools and techniques to aid in his survival. This was where he learned to fight back, rarely with his fists, but with words and an attitude that belied his almost debilitating terror. Make them laugh, make them wonder if you're crazy enough to be dangerous, make them think before they pounce. Their major weakness was the insecurity they concealed behind the bluster. They were clumsy and, for the most part, they weren't very bright. This is where the new persona was born. This is where the dark-haired boy learned how to get by, how to charm and when it would be effective, how to manipulate, how to use his rage, how to be whatever it required to do whatever it took to push through the arid and unforgiving structure under which he'd been withering. What he didn't learn was how to let go of the anger. And he never let his guard down. Anyone could turn. Of course he could learn that, too. He knew now how to adapt. He was still a child.

But really the schoolyard ghosts were powerless now, these memories evoked by force of will. And the exercise was strictly an intellectual one. Here, with these images he'd called forth, some emotion might be appropriate. It just wouldn't come.

The message light was blinking. He pressed the button.

"I'm sorry, but I had to call Aaron to get your number there. I need to talk to you. Is your cell phone broken? Please call me. We need to talk."

Shit. He picked up the receiver and dialed. "It's me."

"Is something wrong with your phone?"

"It's off."

"That's not very helpful."

"That depends on your perspective."

Jennifer sighed. "I'm very sorry about your father."

"Thanks. He doesn't seem to mind."

"What are you doing out there?"

"Helping Aaron, visiting Hannah, taking some time to decide what I want to screw up next."

"Okay, well, I suppose that's good . . . or something."

"I don't know."

"Are you okay?"

He stepped over to the kitchen window. The grass and trees had achieved a startlingly rich shade of green. "Oh yeah. I'm fine."

"I have some . . . some news."

A cat was stalking something in the grass, one paw shooting out then retreating as the animal slinked cautiously forward.

"I'm pregnant."

"No." It was like colliding with a speeding barn.

"Um, yes."

"How?"

"The usual way, Chase."

"I mean, what about the—"

"The pill? I haven't been on birth control for more than two years."

"That little round case in the bathroom cabinet?" There was simply no way to know how he felt about this. He'd thought about children, they'd discussed them in the abstract, but how had he missed this? Of course this changed everything, but it wasn't at all clear how.

"Just a stage prop, I'm afraid."

"Well, gosh, honey. That seems vaguely dishonest."

"I wanted a baby, dear."

"Oh. That's different."

"Save your bullshit. There's more."

"I hope so. This hardly seems worth a phone call." He sat down, rested his elbow on the table and slumped forward.

"Must you be a jerk?"

"Apparently I must."

"I guess that should make this easier."

"Well then." Why couldn't he ever stop?

"It. . . ." He could hear the tremors in her inhalation, knew another bomb was about to come crashing down. "It isn't yours."

Thud. "Oh my."

Silence.

He was totally blind. "I'm just not sure why you're telling me this."

"Do you think this is easy for me?"

"For some reason that particular question didn't occur to me, but I certainly hope not."

Dramatic sigh. "I'm telling you because you are likely to notice at some point. And it seemed like the right thing to do."

He laughed, though his heart really wasn't in it. "Well, gosh. I guess I appreciate it then." This all made the grade school playground seem so very safe and welcoming.

"I suppose there was a time when I found you entertaining. Maybe my tastes have changed, or maybe you've just become more venomous."

"Could it possibly be a question of context?"

"It doesn't matter," she said and hung up.

It seemed unreasonable, unfair, somehow, for her to be upset with him. What reaction could she possibly have expected? Yippee! The entire situation had the quality of a slow-motion beheading. Now what? Brain surgery would be too expensive. Vomiting might offer some temporary minor relief. He rose and looked out the window. The cat was sitting back now, hunched over, its bobbing head buried deep in its nether-regions, one hind leg aimed upward, furry little toes pointing toward the firmament. The simple life.

22

Chase was about halfway through an overcooked cheese omelet when he heard a car skid to a halt on the driveway. Aaron didn't drive like that. Perhaps the cops had come back to kill him. A door slammed shut. Haley was possible but very unlikely. Pounding on the door. This was not a happy person. Chase stood and made his way through the living room. He opened the door. Glaring up at him was a short, muscular man with thinning hair the color of a raw pine board and permanent grease spots on his cheeks. He folded his bulging arms over his chest and thrust his goateed chin forward. "What's your fucking deal, man?"

"No cookies today."

"Don't pull that shit or I swear to Christ I'll pop you one."

"Listen," Chase said, trying to assess the danger. "I'm having my dinner. If you want to come and watch me eat, maybe tell me a little bit about yourself and what you're so pissed off about, I guess that's fine. Otherwise, you can back your pickup out of my driveway and find someone else to . . . pop." He turned and walked toward the kitchen, bracing himself for an attack. It was really just a question of time.

He sat down and the stranger hovered over him.

Chase glanced up. "I didn't make enough for two."

"I ain't hungry."

"You ain't?"

"Naw. And I don't eat eggs."

"Shoulda called ahead. I'd of fried y'up a heap o' spicy mottserelly sticks."

"You really don't reconize me, do you?"

"No. I really don't." He scooped up some omelet and took a bite.

"For a guy who's this close to getting his ass kicked, you got one hell of a attitude."

"I keep hearing that." Chase took another bite and gripped his fork tightly. "Would you happen to have a weapon?" He sipped his water.

"A weapon? For your skinny ass?"

With his left hand Chase clutched the knife. "I'm tired of you now."

"I guess you think you can just breeze into town, screw around with Alice and then breeze out again."

"Oh." Chase scrutinized the man, found beneath the wrinkles and the permanent tan something from the distant past. "Jim?"

He raised his eyebrows.

"Listen, Jim, I couldn't possibly care less about Alice. I truly wish I hadn't run into her. I don't like her, don't ever want to see her again, regret having ever known her. Frankly, Jim, she repels me."

"You insensitive prick."

"What?"

"Repels you?" He shook his head and frowned. "Re*pels* you? She really thought you was into her."

"Let me get this straight. You're pissed because I don't want to—"

"You led her on, man."

"What?"

"You used her."

"You're not jealous?"

"Sure I am. Of course I'm jealous and shit, but you don't just fuck a great lady like that and then act like she don't even exist. That's some real insensitive shit, dude."

"Your time of the month?"

"Oh boy." He rubbed his hands together. "I'm having a real hard time holding myself back."

"Let me help you." Chase pushed back his chair and rose. "If you don't get the fuck out of my house I'm going to prod your forehead with this fork until I locate the defective unit. Then I'm going to pry it out with this knife, spread it on toast and replace it with a . . . with a . . . ," he looked around, "a stick of creamery butter."

"Butter?"

Chase shrugged. His heart wasn't in this.

"That's fucked up, man."

"Cholesterol?"

"What the hell does she see in you?" The question sounded more genuine than hypothetical.

"I have no idea, Jim. Maybe it was just a way to get your attention."

"She pulls this crap all the time, man." He shook his head.

"People tend to be extremely fucked up." Chase put the knife down.

Jim leaned back against the sink. "Tell me about it." He tugged and twisted his goatee and Chase sensed that the danger had passed. This guy was just hurt.

"Maybe she's looking for a reaction, you know, trying to make you jealous."

His mouth dropped open. "Oh wow." He turned his back to Chase and leaned over the sink, his chin against his chest.

Chase watched in terror as Jim's muscular shoulders began to bob. *Oh, Jesus, please don't cry. Please don't.* He tapped his fork against his plate and scratched his head, trying to think of something to say, something comforting or uplifting. He cleared his throat. "What year's your pickup?" Nothing. "Is that custom paint?" Then the sobbing began, the short, high-pitched, doleful whines of a mourning hound. *I'm totally incompetent to deal with this.*

Chase stood up, reached out, then swiftly withdrew his hand. He moved a little closer to Jim. *Give him something.* "Can I . . . ," he took a deep breath, swallowed. "Can I offer you some toast?"

23

It might have been worse, but that wasn't much comfort. He held the ice against his mouth and closed his eyes. The swelling would go down soon enough and his teeth seemed intact. Still, it was difficult to escape the conclusion that he was doing something wrong, his flailing, halfhearted efforts to find a positive direction notwithstanding. Adding to his befuddlement was the fact that he had no idea where things had gone wrong. When Jim had finally calmed down, Chase handed him a napkin. "Here you go," he said. Jim thanked him and wiped his eyes. "Sorry," he said and looked away. Chase saw that he was embarrassed. "Hey," he said. "We all get emotional sometimes. Don't worry about it." Jim blew his nose and shook his head. Then Chase said, "You guys are going to work it out. I'm sure of it. You two belong together." Jim smiled, but there was something wrong with his eyes; they were wide and glazed and they seemed to be staring through him, at something behind him. "Are you going to cry again?" Chase asked.

Just one good blow to his mouth and Chase was munching on the deep pile.

Jim glared down at him. "Asshole." He turned to leave.

Chase looked up and said, "You can forget about that toast." But it sounded like he had a mouthful of putty.

Maybe it was time to reevaluate his entire approach to life. It might not be altogether futile. Indeed there were a few aspects of his behavior that would require very little examination. The temper, for instance; it just wasn't productive. And aside from those brief, giddy moments of pride—oh, how very clever am I—his habitual reliance on acerbic, sometimes vicious sarcasm didn't appear to contribute anything of value to his life. Unfortunately these characteristics came as naturally to him as blinking or jerking off. But by gosh that kind of crap could generate antagonism in even the meekest souls, and it could precipitate serious, sometimes irreparable damage, wounding anyone unfortunate enough to be loitering within the general blast zone. It might not solve all his problems, and it would require some effort, some self-control, which in itself would be a new experience, but it would really cost him nothing to attenuate the expressions of hostility just a jot. And then there was the thing he didn't feel like addressing, the drinking, which, it could be argued, often played a supporting role in his most egregious episodes. And where had his tenderness gone? Something, no, some things had to change.

In the bathroom mirror Chase assessed the damage to his face. Just a small cut on his lower lip and some swelling. Sure, he could have handled the entire thing differently, but still, there was a part of him that wanted to hunt the greasy little shit down, tackle him, push his leathery face into the dirt and hold it there until he was farting dust and regrets. Not a great first step. Really, these violent impulses were new. Or perhaps he just hadn't acted on them before. Either way, his lack of impulse control had become a major source of irritation, spawning behavior with the corrosive force of industrial strength Drano. All this and Jennifer was pregnant with another man's child. Was that his fault, too? The truth was he hadn't been giving her anything she needed.

There was just so much going on, so much to deal with, more than Chase, even at his best, his unremarkable best, could easily assimilate. What he wanted now was someone to talk to, someone who would listen and care, preferably a woman, one who would look into his eyes and see his suffering and his goodness and his need and want to comfort him, want, no, *need* to help him through it all. She would take his hand and lean toward him as he spoke, and he would share everything because, of course, he knew he could trust her, and only when he was finished would she speak, her voice calm and soothing, her face radiating sympathy and love, understanding and—this, frankly, was the most important component—desire. Or if it wasn't the most important, it was a critical element the absence of which would greatly diminish the potency of all the others. The only exception to this was Hannah. If she were with him, conscious, healthy and whole, her presence alone would be a comfort. She would listen, would understand and forgive his flaws and missteps while trying to nudge him gently back on course. She would recognize his potential and see how he'd failed to achieve it without making him feel like a criminal or a compulsive failure. She would bring out what was best in him. But this was just a pointless detour into the land of make-believe. He could spend hours fantasizing, questioning and rationalizing, but that would just be delaying the inevitable. Regardless of the futility, the potential for humiliation and pain, there was no question what he was going to do.

The call had been very brief. He'd said, "Can you come?" and she'd simply said, "Yes, after 9:00." How would she explain it to her husband, or would she? Maybe he didn't care, or perhaps he had lovers of his own. No, she would have mentioned that. Well, maybe. Chase was waiting outside, standing in the mist when her headlights floated off the main road, bobbing toward the house on invisible waves.

She stepped out of her car wearing faded jeans and a baggy sweater.

He moved toward her. "Have you eaten?"

"I'm not hungry," she said. "Are you?"

"Not really. I was just wondering if you'd go out somewhere with me."

"It's a pretty small town."

"You have an impressive ability to avoid direct answers."

"Thank you," she said. Her eyes narrowed. "Are you going to be mean to me?"

"I wasn't planning on it." He reached out and took her hand. "You're not feeling vulnerable?"

"Not vulnerable. Maybe just a little fragile."

"What's the difference?"

"I think vulnerability gives other people too much power. But you're the writer."

"You give me too much credit."

"Perhaps."

He drew her toward him, embraced her. *Please talk to me.*

Why was it so difficult to say? Even now, with her body pressed against him, his will was withering. Yielding to this desire would be so much easier, the outcome more certain, and even beyond the intoxicating excitement and the pure, raw physical pleasure, it had its rewards. Touch carried something with it, something mysterious and wonderful, and then there was the stark candor, the vulnerability of being naked together, the sharing of smell and taste, of saliva and sweat, the magic of commingling, limbs interlocked, pulses racing, letting go and finding the comfort to demonstrate your loss of control. In all of that there was something intangible, incorporeal and deeply intimate. And yet that was easier than simply looking into a woman's eyes and saying what you felt. Somehow there was more danger there, more potential for pain, embarrassment, rejection. Was that because he was a man, because it was burned into his DNA? *I want both. I want it all. Blah blah blah.*

She pulled back. "I could use a drink."

They sat sipping wine at opposite ends of the living room couch, not speaking or looking at each other.

After a few minutes of silence he said, "Did something happen?"

"No."

"Are you okay?"

She shrugged. "I'm okay."

"Do you have any interest at all in talking with me?"

"Maybe I should. I don't know." She studied him. "Did somebody hit you?"

"Yes."

"Why?"

"Because I don't want to sleep with his . . . his wife, or girlfriend, or ex-wife or whatever the hell she is."

"You lead an interesting life."

"It's a very recent trend."

"What else have you been doing?"

"Digging up graves and burying panties, the usual stuff. What about you?"

"I'm afraid I can't compete with that."

Chase swirled the wine around in the glass. "Why are you married?"

"Probably for the same reasons that you got married."

"No. What I mean is, why are you *still* married?"

"My husband is one of the best people I've ever known."

"That's nice."

"Yes, it is. And it's true."

"Okay. Do you love him?"

"Yeah, I guess I do."

"You guess."

"He's very good to me."

"I'm a little confused."

"I . . . I don't love him that way."

"Why not divorce him?"

"It would hurt him."

"What about this?"

"This?"

"What we're doing."

"Well . . . I'm not a very nice person. I know it. I'm selfish."

"And you're determined to prove it."

"I don't need to prove it."

"Isn't it under your control?"

"Maybe. To a degree." He thought he saw the slightest quake around her mouth.

"You just seem so . . . sad."

She looked down at the floor and ran a hand through her hair. Again she shrugged. The wall had ascended.

"I have no idea what to say to you."

"You don't have to say anything."

"No, probably not. But I want to. I can't help it."

"I . . . I can't be anything else for you." She looked up at him. "I mean, if you really do want more than this, I can't. . . . If you knew me better you wouldn't want more from me."

"Because you're so terrible."

"Whatever you think you see, you don't know me."

"Of course I don't. How the hell would I? It's not that I don't cherish our little nonversations. They're entertaining, if not particularly informative. You don't talk about . . . you don't share anything, any hint of what you're feeling or thinking or what you want." He set his glass down on the table. "Do you want anything? Or are you just torturing yourself at my expense? If your life is so awful, if you are such a horrific person, why not just drive off a fucking cliff and let the rest of us get on with our lives?"

She gazed at him, her expression untouched by his attack. "I've thought about it."

His heart was pounding and his jaw was clenched so tight his gums throbbed. There was a scream straining to emerge, to fill the room, shatter the windows and deafen them both. He filled his lungs, held it in. "Why don't you let me get to know you and then I can decide for myself what kind of a fuckup you are? How about that? Or are you afraid of something?"

"I'm afraid of everything." The edges of her face were sinking. She looked like a wilting flower. "I'm afraid of everything." Now the tears came.

He moved toward her and she shook her head. "I'm fine."

"Yeah." He smiled and took her face in his hands. "Me, too."

Their lovemaking was slow and tender, her groans like the whimpering of a child. Twice toward the end she'd hidden her face, and when he tried to turn it toward him she'd resisted. Afterwards, she fell asleep and he held her close. Bright shapes floated across the bedroom ceiling and there came from outside the sound of tires on gravel. A minute later the lights retreated and she woke.

"What time is it?"

"I'm not going to tell you."

"I should be going."

He reached over and turned on the bedside lamp. "What will happen if you don't?"

"If I don't go?"

"For a while. Just for a while."

"I don't know. Nothing. He'll worry I guess."

"I just want to talk, to get to know you. You don't share anything."

"People see what they want to see. Why should I spoil it?"

"What does that mean?"

"We don't see each other."

"Maybe not, but I think we'd have a much better chance if we made an effort to divulge something rather than hiding behind a wall of silence, evasion and . . . and lust."

"People rarely conceal the best of themselves."

"The quill never falls far from the porcupine."

"What?" She studied him.

"Generalizations like that are of no use. They don't mean anything. If you want to tell me that you're hiding some vile, hideous part of yourself then tell me that. Don't give me this vague, theoretical shit."

"Why is this so important?"

"Fuck it." He sat up and leaned forward. With his elbows resting on his legs, he buried his face in his hands. It was time to give this up. But for the sex there was nothing here. She lacked the capacity for intimacy. She was either empty or impenetrable, and from his perspective the difference was irrelevant. If there was anything beyond the little she was willing to reveal, he would never see it, never touch it. A hand on his back, gentle, tentative. Now what?

"Do you think . . . ?" A shudder in her voice. "When we're all so lost, so duplicitous, committing our private acts of treason, do you really think it's so simple to trust?"

He turned around. "What's the risk?"

She wore the weary expression of someone suffering chronic pain. "Annihilation."

He took her hand in his. "Versus a slow suicide?"

"At least the terms are mine."

"What about your husband?"

"He asks very little."

"Does he know you? Do you reveal yourself to him?"

"He sees what he wants to see. I won't deprive him of his illusions."

Then he remembered the car. "Is there any way he could know where you are?"

"No," she said.

"There was a car outside."

"When?" She sat up.

"You were asleep. It drove up and then just left."

"No. I don't see how he could. . . ." The color drained from her face. "I should go."

"If it *was* him it's too late."

"I'm sorry," she said and pushed the sheets aside. "I have to go."

"Would he get violent?"

"No." She moved toward him and reached out to touch his face. "I really am sorry. I don't want. . . . I'll call you."

"Okay."

She looked into his eyes, opened her mouth as though to speak, then got up and began to dress.

He was sitting up in bed paging through the local paper when his phone rang.

"Hello."

"When I got here he was asleep, or at least he seemed to be."

"Could you tell if he'd been there for a while?"

"Not really."

"I don't suppose you checked the hood of his car."

"Checked it?"

"To see if it was warm."

"No."

"Would he hurt you?"

"No," she said. "I'm not sure he'd even say anything to me."

"Call me."

"I'll call you tomorrow."

"Will you?"

"Yes. I'm afraid I will."

The question he'd been avoiding, though it had been fluttering around his thoughts like some elusive nocturnal bird, was if he'd still be obsessed with her if she weren't so remote. It wasn't difficult to imagine that it was the mystique surrounding her inaccessibility that had seduced him—this time I'll get through, this time I'll be loved. But what if he was disappointed by what he discovered if and when the wall finally crumbled? What if he discovered nothing at all? She might be nothing more than a convenient object of his need, the challenge of overcoming her unavailability an added incentive, a trigger for his ready obsession. This seemingly instinctive attraction was really no more credible than his unquestioning faith in his own wife's fidelity. And yet it felt real enough. And there was something sweet and powerful in this agony. Pain as proof: I'm alive.

Chase spent the morning cleaning the house, dusting, vacuuming, scrubbing counters and floors and doing the windows. When the cleaning was done he walked around the house oiling the hinges on all the doors and tightening knobs on the cabinets. After lunch he took the ladder from the garage, leaned it against the side of the house and swept the dead leaves and twigs out the rain gutters. When that was finished he hooked up a garden hose, pulled the car out of the garage and washed it. He swept the garage floor and pulled the car back in. He was stepping out of the car when his cell phone rang.

"Hi."

"He was fine this morning. I really don't think he knows anything."

"Well, that's good . . . I guess."

"It *is* good."

"For you?"

"For him."

"Yeah, well."

"I like . . . I do feel something for . . . for you. But I couldn't stand to . . . to hurt him."

"Aren't you hurting him by staying with him?"

"Am I?"

"Maybe without you he'd find someone . . . someone—"

"Someone faithful?"

"Well. . . ."

"It's not so easy to think in the long term."

"Maybe not, but it could be constructive."

"I know, I just . . . I don't want to talk about this right now."

"Okay." Of course not. "When can I see you?"

During the long silence following his question, he imagined her trying to find an easy way out. The thought of being caught had frightened her, or maybe it was all just a game. Give me all your love. Go fish.

"I'm not going to push you." His throat tightened. "Do whatever you need to do."

24

Maybe her eyes weren't as glassy, as blank, but she looked even more depleted now, as though the gradual approach of reality were draining her, wearing her out. Or was he just imagining all of this? No, she did look exhausted.

"Are you at least getting used to me?"

There were always little random movements, so it was impossible to know if she was reacting to him when her eyes shifted or a corner of her mouth seemed to rise slightly.

"I'm doing what I can for you. I'm trying." He leaned down to pry her eyes from the floor. She didn't follow, but she didn't appear particularly frightened either. "I asked them to adjust your medication to see if maybe you could feel a little better, maybe have some contact with someone, with me, with anyone. You must be so lonely. I think . . . I hope this will help."

She frowned, or did something close.

"I'd really like to talk with you, to be able to . . . to hold your hand and tell you about my life and ask your advice. And we could laugh." And I could hold you close and show you that you're loved. And you could tell me what a jerk I am and help me get my life together and remind me that I'm not just a jerk, that I'm more than that, better than that, too, sometimes. And then we could skip merrily through the woods they hacked down to put up those hideous apartment buildings and the lifeless parking lots that abut them. We could frolic hand-in-hand like the sweet young children we could have been if not for everything that went so very wrong, everything that's always gone wrong and will always go wrong because . . . just because that's the way it is was will be. But we were okay. We were fine for a while. Weren't we?

Why was he doing this? Who was it really for?

When the attendant stepped into the room, Chase rose and approached her. "How do you think she's doing?"

"Well, I'm not a doctor."

"That's why I'm asking you."

She smiled. "She's a little different now. Sometimes she'll look at me. But then, too, there's something else. I don't know quite what to call it."

He waited.

"I'm sorry. I just don't know."

"Thank you," he said, and for the first time he noticed her nametag. "Thank you, Eleanor."

"You're welcome, sir."

"Chase."

"Pardon?"

"Chase, call me Chase."

"Okay." She stepped toward Hannah and leaned down. "Come on, dear," she said and extended her hand.

Chase wasn't ready to go back to his father's house, to stare at the walls or to spend hours obsessively scrubbing them. He needed a distraction, something to jar his thoughts onto some other path. Without a plan or a destination, he headed toward downtown Stroudsburg.

The traffic on Main Street was heavier than he'd expected, and the population, while still elevating the national standard for obesity, now included a generous mix of darker shades. Old buildings with new faces, already dull and worn with age, neglect or both, flanked the narrow, two-lane street: a sporting goods store, gift shops, stores selling sewing machines and vacuum cleaners, a flower shop, two or three clothing stores, bars, cafés, a coffee shop and a hotel; a mix of mom-and-pop stores with a few representatives from the minor chains. In spite of the facelifts everything looked dirty and cheap. Without shedding a single layer of its shoddy atmosphere, his hometown had evolved from a gloomy small town to an ugly little city. It certainly wasn't home. The town where he grew up no longer existed. It had vanished along with his childhood.

Certainly most of what was gone wouldn't be missed, not by him or anyone else, but there were aspects of his past that he would welcome now: images and scents, sounds and sensations that might provide some sort of comfort, a feeling of home—not his true home, not the place where he'd lived, with all the oppression and unspoken tension, but the home that exists in that faint but compelling feeling of security and belonging that can be triggered by memories of those transient moments and the sensory stimuli that somehow made them shimmer. There were the thunderstorms he would watch—sometimes alone, sometimes with Aaron or Hannah—from the illusory safety of the front porch, the violence of the noise and light, the power of the rain, inexorable and insistent as the passing of time—as his mother's silent anger—and the crisp, cleansing scent that remained when it was over. The nights when he slipped silently out into the backyard with his blanket to lie on his back and stare up at the sky watching the stars multiply, and then to wait, sometimes for hours, in hopes of glimpsing just one shooting star, and then, spurred on by his success, to see another. Those same stars were still there, but they looked duller now. Most of their magic was spent, or if it was there, it was no longer available to him. If his memory could be trusted, which wasn't at all clear, there'd even been a few pleasant family moments: sitting around a tree opening presents on Christmas morning and acting for a couple hours as though everything was just fine and dandy; the few times his father laughed, and then, forgetting for a moment how terribly unhappy she was, his mother joined in, her laughter staggered and uneasy, as though she was trying to choke it back, as though it confused her or caused her terrible pain. The fireplace where they roasted marshmallows and popped corn; the neighborhood cat, the one nobody owned and everyone fed and cared for, fat, fluffy and orange as a Creamsicle; the big weeping willow in the front yard and the crooked tree out back that was made for climbing. Those trees, that fireplace, the cat, the laughter and the stars had meant something, had produced in him a singular warmth, something separate from home and family but somehow representative of what some part of him knew it *should* have been.

But perhaps what he'd found was of his own making, generated to fill a void, the feelings merely artifacts of some frenzied subconscious search. Perhaps everyone found comfort in convenient little myths created out of need, out of desperation. Or maybe some lives were truly wholesome, replete with the rich, sustaining byproducts of love. But what did it matter? Searching for answers was like studying a map after arriving at your final destination. All the information in the world wouldn't alter where he was or what he'd become.

At Ninth and Main Chase stopped for a red light. Hobbling across the street pushing a shopping cart was a man in tattered jeans and a baggy green T-shirt that looked as though it had spent a week balled up in his back pocket. He was tall and broad-shouldered, with hair the color of used motor oil. As he crossed in front of the car, Chase noticed the prominent forehead, the Roman nose and wide, extended jaw. That distinctive profile was etched in his memory. In a town this size, how could it belong to anyone else? His gut churned. It had to be his old high school friend. Tim Staples had been bright and talented and far more popular than any of Chase's other friends, but now he looked as though life had collapsed in on him.

Chase pressed the button to lower his window. He was about to call out when a horn blared behind him. He looked up at the light and drove on. When he was on the north side of the intersection he craned his neck around to look back. Tim was leaning over, rooting through a trash bin in front of Dunkin' Donuts. It didn't make sense, didn't seem possible, and it was sad, but it really had nothing at all to do with Chase. Tim was just another piece of a past that no longer existed.

Chase didn't want to be here, in the land of the terminally corpulent, where almost everyone smoked and where among even the most cultured, motor vehicles had a more prominent position, and were more likely to spark animated debate, than literature, art or music. But neither was he eager to go back home to the overpriced strip mall that New York City had become, or to the suburbs, where people hid behind the perfect clothes, the perfect hairstyles, the perfect toys, the perfect cars, the myth of sophistication and simulated depth, which, for those few who cared or dared to look deeper, was totally unconvincing, but which no one ever challenged. But was everyone so deeply flawed, or did it serve the needs of Chase's ravenous ego, did it make him feel better about himself, to view them that way? At least I'm not *that* bad. Of course that didn't work. Not at all. Nor did this ceaseless self-examination bring him any answers. And with his sister in yet another form of limbo, there really was no question where he needed to be.

In spite of his attempt at a cognitive detour, he couldn't excise from his thoughts the image of Tim and the shopping cart. Chase rubbed his temples, checked his mirror, cursed and made a U-turn.

Tim was still in front of Dunkin' Donuts arranging the contents of his cart when Chase pulled into the lot. After parking his car, Chase stepped out and approached his old friend.

"Hey, Tim. It's me, Chase."

Just a cold, empty stare.

"Chase Stoller. We were in high school together, Stroudsburg High."

Tim narrowed his eyes and scrutinized Chase, inspecting his clothing, his hair. The suggestion of a smile, the slightest nod.

"You remember?"

The smile blossomed, though there was something peculiar about his face. It was a little difficult to look at. Maybe he'd been in an accident and suffered a head injury. That could explain the vaguely contorted shape of his head when viewed from the front, and the way he stood with his shoulders hunched.

"What's going on?" Why not ask where he got the nifty cart? "It's been such a long time." Ugh. "Listen, let me buy you some lunch or dinner or whatever. What do you think?"

Tim shrugged, then nodded.

Chase surveyed the area. "Is there some place around here?"

Still silent, Tim pointed to a little tavern on Ninth Street, just east of Main.

Chase smiled and reached out to grip his friend's arm. "Can you speak, Tim?"

Tim looked down at the ground and shook his head.

The bar was dark and, but for the bartender, unpopulated. The odor, a musty mélange of beer, cigarette smoke, fried food and aged eighty-proof urine, was overpowering. They sat down at the table nearest the door and a minute later the bartender, a tall, blocky man with a face full of potholes, plodded over.

He glared at Tim and then turned to Chase. "I take it *you're* paying." His arms were carpeted with a heavy black pelt.

"Yeah, I'm paying."

He rolled his eyes. "What'll it be?"

"Can we get some food?"

"You can if you want burgers and fries."

Chase looked at Tim. "Is that okay?"

Tim nodded and pointed to a card on the table that showed a bottle of Pabst.

"Two burgers with fries and two bottles of Pabst."

"No Pabst."

"What do you have?"

The bartender sighed. "Why'nt you ask your pal?"

Chase swallowed his anger. "Just tell me what you got."

"Bud, Schaefer and Rolling Rock."

"Two Rolling Rocks. And can we get cheese on the burgers?"

"Cheddar or American?"

Of course. "Cheddar okay?" he asked Tim.

Tim nodded.

The bartender shook his head and walked away.

There was something ludicrous about the entire situation, and the symbolism wasn't lost on Chase. Here he was again, trying to communicate with someone who sat across from him unable or unwilling to speak, to give anything back. Feeding him was, perhaps, a gracious gesture, but it was also a self-serving act, the effects of which—beyond the mollification of his own conscience—would be no more lasting than a strip of duct tape on a freshly severed limb.

"I've been away for a long time," he said. "I have no idea . . . I don't know anything about what's gone on here, about what you've been through. I came for my dad's funeral and just sort of stayed on. I live in New York now, but, I don't know, I'm getting a divorce and I'm not working, I lost my job, and my brother and sister are still here, so I don't know . . . I really don't know what I'm doing." Chase laughed. "Not very enlightening, is it?"

Tim seemed to be paying only partial attention. His head was in constant motion, as though he was looking for something, and he kept pushing his hair back, but he occasionally nodded and grinned in Chase's general direction.

In a few minutes the food came and Tim gorged himself. He'd eaten everything in front of him and finished his beer before Chase had swallowed his third bite. Chase slid his plate across the table and Tim grabbed it.

The bartender came over and Tim held out his empty glass. "Two more?" He directed the question at Chase.

"Sure."

Tim's second beer went down in two long, noisy gulps and Chase reluctantly bought him a third.

"Take your time with that one, buddy. I don't want you to overdo it."

Tim stared into his eyes and opened his mouth as though to speak. It was then that Chase realized what was wrong, really, glaringly wrong. Tim's eyes, a deep sapphire blue, had always drawn attention, particularly from girls. The man sitting across from him had brown eyes.

It wasn't the money that bothered him or the time he'd wasted. It was the fact that he'd been such an easy mark, that a vagrant with a vaguely misshapen head could so effortlessly dupe him. He'd just stood there looking like a serial killer while Chase did all the work. He wanted to break his glass over the man's head. But no, he was controlling his impulses now.

"So, old buddy," he said, trying to conceal his anger. "Tell me about yourself."

The man tilted his head and shrugged.

"What kind of work are you doing these days? Still trading stocks and bonds?" Chase turned toward the bar. "Could I have one more beer please, and a prune juice and vodka for my old friend?"

"Prune and vodka?" The bartender screwed up his face. "You serious?"

"Yeah. It's called a pile-driver," Chase said. "Heavy on the prune juice." He turned back to his guest. "You always loved your pile-drivers." He grinned. "See how much I remember, buddy?"

When the drinks came Chase raised his glass and held it out. "To old friends." He swigged his beer, put the glass down. Then he motioned to the mixed drink. "Drink up, pal."

The stranger lifted his glass, took a tentative sip, swallowed. He wiped his mouth and said, "Not too bad." Another sip. "Not bad at all."

"It's a miracle!" Chase stood up. "He's talking. Another pile-driver for the new, improved Tim, bartender."

"Make it a double, Frank," the stranger said.

Chase leaned closer. "I hope you shit your only pants."

"That's not very neighborly." He chugged the rest of the drink.

"What about what *you* did?"

"I really didn't have to do a thing," he said.

"You could have said something."

"Yeah, I guess I could have. But I was kind of hungry and, well, you *did* offer."

The bartender brought the drink and walked away.

Chase glared at the stranger as he raised the glass to his lips. "I hope you wake up in a swamp of deep-fried diarrhea."

The man shrugged. "Truth to tell, I could use a good crap."

"That's good to know."

Wide grin. "Save it for you if you want."

"Photos will be fine."

"I'll need the money for developing and postage."

"You have a camera?"

"Nope. I'll need that, too."

"Why don't I just give you my American Express card?"

"How about transportation?" He motioned to the drink. "Want some?"

"No. Thanks. Cessna okay?"

"Cessna?"

"It's an airplane. You could parachute out over the mall. I'll make sure your equipment's properly ventilated."

"Wouldn't want to take advantage."

"Of course not, you fucking prick."

"What are you so pissed off about?"

"I thought I was talking to my old friend."

"Probably didn't like you much anyway."

"Jerk."

"Don't be that way. You had the pleasure of my company, a bad meal, a couple beers, and you got to open up your heart to an old friend without any unpleasant complications. You don't even have to take me home and clean me up."

"Gee thanks."

"And you got to feel good about yourself. That's worth a hell of a lot in these difficult times."

Chase sat back and assessed the man. He could almost see the humor in this. "You seem fairly bright, you're reasonably well-spoken, you're not crippled in any way I can see, you have a sense of humor that people who don't happen to be me might appreciate. . . ."

"Thanks. You have a very nice shirt."

"It's yours." He reached for his top button.

"Too small."

"Well. . . ."

"So what's your point?"

"I just don't understand what you're doing pushing a shopping cart around."

"I work at the ShopRite."

"You what?" Chase shot forward.

"I'm kidding."

"I really hate you." He couldn't restrain a smile.

"So does my ex."

"So listen. I treated you to a lovely dinner and drinks and I've nearly decided not to beat you to death. Just do me the favor of telling my why you're doing . . . whatever you're doing."

"I got sick of the bullshit."

"Everybody gets sick of the bullshit. There's got to be more to it."

"And I was bored. Still am most of the time."

"That still doesn't explain it."

"And I'm a dedicated alcoholic." He raised his glass.

"Ah," Chase said and picked up his own glass. "I suppose I can take some solace in the knowledge that I'm contributing to, perhaps even accelerating your slow suicide."

"Me, too," the man said, and they both drank. "Name's Tom." He wiped his hand on a napkin and extended it.

Chase shook his hand. "Just one letter away."

"Sorry."

Chase studied the man. "Can I ask you one more serious question?"

"Why not."

"Well, can you look back and see some point when you stepped over a line, or, I'm sorry, but is there something you could have done that would have enabled you to . . . to avoid this?"

"I guess it was probably a process, not inevitable maybe, but pretty goddamned likely, given my fondness for drink and my general nature. But I really don't give it much thought. No point." Then suddenly he wrinkled up his face.

"You're obviously thinking of something."

One hand pressed against his gut, the man struggled to his feet. "Batten down the hatches."

"Excuse me?"

"Soup's on," he said. Then, legs clenched together, he shuffled toward the bathroom.

25

They were on the corner waiting for the light to change when Chase noticed the big burgundy tow truck in the Dunkin' Donuts parking lot.

"Looks like they're towing your shopping cart."

"That's pretty funny," Tom said. "But isn't that your fancy car hanging off the back of that rig?"

Chase laughed. Then he saw his car's headlights peering up over the roof of the truck. "Fuck." Hands waving over his head, he sprinted across the street.

As he neared the truck he called out. "Stop. Wait."

The driver looked down at him from the cab, his eyes at half-mast.

"What are you doing with my car?"

The man shrugged. "Looks to me like I'm towing it."

"Why?"

"S'what they pay me for."

"Who's paying you to tow my car?"

"Well." With a grimy finger he rubbed the side of his nose. "I guess you are."

"Not a chance." Chase stepped toward the truck. "Now take my car off this piece of shit."

"'Fraid I can't do that."

He stifled the urge to reach into the window and grab the driver. "Why?"

"Look, pal, they call me and I come. Once the car's on the truck I got no choice but to take it."

"*Who* calls you?"

"Well, in this situation right here it was the manager of Dunkin' Donuts."

Chase surveyed the lot. "The parking lot's not even half full."

"Got a sign back there." He motioned with his head. "Says right on it, customer parking only, violators towed at owner's expense."

"This is bullshit."

"'Fraid you'll have to take that up with them." He shifted the truck into gear. "I'm blocking the entrance here."

"Don't do it." Chase took another step toward the truck. "Please." Without his rage he felt helpless.

The driver shrugged, the engine revved and the truck lurched forward. From the far side of the truck came the sound of metal grinding, then a scream. Chase ran around to the back of the truck. Tom was lying on the ground, his legs wedged between the tires of the truck and the crushed shopping cart. He grinned up at Chase. "Now how the hell is anybody going to get into the parking lot?"

When the driver appeared Tom began to moan. "I can't feel my legs. I can't move. Dear God in heaven, I'm crippled."

"Just take it easy, buddy," the driver said and pulled a cell phone from his pocket. "We'll get you an ambulance."

"What about my cart?" He began to weep.

Chase suppressed a laugh.

Hands trembling, the driver poked at the keys of his phone. "We'll take care of it."

"Wait," Tom called out.

"What?" The driver's face was dripping perspiration.

"I need a potty."

"What?"

"I think I have to make a poo."

The driver looked around. "What do you want me to do?"

"Get me a bowl or something, a big one. Just please don't make me soil my favorite trousers."

"Harry." A short, bald-headed man peered out of the Dunkin' Donuts doorway. "How in heck are my customers supposed to get in and out?" He looked and sounded like Elmer Fudd.

"I got a situation here," the driver called back.

"Just get that thing out of the entrance."

"Jesus Christ, Jim. I got a real bad situation."

"Well I got a gosh-darned business to run." He stepped out and planted his hands on his hips.

"Oh no," Tom groaned.

"Just move it up," the manager called out.

"I can't."

"Do I have to have *you* towed now, too?"

"Just give me a break, you goddamned bubble-headed dwarf."

"Bear's at the cave door."

"What?"

"It's coming out."

"Jesus Christ." The driver sprinted toward the entrance of Dunkin' Donuts and went inside.

Tom smiled up at Chase. "I have a feeling you'll be out of here in a couple minutes."

"Do you really have to . . . ?"

"Are you kidding? There's nothing left in my colon but dust."

"What are you going to do?"

"Have a little rest here until you're on your way and then either limp into the sunset or get some of that delicious hospital food."

Chase extracted a twenty-dollar bill from his wallet.

"No. This was my fault. You can buy me a drink . . . well, a beer next time you miss your old friend."

"Hold on, I'm coming." Running toward them was the driver, a large paper cup in one hand, a roll of toilet paper in the other, the loose end wagging in the breeze.

26

Chase was restless now, eager to do something, to feel a sense of accomplishment. The afternoon's events, just a minor detour in terms of his life, had energized him. But what was there to do? Perhaps what he needed was just some forward motion, measurable progress in some clear, predetermined, positive direction; not this arbitrary motion, this twitching and fluttering and rash reacting and maniacal overreacting, this sense that he was always so busy girding himself for the next random assault that he was incapable of independent action. Somehow he was losing himself in all the noise and thrashing about. He'd been losing himself for years. Maybe part of what he was missing was silence and calm and a connection to the Earth, to nature, to himself. Ride a bike, row a boat, pet a squirrel, lie beneath a weeping willow chewing on topsoil and bark and jerking off with uncommon fervor. And he needed a friend, a comrade, someone who wouldn't ridicule him for his weakness and his need, who would forgive his incompetence and indecision and his masturbatory impulses. He needed everything but what he had. Of course he did. He was absolutely giddy with need.

As Chase approached his father's driveway, he glanced at his rearview mirror. A short distance behind him was a black Range Rover. When he slowed and put his signal on the other vehicle did the same. He squinted into his mirror but the Range Rover's tinted windows obscured his view of the driver. There was no reason to assume that whoever was behind him intended any harm, but it really didn't matter. Even a benign visit would be an imposition, an interruption of whatever he was failing to accomplish. He passed the driveway and resumed his speed and the other vehicle did the same. About a mile beyond his father's house, Chase made a series of random turns, the Range Rover remaining a respectful distance behind. Perhaps it was a real estate agent or someone from the bank, though it seemed extremely unlikely they'd follow him through this haphazard maze. Chase drove carefully, keeping his speed down, coming to a complete stop at all the stop signs and using his signals before every turn, hoping, as he roamed through increasingly unfamiliar neighborhoods, that the other driver would simply run out of gas or interest. After a few more minutes he found himself in an area he didn't recognize. He was disoriented and his mouth was dry; the muscles in his jaw were throbbing. He wanted to put his car in reverse now and jam his foot to the floor. Tamp down the anger. He made the next right and then a quick left onto a narrow street that ended at its intersection with Park Avenue. He stopped and looked around to get his bearings. Downtown Stroudsburg was to the left, Delaware Water Gap a few miles to the right. He made the right toward Foxtown Hill, adhering to the speed limit until he reached the crest, but as soon as the descent began, he pressed his foot to the floor and went through the gears. At first the Range Rover shrunk in his mirror, but before he reached the bottom of the hill it was with him again, staying close as he skidded around the right turn onto Main Street, flew through the red light in the center of town and continued up the hill, past the post office and the municipal building. When the Deer Head Inn appeared, Chase remembered the steep, tight right turn just beyond it and the narrow dirt road that went off to the left at the top of the hill. He passed the Inn and twisted his wheel hard. The undercarriage bottomed out and when the steering wheel lurched he nearly lost his grip. A flash of broken glass and torn metal, blood pouring from a deep gash on his forehead. Rats eating his brain. Cocksucker. At the top of the hill he turned onto the dirt road and when the lake appeared on the right he slammed on his brakes, skidded into the gravel parking lot and leapt out of the car. He was breathing hard and his heart was racing.

The Range Rover gradually slowed to a stop. The passenger's window lowered but the driver was cloaked in shadow.

Just the ticking of Chase's engine and the other vehicle's idle, then the man said, "You're burning oil."

Chase folded his arms over his chest, swallowed. "Can I do something for you?"

"Hop in and we'll take a ride together, maybe have a talk."

"I think I'll just enjoy the clean, fresh air."

The man leaned toward the open window. His hair was dark and he wore sunglasses. "I'd like you to leave my wife alone."

"Let's assume I know what you're talking about."

"Yes, let's."

"Why don't you tell *her*?"

"I'd prefer to resolve this between us."

"Is there a threat in there somewhere?"

"This is a request, a plea, man to man."

"What if I don't feel like complying?"

"You're not a bad-looking guy. I'm sure you can find someone else to screw."

"Is that what I'm doing?"

"Do you think this is something special?"

"I don't know what it is."

"No, you don't."

"You seem to be trying to tell me something."

"I'm just asking you to respect our marriage. Do you think you can do that for me?"

"I get the feeling there's something else you want to tell me."

His face dissolved as he slid back into shadow. "You're just a minor player in an old routine." Silently the window rose.

Chase leaned back against the hood of his car contemplating the lake and trying to estimate how far into it he'd need to travel before his car became totally submerged, the approximate speed he'd need to attain by the time he reached the shore in order to travel that distance through or over the water, whether or not he could reach that speed without ending up in a ditch or running over some innocent puppy and if he really gave even the most insignificant lump of excrement about innocent puppies right now. Too many variables.

Well, her husband knew—that seemed evident—but what else had Chase learned today? That perhaps she'd done this before? Oh yes. That had been the subtext of her husband's parting comment, delivered without any attempt at subtlety. He could try to beat up his car again, but another defeat by an inanimate object would sting right now, and anyway, he might need his hands to strangle someone. He pulled his phone from his pocket.

No, don't.

But I want to.

No sirree.
Why?
Because whining is extremely unattractive and if this becomes too unpleasant she can just end it.
Great.
And because knowledge is power.
What the hell is that supposed to mean?
At the moment she's got all the power here. That's just no good at all. Telling her you had this conversation with her hubby might alter her responses to any questions you ask.
It's not like I'm trying to trip her up.
Of course it is. How else do you expect to get to the truth?
I hate me.
Yeah, well, me, too.
Blow me.
I'm not sure I'm that flexible, but buy me a nice dinner and we'll see.

He knelt by the lakefront and sifted through the detritus until he found a smooth, flat stone. Facing the water, he leaned hard to the right, cocked his arm and with a powerful thrust he launched the stone, which pierced the water like an arrow and disappeared in the murk. A stabbing pain shot up his arm. *Shit. Pain is your body's way of laughing at you. Traitor.* He kneaded his bicep.

As a teenager Chase had passed this lake dozens of times, sometimes with his buddies and occasionally with his girlfriend or some auxiliary lust object. Another two or three miles up the road was the rocky mesa most people knew as the vista and Chase and his friends called the fingerbowl. Bordered by trees and a scenic overlook, with only one point of access, it was the perfect setting for hard drinking and heavy petting and, occasionally, profoundly inelegant coitus. Some nights he and his friends sped up the hill with a sense of urgency and enthusiasm he hadn't felt more than a few times in the years since. After a couple beers the jokes and stories would begin, and sometimes, after a couple more, they'd sing, striving, with only marginal results, to reproduce the harmonies they'd heard on the radio. If they got drunk enough they might become rowdy; occasionally there would be a shove, a fist would rise, or there might be another group standing around another car, a verbal taunt from one camp or the other, some hint of aggression, more words, strutting and posturing and swiftly mounting tension as the two sides tried to find an honorable avenue of retreat. Once or twice, when the other group was doing more than posing, when the scary bastards really wanted an actual goddamned fight, blows would be exchanged, producing a dull, meaty thud that always made Chase want to run and hide, though his pride would never permit it. Overall they'd been lucky: just a few minor skirmishes, a bloody nose or a split lip. But there had been teeth lost out on that mesa; there'd been deep bruises, lacerations and broken noses, fingers slammed in car doors and clothing shredded. On a Saturday night one summer, a fifteen-year-old boy from Jersey had lost an eye. Once or twice knives were drawn, and some guy from Snydersville had been cut up pretty badly with a broken bottle. There were rumors of handguns and packs of wild dogs, but those might have been designed to limit the population.

If you were underage and you were drinking you'd always face the road, watching for headlights and listening for an approaching vehicle. The local cop would come up and shine his spotlight around, but he soon left if there wasn't any serious trouble. He'd once told Chase, with a wink that had made Chase feel like a serial rapist, to let him know if he ever had any "action" he couldn't handle.

The State Police, on the other hand, were not entertained by the activity up there. They made frequent arrests for underage drinking and disorderly conduct, though what they really craved was something that would make the local papers and aid them in their constant battle against the real threat to the American way of life: an actual drug bust.

Chase recalled how, when their supply of alcohol ran out, he and his buddies would careen down this rutted, winding, one-lane road, fueled by inebriation and testosterone, primed now to bring civilization to its knees, or at least to laugh until they vomited. Had he driven the road once with his lights off or had that just been a story he'd invented? Sometimes, with the passage of time, truth and the fiction ran together. But real memories, those that reflected actual events, were generally supported by the type of detail one rarely takes the time to fabricate.

One night, after a particularly rancorous argument with his girlfriend, Chase asked one of his friends to punch him. Burt, who had been a faithful drinking and carousing partner for several years, was short and a little overweight, but his arms and chest were packed with bulging cords of solid muscle. He really didn't want to hurt Chase, but they were both drunk and Chase just kept pushing until he complied. Numbed by alcohol, Chase rubbed his jaw and then asked him to do it again. Later that same summer, Burt's girlfriend said she was tired and he offered to drive her home. As soon as they were in the car Jacki slid her hand between his legs, giving him the gentlest of perineal caresses through his jeans. By the time they got to her house he was so hard he couldn't stand up straight. She was skinny and a little sluttish but incredibly sexy. He lasted about three minutes and never got over his shame. If she were here with him right now, Chase would attempt to demonstrate that his performance that night had been an aberration, to compensate her and vindicate himself.

Standing next to his car, Chase surveyed the area. About fifty yards beyond the north end of the lake, the road began to climb. There was a gate across the road now, broad diagonal bands of black and yellow proclaiming its authority. Still rubbing his arm, Chase made his way to the gate: *No unauthorized vehicles beyond this point.* He stepped around the gate and continued along the path, overgrown now with the products of nature's reclamation.

For a few minutes he trudged forward, blindly following the road as it wound upward. But soon, chilled by the breeze and energized by the sweet vegetal scents, Chase increased his pace, pebbles, twigs and leaves crunching underfoot. Soon he could feel his heart pounding, hear the rhythm of his breath, feel his leg muscles burning with the effort, the road ahead bouncing and trembling as it rushed toward him. The trail became rougher and again he increased his pace, dodging rocks and puddles and hurdling downed branches. He was invigorated by the effort. His chest was tight and his throat felt like sandpaper, but still he ran, pushing himself harder and harder. He could do this forever, find his rhythm and run until the bottoms of his feet wore out. Patches of light shone through now and as the road began to level Chase broke into a hard sprint, swinging his arms to propel himself forward. He felt good, strong, indestructible. He looked up and smiled as the canopy split apart, the two sides pulling away from one another to reveal a perfect cloudless sky. He let out a scream of joy, his foot caught on something and he went down like a sack of wet sand.

For a minute he just lay there waiting for his breathing to slow and trying to assess the damage. When did he become such a clod? Cautiously he moved his legs, then his arms. No sign of a break. He gradually raised himself into a sitting position. His pants were torn at the knees and his right elbow was bleeding, but the worst of the pain was where he'd landed on his ribs, and even that was tolerable. He closed his eyes and listened. At first all he heard was the distant whisper of the breeze. Then a bird chattered, stopped for a moment and began again. The sounds were calming. Chase opened his eyes and turned to look around him. The scene was fairly close to his recollections, though some of the distances were wrong and the shape was a little off. And it had grown wilder.

At the edge of the clearing was a grassy patch, the perfect scene for some symbolic vision, something that would provoke a deep realization, perhaps a fallen nest. No, too obvious. A doe with a wounded leg sniffing the underbrush. Chase would carefully adjust his position to get a better look and she would turn her head toward him and freeze. For a few more seconds she'd remain there, and he'd be moved by the moment. Finally she would turn and bound off, disappearing into the forest. There would be several possible interpretations, all of them relevant. Another sound drew him from his thoughts: the low, steady hum of cars and tractor-trailers speeding along Route 80. Chase rose and brushed himself off. Then he noticed all the litter: bottles and cans, bags, cigarette packs, matchbooks and candy wrappers, shreds of tin foil and cellophane.

Desolation lurking in the shadows like a contemptuous stalker, Chase worked his way back down the path. About halfway to the bottom he heard the distant purl of flowing water. He turned off the trail and followed the sound until he came to a treeless patch of ground covered with hundreds of plants, their broad heart-shaped leaves a rich, luminous green. It was as though he'd slipped into some other latitude. On the far border of the patch was a grassy escarpment overlooking the lower tier of a waterfall. To the right it rose up, a glistening cascade of liquid jewels, following a steep rocky slope toward its source, and to the left it dropped down below the escarpment and slowed before spilling into a pool that released its overflow into a narrow stream. Chase clambered down the bank, peeled off his clothing and eased himself into the water. It was so cold it burned his skin and sucked the oxygen from his lungs, but it also seemed to draw the pain from his injuries and some of the clutter from his mind. He just sat motionless in the frigid pool letting his thoughts evaporate. Soon the thought of freezing to death wasn't entirely unpleasant. There was peace here. He could just stay. He remained there until he sensed some essential part of himself beginning to slip away. Then he lifted himself out and for a long time he sat trembling on the bank, his knees pulled up snug against his chest, his arms wrapped tightly around them.

27

By the time Chase reached his car, the shadows had all begun to huddle together. His stomach seemed to be crawling around inside him in search of an organ to consume, but he felt grubby and disheveled and acutely antisocial. Dinner out was not an option. Shuddering and faint, he drove down the hill and pulled into a parking space on Main Street.

"Good evening. Deer Head Inn." If not for his hunger and the fact that it had taken him ten minutes to get the number, he might have hung up as soon as heard her voice.

"Hi, Zoë. It's Chase."

"Hey, how are you?"

"I'm sitting outside in my car starving to death."

"Well, come on in. We have food."

"I'd almost like to, but my clothing's dirty and torn and I'm covered with cuts and bruises."

"Oh my gosh. What happened?"

"I tried communing with nature, but nature wasn't interested."

"Just come in."

"I'd really rather not."

"Okay. Well. . . ."

"I was wondering if I could order something to go and maybe you . . . maybe somebody could bring it out to me."

"Are you okay?"

"I think so."

"What would you like?"

"Are you absolutely certain you don't want to fall in love with me?"

"I'm afraid that's not under my control."

"How about if we just lie together naked." Chase's phone beeped. Someone was calling.

"I guess you're not in too much pain."

"I am. It's horrible. You could cure me."

"Well, I *could* probably make you forget the pain for a while, but I'm not a big believer in stopgap measures."

Another beep. "*I* am. I *love* stopgap measures. They're my all-time favorite measures."

"You're very funny."

"You're very forgiving."

After ordering his food Chase checked his messages. Earlier in the day Aaron had called, employing dozens of words in service of a message that had apparently jumped ship. Haley had left a two-word message: "Call me." He didn't feel up to either call.

Zoë brought his food out to his car and handed it through the window. The bag was heavy and it bulged in several places.

"Is this a coordination test?"

"You sounded like you could use a beer," she said.

"A beer?"

"Or two." She smiled.

"You'd be much less of a problem for me if you weren't so fucking nice."

"You'd probably like me more."

"Probably. What do I owe you?"

"Take better care of yourself." She leaned down and kissed him on the cheek before going back up the steps to the Inn.

She was so pretty, so young, and she was genuinely sweet. In fact that was the problem. She was too nice, too emotionally fit to be interested in someone as hopelessly lost and chronically confused as he was. It made sense that he'd appeal to a woman who was emotionally distant and unavailable, someone who'd only feel at ease in the company of another desolate, suicidal wreck. But Haley *had* called; that was something. Between that and his encounter with her husband, it was almost like having the upper hand. It would require more willpower than he was accustomed to exercising, but he resolved not to call her until he'd eaten and cleaned himself up.

She was leaning against her car when he pulled up the driveway, her face turned toward the ground. Lit by his headlights, she looked like an actress feigning sleep.

He got out of his car and took a few steps toward her. "This is a nice surprise."

"I hope you don't mind."

"Of course not. You can even share my yummy dinner."

She didn't respond.

He tried to read her expression but his eyes hadn't adjusted to the dark. "Is everything okay?"

She shrugged. "I'm not crazy about the fact that I . . . that I'm here."

That was probably as close as she'd come to acknowledging feelings for him. Better than nothing. Or was it? She could keep him off balance forever like this.

"I'm glad you're here," he said.

"Really?"

Now he could see her face. She really didn't believe it. "You don't get it, do you? I want to be with you."

She winced, as though she were expecting a blow, as though the thought of being loved caused her unspeakable pain. And maybe that was it. On the one hand she felt unlovable and on the other the prospect of being loved terrified her. But even if he was right, there was nothing he could do about it.

"Someone might drive by later to take a look at my father's car," he said, his spirits plummeting further. "If I pull it out of the garage would you mind pulling yours in to make room?"

"You're still worried about the other night."

"I'd just rather not take a chance."

"Okay." For the first time since he'd arrived, she looked directly at him. Her eyes widened and she gripped his hand. "What happened to you now?"

"I cut myself shaving."

Chase devoured his food and then took a hot shower. When he stepped out of the bathroom, Haley was waiting on the bed. He gazed down at her naked body. Yes, she was beautiful, and self-restraint was, at best, only the most microscopic component of his character. It would be so easy to postpone the discussion he'd been planning, or to forego it entirely. More than anything else, he wanted to sink slowly in, to lose himself in her, in the softness and warmth, in the gentle motion, to accept as spontaneous, genuine and unambiguous the indecipherable gasps and shudders that would come, the earnest utterances and urgent embraces, to cling for just a little while to all the manifestations of love. And yet he knew that searching for truth there, or for answers, was a futile and potentially perilous undertaking. *Just let yourself feel loved, even if it's only an illusion.* But perhaps he had it backwards. Perhaps what he needed was not to be loved, but to believe in his own capacity to love. Was he his father? Was he alive?

He sat on the edge of the bed clenching his fists, trying to fend off the urge to touch her. "I'd like to ask you something that's probably none of my business."

"Okay."

"Before me. . . ."

"Before you, what?" She was going to make him say it.

His body tensed. "Am I . . . is this something you've done before?"

"No."

"You've never been unfaithful to your husband before?"

"That's not what I said." She sat up and wrapped the blanket around her shoulders.

"I'm a little confused."

"I did have another affair, Chase. But it wasn't like this."

"What was it like?" Without a conscious invitation, sarcasm had crept into his tone.

"For one thing, he was an asshole."

"So it was just about sex?"

"No. I thought I loved him at first. Okay? But he was . . . he was insecure and he took advantage of . . . of my weakness. I don't mean that the way it sounds. I mean he knew about my self-doubt, my vulnerability, where it came from and how to use it. He wanted to keep me, to own me, even if it meant destroying me. He was selfish and insecure and ultimately very cruel."

"Do you ever—"

"God, no. I ended it. It's over."

"But why would you get involved again?" He didn't remember her arms being quite that short. Why was he finding flaws now?

"Because I'm fucked up and selfish, too, Chase. Can't you see that yet?" She sighed. "And because . . . I don't really know. You wanted me. I don't know."

"A fairy-tale romance."

She didn't smile.

"I need to tell you something."

She studied him. Her lips were trembling.

"Your husband knows."

"No." She shook her head frantically, like a little girl denying some shameful misdeed. "He can't."

"I'm sorry."

"How? How do you know?"

"He . . . he followed me, and we had a . . . a brief discussion. I should have told you right away, but he said something . . . something that upset me. I should have called you. I'm sorry. He knows about us, Haley."

"Oh God."

"And he told me . . . he insinuated that you'd done this before."

"What did he say?"

"He asked me to leave you alone and said this wasn't anything new. The message seemed fairly clear."

She closed her eyes and let her head fall forward. When the sobbing began, Chase moved toward her and put his arms around her. Just hold her. Just give her whatever she needs. There's nothing else to lose now.

"I . . . didn't want . . . ," she said through staggered sobs. "Oh God, I didn't want to do this. I didn't want to hurt him."

"You must have known he'd find out."

"No. I didn't." Again she looked like a child. "I really didn't. He's so innocent."

He brought her head to his chest and stroked her hair.

She pulled away, put a hand behind his neck. Lips parted, she pulled him toward her.

He drew back and took her face in his hands. "Will this make it better or worse?"

She shook her head. "Neither," she said, and pressed her lips to his.

There were at least a dozen points of contact and yet Chase wanted more. He couldn't remember the last time he'd felt such powerful, overwhelming hunger for touch. Just be here. Just stay.

"Just stay here."

"Tonight?"

"And tomorrow and—"

"I can't."

"He's already hurt. The damage is done." Was he serious?

"It's never done."

He pulled back to see her face. "What does that mean?"

"I don't know. I always find a way to hurt people."

"Isn't that a little melodramatic?"

"It's how I feel."

"You have choices. If you really don't want to hurt him you can be the faithful wife he wants. Or you can leave him and be done with it. At least that way he'd have some chance of finding someone who wanted to be with him, and maybe you could actually be happy."

She squeezed her eyes shut.

"Don't you *want* to be happy?"

Her eyes flashed open. "What makes people think they should be happy all the time?"

"What people?"

"Everybody."

"Fuck everybody. I'm talking about you, and I'm not talking about being happy all the time. I just don't think you should always have to feel like shit. I mean unless you actually prefer that."

"Why are you angry?"

"I think you use that crap about not having any choice to justify your behavior."

"My behavior?"

A burst of white, geometric shapes gliding across the ceiling, the sound of gravel crunching.

She sat up. "Shit."

"He won't see your car."

"Oh God."

"It's probably not even him."

The lights went out. Silence, then a knock on the front door. They waited. Another knock, louder.

He got out of bed and grabbed his jeans. "I'd better go down."

"What are you going to do?"

"I have no idea."

The first thing Chase noticed was the bulky suede jacket, the perfect place to conceal a firearm, even a grenade. If he tackled him now he'd at least have the element of surprise on his side. "What can I do for you?"

"Is she here?"

"I'm afraid I'm all alone," Chase said, then wished he hadn't.

"Do you mind if I come in?"

Chase backed away from the door and the man stepped in.

He was perhaps an inch or two taller than Chase, possibly a couple years younger and apparently fit, and he seemed to be trembling, which might mean any number of things, none of which were encouraging.

"Can I get you a drink?"

He shook his head. "I'd better not."

Chase led him into the living room, eased himself down onto the couch and motioned to the recliner across from it.

The man sat down and leaned toward Chase. "Do you know where she is?" He allowed his eyes to meet Chase's, then quickly looked away.

"I'm afraid I can't help you." Chase scrutinized his lover's husband. Not quite handsome but certainly not unattractive. Chase was jealous of the man's relationship with his own wife. "Look. . . ."

"Julian," the man said.

"Sorry."

Julian slumped back in the recliner and sighed. Earlier in the day he'd seemed hostile, faintly threatening; now he was almost pathetic. "Haley's more sensitive than she seems. She's gone through. . . ." He paused to inspect the room, as though he might find some sign of his wife there. "She's been through a lot."

"That's a little vague."

"I don't know how much she's told you."

Chase was silent, waiting, eager to learn more.

"She had a rough time when she was young."

"It's a big club."

Julian frowned, shook his head. "I had a pretty good childhood."

"Really?"

"Most people did, I think."

"I guess we travel in different . . . universes."

"Yeah, well."

"Why are you telling me this?"

"I'm sure this is fun for you, but for her—"

"You're concerned about her. Is that what this is about?"

"Of course I am."

"I'm sure she's fine."

"She's vulnerable. I don't want her to be hurt."

"Or are you asking me what my intentions are?"

"Why are you being sarcastic?"

Chase shrugged.

"You're having an affair with my wife and you're being sarcastic while I sit here trying to have a man-to-man discussion with you." His eyes narrowed.

"Something about that phrase, 'man-to-man'—something about that just bothers me."

"Okay. I'm trying to have a *frank* discussion with you. Is that less . . . threatening?"

"Threatening?" Chase produced the grin that generally made people want to step on his face.

"Is there some reason for you to be pissed off at me? I mean, under the circumstances that seems a little backwards. Am I just supposed to mind my own business while you destroy my life? Does that seem reasonable?" He leaned forward and tilted his head. "Would you do that if our situations were reversed? Would you?"

"No." Suddenly Chase was exhausted. This part just wasn't fun. "At least I don't think so." He rubbed his eyes. Her scent was on his hands. All he wanted was to go back up to her. "I honestly don't know what I'd do."

"Your actions don't occur in a vacuum."

"I'm not . . . I haven't forced myself on anyone."

"But if you weren't here. . . ."

"But I am here."

"What you're doing is wrong."

"Wrong." Chase let his eyes fall shut. This was a man, not just an obstacle to his happiness—his purely theoretical happiness—but an actual human being, someone he might not be able to force himself to abhor without more effort than he was able to expend right now. This was going to be sad for someone, maybe for everyone. But what was he supposed to do about that? It couldn't be undone now. What was he supposed to do with the sympathy, the sadness he was beginning to feel for this man? *Please be gone when I open my eyes.*

"I'm sure you've heard of right and wrong."

"Moving targets with an infinite reserve of disguises."

"You're sarcastic and glib."

Chase pressed his fingertips into his temples. "Look, I'm sorry. I'm really not trying to be a jerk, and I have no desire to cause you . . . to cause anyone pain. What you're accusing me of isn't particularly nice, no. But I really don't need you to teach me about morality. This stuff is nothing new. People get caught up in their own needs."

"Don't you mean desires?"

"Whatever word you prefer. We're all selfish animals." What a transparent justification.

"Why can't you just go back to New York and leave us alone?"

"I don't know what to say to you."

"This is just a diversion for you, an entertainment."

"How do you know what it is?"

"Are you in love with my wife? Am I supposed to offer you my blessing, maybe give the bride away?"

"I don't want your blessing."

"No, you just want my wife."

"This isn't helping anyone."

"Just get out of the way so Haley and I can get back to our lives. That's all I'm asking."

"What if she doesn't want to get back to that life?"

"When you get married you have an agreement, you have responsibilities to someone else."

"I'm familiar with the theory."

"It's not just a theory. It's the way people live, decent people, that is, people who don't think whatever serves them is right and fuck everybody who gets in their way."

Chase sensed the anger now, and he felt energized by it. This, at least, was familiar territory. "Is that what I'm doing, Julian?"

"I'd say that's what you're doing, fucking anybody you want to and to hell with decency and screw the victims. Yeah, I'd say that's exactly what you're doing. And on top of that, you're arrogant and snide."

"Okay."

"You're *okay* with my assessment?" He laughed. "How *big* of you, city boy." He slid forward and leaned closer to Chase. His jaw was moving from side to side and his forehead was beaded with perspiration. "You don't give a shit about Haley. You don't give a shit about anybody but yourself, you fucking arrogant cocksucker."

Was this what he'd been waiting for? Had he pushed him far enough to make him hostile enough to ease Chase's inconstant conscience? Were they equals now, or was Chase still awaiting the life-affirming collision of the man's knuckles and his jaw? *Hit me.* "You don't know anything about me." *Go ahead.*

Julian sat up, eyes glazed, hands writhing on his lap. For what seemed like five minutes, he glared into the distance. Chase was waiting for the explosion. If it didn't come soon, Haley might think they were alone again and come down the stairs. He was ready to react, watching for some sudden movement. Julian's eyes suddenly widened. He grinned and nodded. "Okay," he said and rose. "Okay." Without another word he walked out of the house.

When Chase got back upstairs Haley was sitting on the edge of the bed buttoning her blouse.
"Where are you going?"
"I have to go home." She stood up.
"I don't think that's a good idea."
"I'll tell him I was driving around."
"He won't believe you."
"He needs me."
"He seemed . . . on the edge."
"Of what?"
"I don't know, but I think you should stay away."
"Is the garage unlocked?"
"Yes, but I don't think—"
"He would never hurt me."
"Call him from a hotel, tell him you just need some time, at least get a sense of his state of mind before you go home. He didn't look like he was in control when he left."
"He needs me."
Chase moved toward her. "Please don't go." His words just floated between them like fog. When he reached out to take her hand, she shook her head and rushed out of the room and down the stairs.

28

Disoriented and drenched with perspiration, Chase disentangled himself from the sheets and sat up. He'd had a terribly disturbing dream. He was checking his hair with two mirrors when he noticed a large bald spot in the back of his head. His heart dropped into his stomach and his knees buckled. When had this happened? Why hadn't he seen it before? Why hadn't anyone said anything? He was at least a foot shorter, too. He'd had to stand on tiptoe to see his face in the mirror. It was like awakening to find his arms were gone, and it was so real. What the hell did it mean?

He inspected the room. Well, here he was. Haley might be gone forever, back with her husband or off somewhere with the next lucky contestant. Of course he'd survive if he never saw her again, but survival was not the loftiest of goals and certainly not what he thought he'd been aiming for. That her husband had been right did nothing to diminish his distress. Chase had been sarcastic and snide and totally unsympathetic. But why? What was the point of trying to prove that the man whose wife he'd just screwed from several different angles was a jerk? This was not something to be proud of, and he hadn't always been this way. He hadn't always been so cruel and hostile. He used to be tender and caring, a lover of small furry creatures. Where had that part of him gone? He wanted it back. On the other hand, what he didn't need now was yet another reason to feel like a glob of excrement. He needed something more, to feel good about being alive, about himself, to actually do something, something good, whatever that meant. But what *did* it mean? Should he read to a blind man? Smile at a child? Help a cripple across the street, castrate a telemarketer, shoot an accordion, bomb a bagpipe, light a congressperson on fire? He showered, picked at a couple hard-boiled eggs and called his brother.

"Any plans for the kids today?"

"Nothing that can't be changed."

"Can I borrow them?"

"Yeah, sure. What's the plan?"

"We'll make it up."

"What is this place?" It was Bradley who asked the question.

Chase pivoted around to face them. "Haven't you ever been here before?"

"I don't think so. What is it?"

All he'd told them was that they were going to have an adventure. That had been enough. "It's sort of a hospital."

Sophie wrinkled up her face. "Do you feel sick, Uncle Chase?"

"Well, a little." He smiled and took her hand. "But that's not why we're here."

"Then why are we?"

"This is where my sister lives."

"You have a sister?"

"Yes, and she's your aunt."

"Really?" Bradley turned and grinned at his sister. "Awesome."

Chase hadn't expected them to have a great deal of information about their aunt or where she was, but he'd been certain that they'd at least be aware she existed.

"She's not feeling so well, so she might act a little funny. She might not even look at you or say anything, but she's really very nice." Any way he looked at it this was risky, and yet it seemed critically important for the children, and perhaps for Hannah as well. Aaron would be upset when he found out, but with Chase as his only acknowledged living blood relative, he'd eventually come to appreciate the pragmatic value of forgiveness.

He stepped out of the car, opened the back door and leaned down to look in at them. "We don't have to go in if you guys don't want to."

"I want to," Bradley said.

"What about you?" Chase smiled at Sophie.

"Me too."

"Promise to be especially nice to her, okay?"

They were both eager to get out of the car and go inside, but as soon as they stepped through the doorway, Bradley adopted the rigid posture and cold stare Chase had recently noticed. But perhaps it was just a reaction to the place. Between the dull, worn appearance and the pungent institutional smells—disinfectants, body odors, food processed to the point of irrelevance and medication—it certainly wasn't an inviting atmosphere. After checking them in, the woman at the desk led the three of them to the waiting room. A few minutes later Eleanor delivered Hannah, who glanced at the children and then at Chase before allowing her eyes to drift toward the drab and permanently stained linoleum floor.

"Hannah, these are Aaron's children, your niece and nephew, Sophie and Bradley. I thought you might want to meet them." He knew by now not to expect anything, but it didn't really matter. For the moment they were all there together. Here is your family. Here is our family. Here is whatever it is.

Sophie sat off to the side furtively observing her aunt, but Bradley, after a very tentative start, seemed to sense Hannah's fragility and to be drawn to her. As Chase spoke, Bradley moved cautiously closer toward his aunt, and once, when she looked away, he reached out and touched her robe. Chase nearly wept. Although there were no significant changes in Hannah's behavior today, Chase was sure there was some subtle difference in her affect. And though they only stayed for about fifteen minutes, more than once she seemed aware of the children, and at one point she looked into Chase's eyes for a couple seconds. But if she seemed a little less remote, there was also in her eyes something else, a trace of distress, or anguish. Of course he was guessing. She could have been watching naked pirates doing ballet.

There were no breakthroughs, no dramatic signs of improvement, no miracles. It really wasn't much at all—perhaps it was nothing—yet it felt important, it felt right, which was an increasingly rare experience. Wrong, on the other hand, was generally easier to recognize—though often not until it was too late to elude—and it was certainly far more familiar. So many things were wrong and so few clearly and unambiguously right. Maybe this was as close as he could get to good. *I'm not going to cry. This belongs to them.*

"How dare you put my children through that?" Aaron's face was swollen with rage and Chase wanted to slap it, spit at it or step on it, maybe yank off an ear or a lip.

"I just thought it would be good for them . . . and for her."

"They aren't *your* children. *You* don't get to make these decisions. If you want to screw up some kids, feel free to have a couple of your own."

"I assumed they'd been there before."

"You could have asked." They were standing in the study while Bradley and Sophie played outside and Sarah worked in the garden.

"It really never occurred to me that you'd be so ashamed of your sister that you'd conceal her from her own niece and nephew." Of course that wasn't entirely true, but it was a credible argument.

"Ashamed?"

"I just can't seem to find a less-incriminating explanation."

"Well fuck you."

"Can *you*? Can you give me another reason that makes any sense at all?"

"Don't try to turn this around. I'm the injured party here."

"Oh, golly. I thought this was about the kids."

Aaron was pacing now. He wasn't accustomed to this sort of confrontation and he didn't like it. The directness seemed to twist him up.

"You're the one who thinks family is so important. Hannah is family, yours and mine and theirs, and they have a right to know her, and she has a right to—"

"So after years of a total lack of interest you suddenly care about everyone. And we're all supposed to accept your judgments and respond to your dictums. You want to take over our lives and teach us ignorant novices how to raise our children. Meanwhile you can't keep a job or a wife. You're a joke."

"I've always cared, Aaron."

"Maybe in theory, from a comfortable distance. But that's really of no use to anyone but you. That's not caring. That's just a way of assuaging your guilt."

Still, he wasn't doing too badly. "Okay. I'm an asshole. I won't argue with that. But isn't it possible that my distance has enabled me to see things you can't?"

"What things, Chase?"

"That your children might be slipping away."

"Christ."

"We pass it on, like baldness, like a heart disease."

"Pass what on?"

"The damage, and the fucking genetic mutation that turned our home into a . . . a giant petri dish for culturing powerful new strains of dysfunction and depression."

"That's cute. But you're the damaged one, little brother. Not me."

"Once again, you've forgotten your sister."

"You two can be as fucked up as you want. I'm fine and my children are fine and they don't need either one of you."

"I think you're wrong."

"So now you know more about my kids than I do."

"No, that's not it. But you see them every day. You probably don't notice when they grow a quarter of an inch or gain a few ounces. It happens gradually and you get used to it and you miss all the little steps and then you realize they're bigger and they know things you've never heard them talk about before, things you didn't teach them, and they've got problems you could have helped them with if you'd only noticed them before it was too late."

"Okay, doctor. Tell me all about my kids. Tell me what I've missed."

"I wish you'd try to listen, or just look for yourself, without all this defensive bullshit."

"Go ahead. I'm listening. I want to learn from your expertise."

Chase could see it wasn't going to get through, but he persisted. "Bradley just tunes out sometimes. He goes away and shuts everything out."

"Who doesn't?"

"And he's afraid, Aaron. I mean really afraid, of life or death or something far more real than ghosts and bogeymen."

"And how did you figure all this out?"

"By watching. And by knowing how it feels to be afraid, by knowing how awful it feels to realize that the scariest stuff is really out there."

"You see yourself. He's just the . . . the screen you're projecting your own distorted image on."

"I wish that were true."

"This is all about you."

"Maybe I *can* see it because I've felt it, but what if I'm right, Aaron? What if he's scared or depressed or just needs something he isn't getting, or a little more attention? What if it isn't just me? Isn't it worth a little time and effort to find out?"

"All kids have problems. I see it every day. They go through all sorts of shit. Then they get over it. Maybe it's time for you to get over it."

"Is it too much work? Is that the problem? Are you really so selfish you'd sacrifice your own kids for a gig at the Deer Head?"

"You're really fucked up."

Chase shook his head. "It never even occurred to me that you just didn't care."

"I've had to do everything," Aaron screamed. His face looked as though it was melting. "You weren't here," he said, his voice faltering. "You were never here." And then he began to cry.

This was the part of Aaron Chase so often forgot about, the fragile, sensitive child who lived his life in the shadow of the terminally narcissistic adolescent who stumbled around knocking over family, friends and strangers in his ceaseless effort to prove . . . what? And to whom? But this was real, too. Something was going on in there. Chase knew he should embrace his brother. That just wasn't something they did.

"You left and I had to do everything myself."

"What do you mean? You mean with Dad?"

"*Every*thing. I *do* love my children, but it's hard. I have to work and keep up the house and the car and help with their homework and try to be a husband. And Dad just needed more and more."

"I'm sorry I haven't been here."

Aaron wiped his eyes. "Sarah and I don't really get along that well and there's nobody else."

"I'm sorry, Aaron. I know you love your children."

"I miss you, Chase."

"I miss you, too." *Or something like you, or what you could have been to me, or perhaps it's just the abstract idea of you. I miss who you'd be if life were a TV movie.*

Aaron took a tissue from the desk and blew his nose. "Bradley *is* sensitive. He can tell when Sarah and I aren't getting along. He doesn't talk about things, but I know he feels them."

"Look, I don't know anything about this stuff. All I know is the feeling I have. Sometimes my instincts are good. If I'm wrong . . . well, that's great. I really hope I am. But I care about them, too. They are incredibly bright, sweet kids, and they allowed me into their lives without any question. They made me feel like family. Now I'm worried about them. I just want them to be okay. I love them, too, Aaron, and I'd never do anything to harm them."

"I know you didn't mean any harm. I know that."

"And they really didn't seem at all bothered by seeing Hannah. They were great with her. But you're right, I should have asked first. I just thought it was important. I wanted us all to be okay, to be close. I screwed up."

"I was afraid she'd scare them."

"There weren't scared at all. Really they weren't."

"I just had to figure it out for myself. Nobody was here to help me."

"I'm sorry you've been so overwhelmed. I'm sorry I wasn't around to help with Dad, and. . . ." It was true, of course. He'd been hiding, avoiding them.

"I'm glad you're here." Aaron smiled and sniffed. "Maybe we needed a fight."

"I wish I could be better at this. I wish I could make it easier for you."

Aaron wiped his eyes. "I hardly have any time at all for my music."

29

The only thing Chase wanted more right now than to be with Haley was to not want to be with Haley. She was remote, inaccessible, depressed and, well, there was that marriage thing. If she weren't so inaccessible the list might well be twice as long. Probably lurking beneath that protective wax sheen was a Pandora's box of unaddressed issues waiting to manifest themselves as facial tics, unreasonable prejudices, irrational hatreds and sudden mindless acts of violence. They could be related. What was it about her that he thought he loved? Yes, she was bright and beautiful and sexy, but was there anything else, anything . . . well, deeper? Most likely what had drawn him to her was the Stygian bleakness she silently conveyed. Maybe the only true subconscious desire anyone has is to go home, no matter how ugly and forbidding, no matter how deadly. Beat me, burn me, ignore me, hate me and I'll be yours forever, lucky you, lucky me. Who better to replace a mother who disappeared than a woman who was already invisible? She just skipped right to the gone part.

Chase scoured the stove, the oven and the refrigerator. He scrubbed the kitchen sink with cleanser and then, armed with a roll of paper towels and a bottle of Formula 409, he searched out and destroyed dust, dirt, odors and bacteria in closets and corners. He launched an assault on the downstairs bathroom and started on the one upstairs. He was cleaning the mirror when he got a close look at his face. His eyelids were folding over on themselves like tiny double chins. Not good. He moved closer to the mirror: several rogue whiskers had sprouted under his left nostril, a nest of festering ingrown hairs had set up camp under his chin and his complexion was the color of Cream of Wheat. *Dear God, who is this hideous ghoul? Somebody bury him before he begins to stink.*

He grabbed his father's shaving cream and his razor from the cabinet and ran the water. When it was hot enough to cook a chicken, he soaked a washrag in it and pressed it against his face until his skin felt as though it was resting on a bed of charcoal briquettes. Then he applied the shaving cream, grabbed the razor and, with an ardor bordering on mania, he began to shave, minute blood spots becoming streaming rivulets as he scraped, shredded and flayed his skin. After shaving he took a pair of tweezers from the cabinet and stormed the ingrown hairs, digging and tugging until he couldn't see anything through the puddles of blood. He washed his face and rinsed it with cold water, rinsed it again and again, but his skin was mottled now with dozens of little nicks and the bleeding wouldn't stop. There was no styptic pencil, so he tore a sheet of toilet paper into scraps and to each wound he pressed a piece of tissue. When they were all covered he stood back from the mirror and surveyed the pasty face that stared back at him with an expression of abject horror, its cheeks, chin and neck specked with bits of tissue flecked with blood, a battlefield strewn with crude little Japanese flags. Here I am, women of the world. Come and get this handsome son of a bitch before he bleeds to death.

By early evening he didn't look quite so hideous, though there were still a few red spots on his cheeks and neck and a small scab the color of a ripe boysenberry had formed under his chin. After a quick shower he put on some clean clothes, squinted at himself in the mirror and headed out. This was as good as it was going to get.

The Stone Bar Inn was the only place in the Poconos where Chase could recall having had seafood that tasted as though it might at some point have been near a natural body of water. He'd taken Christine there once, or she'd taken him. They drank too much, had an argument about the salad dressing—an argument that was so vehement the manager had had to ask them to tone it down—and then engaged in feral sex in the parking lot. Not a bad night for them.

"Just one, sir?" Her nose was just a tad long, but it was a nice nose, a handsome nose, and somehow it worked with the rest of her features. This was gangly done right.

"That's it."

"Dinner?"

"I hope so." And thank you for not glaring. In fact no sign of pity or distress. Just a warm smile that he'd happily delude himself into believing had been a specific spontaneous response to his charm and good looks rather than a critical but occasionally repugnant component of her job.

"Right this way." She grabbed a menu and led him to a table. "Is this okay?"

"Perfect."

"Have a great dinner."

Viewed through her gray slacks, her thighs appeared to be on the ample side, but the shape and the virtual absence of gelatinous quivering when she walked away suggested that any excess bulk was more likely muscle than fat. Although she wasn't a classic beauty, there was something very appealing about her.

A middle-aged busboy (shouldn't there be another name for them when they reached forty?) with a hairpiece so bad it might have been homemade, poured him some water. A minute later a waitress appeared, thin with a compact figure, everything in the proper proportions. Her short black hair and big dark eyes gave her a severe, detached appearance, just this side of goth, though she barely looked old enough to be in college. Of course that had its advantages, too. Perhaps she hadn't been hit on thousands of times by jerks like him. *Let me be the first to trick you into going home with me, and feel free to bring the hostess. Can I ever stop?*

"I'm Michelle and I'll be your waitress this evening. Can I get you a drink to start?"

"I'd love a good single malt if you've got one."

Her eyes widened. "Glen Ord!"

"Who?"

"Glen Ord! It's the sh—" Her cheeks flushed. "It's the best."

"You drink it?"

"Well, only twice, cause it's really expensive, but. . . ."

"It's the shit."

"Well . . . ," she shrugged, "yeah."

"Okay. The shit it is."

"I'll be right back with your drink and the specials."

When she placed the drink in front of him, he inspected the glass.

"Is anything wrong?"

"I was just checking to see if you'd gotten any lipstick on it."

She stared for a second, then smiled. "I carry a straw."

Chase had just finished his mussels when he heard a familiar laugh and looked up. Christine and a tall square-headed man in a nicely tailored suit were following the hostess toward a vacant table at the opposite end of the room. When they reached the table the man reached up as though testing the wind direction, shook his head briskly and pointed to another table. The hostess shook her head and smiled. He was deliberating now, frowning with impressive gravity as he surveyed the room. After a minute he pointed toward an empty table. Shit. They could all hold hands. They headed toward the table and then she saw him. He pasted on a grin and raised his drink to her. The guy had a moustache. She raised her eyebrows, shook her head. A Robert Goulet moustache. And his hair was just a little bit too lustrous. And she looked breathtakingly beautiful. Would she actually fuck this guy, or even let him fuck her? They sat down across from one another, their beaming faces in profile. *I wish to perish forthwith.*

The swordfish steak was excellent, but he ate it far too rapidly to truly savor it. It was difficult not to watch Christine and her oversized executive, and impossible not to feel the entirely illogical but incredibly potent shame of dining alone, particularly with Christine's occasional blasts of laughter, little comets of joy shooting across his darkening mood. Now the man was leaning in, grinning like a masturbating monkey as his right paw slinked and slithered across the table. She lifted the hand he was going for and picked up her napkin to dab her mouth. Chase tried to disguise his laugh as a cough but Christine apparently wasn't buying it. She glanced toward him and wiped her chin with her middle finger.

She was stunning in her long, formfitting indigo dress and she had a sense of humor and an exciting, almost dangerous edge that had always been appealing, at least when she wasn't slicing him up with it. What was she doing with the gallump with the reflective hair? Why isn't she with me? He searched for the waitress, located her, got her attention.

"Was everything okay?"

"Very good, thanks."

"Can I get you an after-dinner drink or some coffee or dessert?"

"I'd love another one of these." He raised his glass.

"I told you." She folded her arms over her jaunty little breasts.

"Bring your straw and we can share."

"I wish."

"So do I."

Christine cleared her throat.

Chase spoke a little louder. "You are extremely adorable."

"You're pretty cute yourself." She was just playing along, but it still felt good.

Christine turned toward them. "Excuse me."

The waitress spun around. "Yes."

"I'm trying to figure out what I taste in this salad dressing. It's not tarragon is it?"

"No. It's dill."

"Ah." She nodded. "Dill. I *thought* so."

"Christine?" Chase leaned toward her. "Is that you?"

"Frank?"

"No. It's Chase. Dr. Stoller. I assisted with the . . . well . . . the surgery."

The waitress took his empty glass. "I'll get your drink."

Christine pouted. "Oh yes. I'm afraid the poor little puppy died only a week later."

"Gosh, I sure hope that sweet little crippled orphan isn't suing you. I mean, I can't imagine you actually intended to do *that* much damage to her poor puppy just because—"

"I'm sorry," she interrupted. "This is Don Barlow. He's a corporate attorney, and quite an athlete." She winked at Don.

"Are you competitive, Don Barlow?"

"I do compete a little, but—"

"Well, that'll sure come in handy."

"Excuse me."

"Christine is quite a competitor herself," he winked, "and something of a gymnast."

"Oh, Fred, I wanted to let Don discover my secrets for himself."

"One thing I know," Don Barlow said, "she's one hell of a pretty lady."

"A real cute tomato, Don Barlow."

"You two are making me blush."

"I didn't think that was possible?"

Don scowled at Chase and turned back to Christine. "So anyways, as I was saying, when I was over in Paris the last time I ended up with an entire week to myself."

"Here you go, doctor." Michelle was back.

"Thanks so much."

She leaned down and whispered, "I stole a sip."

"You don't know how incredibly happy that makes me." He held up his glass. His penis stirred. *Relax.*

"Not from yours."

"That's disappointing."

A playful scowl. "Are you always this much of a flirt?"

"Only when I feel irrepressibly drawn to a ravishing woman."

"How often is that?"

"Believe it or not, this is the first time all evening."

"Sure." She rolled her eyes. "I'll check on you in a few minutes."

Chase stared at his drink, amber deliverance with a side of slow suicide. There was in everything he was doing an unnerving intensity, a level of desperation so perilously elevated it made him faint and bilious. His acute and constant need for reassurance, for proof that he was attractive and desirable, drove all his thoughts and actions, made him a blithering slave to those he wished to entice and, for a time, enslave. The one with the need always loses and his well was dry and bottomless, bottomless, bottomless, bottomless. He sipped his drink, put it down, sipped it again. The slightest hint of interest from an attractive woman raised his temperature and made him giddy. A smile, a comment that with some effort could be misinterpreted to suggest an infinitesimal trace of attraction, and the beginnings of arousal were upon him like a rabid grizzly on a honey-dipped toddler. He was tingly and hot. His sensors were always on the alert. Hi. Boing. Gimme sum dat. I want. Well fuck you. Fuck you and Christine and Jennifer and Dad and Aaron and Haley, especially Haley, and the beaky hostess and young Michelle and especially those who have the wisdom, the discernment or the good taste to stay away. Fuck me and my pathetic whining needy grasping overwrought flailing drunken stumbling bumbling blaming lashing crashing rehashing pitiful hostile craven cowering devouring deflowering feeble sham corny ham pseudo-simulacrum of a life. Sing it to me, brethren and sistren!

Another sip.

My life is missing.
"Another drink?"
Where did it go? "Oh yes."
"This one's on me."
It would taste much better that way. "Would you care to go home with me tonight, Michelle?"
"To*night?*"
He laughed. "What a perfect response." *I love you.*
A moment of confusion. "Well, I mean, that's a little more direct than I'm used to."
"We could talk." About genitals and so forth.
"I think I'd have to know you a little better."
"If you knew me better you wouldn't want to go home with me."
"I doubt that."
"That's because you don't know me better."
She wrinkled her brow. "So, what kind of doctor are you?"
"I'm . . . I'm a doctor of despair."
"What, you mean like a psychiatrist or something?"
"I'm not a doctor. I'm a journalist."
"Really?" She glanced back at Christine, who seemed captivated by her date's babbling or the concomitant dancing of the purloined moustache.
"Yeah, she and I are old friends," Chase said.
"I see." Thinking . . . processing. . . . "Oh." Bingo!
"We weren't much of a couple."
"Well, she doesn't like him anyway."
"How can you tell?"
"It's not so hard."
"If it's not, she won't like him at all."
"Excuse me?"

Chase raised his glass, drank, set it down. "So what do you think?"

"About . . . ? Oh. I usually go out with guys closer to my age, but, you know, I don't think age is that important, I mean to a point. I just think it would be better to get to know each other a little before we start steaming up windows."

"Would you be willing to give me your number?"

She scrutinized him. "You're not like a stalker or anything are you?"

"Not yet."

"Okay, sure." Lovely smile. "But first I better take care of my tables."

Did that help? Not much. Most likely she was just being nice, or trying to avoid an uncomfortable situation with an annoying customer who'd eventually have to leave anyway. Maybe it wouldn't be her number, or when he called she'd say she'd decided it wasn't such a good idea. Maybe he was just another jerk. He chuckled. Maybe? How could he be anything else? That was what his desperation had produced. That's what he'd become. Did everyone feel this way? Do we all think we're different, better, that ours is a special case? Ludicrous, contemptible clowns, all in a row, aim pistols at your heads and blow, blow, blow.

He leaned forward. "Would you like to go home with me?"

"Excuse me?"

"Not you, Don Barlow. Your date."

"Chase, don't."

"Would you care to take it outside, doc?"

"Already did that. I was thinking of a more traditional setting this time."

"Chase, please." She looked more sad than angry. It was almost enough to make him stop.

"I just want to take you home and cuddle."

"Please stop."

"You're drunk, pal."

"Yep, but I'll be hung over tomorrow and you'll still be living in the shadow of Robert Goulet's moustache."

Don stood. "Get up."

Christine glared at her date. "Sit down."

"Get up, doc."

"I haven't finished my drink."

"Don, you're making an ass of yourself."

"*Me? I'm* making an ass of myself?"

"Yes."

"What about him?" He pointed a meaty digit at Chase.

Chase laughed. "He started it, mom."

"Chase."

The few remaining customers were staring now.

"Get up."

"Don. Stop it."

"You like this jerk?"

"I *don't* like the way *you're* acting."

"Well screw you."

"No." She sighed. "That won't happen."

"You're too skinny anyway, you fucking whore."

With no course of action in mind, Chase rose and faced him. "You are one classy primate."

Don raised his fists, turned his left shoulder toward Chase and carefully moved his feet into an approximation of the classic boxer's stance.

The hostess ran over. "Please calm down, sir."

"He's just posing," Chase said. A blow to the side of his face, an explosion in his gut. The world rose, twisted. Shoes on the wall? No, it was the floor, a deep voice from somewhere far away. "Have a good life, loser."

"Fire your writers," he said to the floor as the big black shoes trudged off. Another goddamned sucker punch.

Chase looked up. Michelle and the hostess were waiting by his table and Christine was standing over him offering her hand. He hoisted himself onto his chair. His left ear and cheekbone felt as though they were pressed against a steaming radiator. "I'm really sorry."

Christine was staring at him. He couldn't read her expression.

"I'm fine." He rubbed his cheekbone and ear, looked at his hand. No blood, but this was becoming very tiresome. Another week here would probably cost him a limb.

"What a jerk." Michelle glowered toward the door.

The hostess was pale and glassy-eyed. "What happened?"

"I—"

Christine interrupted. "We were having a nice calm conversation about the salad dressing and the guy just went nuts."

Michelle and the hostess spoke in unison. "The *salad dressing?*"

"I am so sorry." He looked at Christine. "Your dinner's on me."

The hostess leaned down. "Do you want me to call the police?"

"No, thanks. I've met them." He smiled at Michelle. "But a glass of water would be nice."

Michelle and the hostess walked away and Christine sat down at his table. "What are you doing?"

"Dying."

"That's not funny."

"I'm sorry about your date."

"That's not what you should be sorry about."

The busboy poured them both water.

"Okay." He swigged the water. "What should I be sorry about?"

"What you're doing to yourself."

Michelle brought another Scotch for Chase and a glass of wine for Christine. "On the house."

"Thanks," Chase said.

"My pleasure."

When she was gone Chase turned toward Christine. "What do you want me to say?"

"Say that you're finished with this shit. Say that you're going to be okay."

Chase felt the tears coming. "I need someone . . . ," he reached for her hand, "I need someone to help me."

30

In his father's bed she held him close, his head resting against her chest, her hands caressing his face. "It's alright," she said, but his sobbing wouldn't stop. Late in the night he spoke for a while about his sister, but that only brought more tears. Sometime later he got hard and she said, "No, not now," and pulled him closer. When he thought he was finished crying he pulled back. "Thank you for being . . . ," and then the crying started again. "Let it out," she said. "Just let it out." "I'm sorry," he said through his sobs, and he shook and trembled with the accumulated grief of a lifetime spent in terror of being alone. "Why is this happening to me now?" "Your father just died." "I started acting out months ago, before any of this. I just don't understand why." "Maybe that's the wrong question. Maybe you should be asking why it didn't happen a long time ago." Throughout the night he wept and in the first glow of morning he tried to hide his face. "Yes, you look awful," she said. "Oh, God. Am I all red and splotchy?" "Yeah, and a little swollen on the left side." She touched his cheek. "I'm sorry," he said. "Not now," she said and reached down and took him in her hands.

"Why don't we find out if the two of us can make love together?"

They sat at the kitchen table, neither one eating the breakfast she'd cooked.

"Now what," he said.

"I don't know. Maybe nothing. I don't know."

"Why?"

"Because I just don't know if we can learn to live with each other, I mean, assuming we'd actually want to. And I'm not sure either one of us needs another needy person to deal with. You're a wreck and I'm not that far behind. I just don't know if we can do it."

"How does anyone ever know?"

She reached out for his hand. "You're asking the wrong person."

Was that sorrow in her eyes? Of course she must have her own grief, and yet he'd never seen it before. He'd never asked, never even looked.

It was impossible not to hope their night together had been more than a sweet digression, impossible not to want more than the memory of a closeness that seemed for a few hours to eclipse his desperation and the free-floating lust it generated so prolifically. It wasn't that he was unable to appreciate it in that limited context; he simply wanted it to mean more, even if that robbed the night of some of its magic. He'd be willing to sacrifice that for something he could hold on to, for some sense of permanence. But would everything he felt now dissolve if they attempted a conventional adult relationship? And was this any more real than his feelings for Haley? If this was genuine, what was that? And if that was genuine, what was this? Or were they just different means of satisfying a need, of filling a space whose emptiness induced an anguish so intense it clouded his thoughts and made Truth—if such a thing existed—only a negligible concern?

What would he do if Haley came to him now and said she was his? What if Zoë called and confessed her love for him? What if last night's waitress were to appear before him right now, naked and ready? That one wasn't so difficult. But where was his heart? Do we all just eventually give up, take what comes to us, convince ourselves it's what we've always wanted and get on with whatever our sad little lives have become because, well, because that's what we do? It wasn't terribly difficult to distinguish sexual attraction from an emotional connection, though there certainly was, at least in the most rewarding instances, an interrelationship. The real problem was identifying healthy responses, those that reflected a genuine emotional and intellectual interaction, those that weren't generated by unalloyed need. Need was a powerful, dangerous and sometimes destructive influence, a single-minded force indifferent to morality and devoid of discrimination. Or could it just be him?

Chase tried to get some sleep but his erection was impossible to ignore. He began to masturbate but then he remembered whose bed he was in and lost his erection. He thought of Christine and back it came, but then every time he felt an orgasm approaching he stopped himself. It seemed like an insult to think of her while he was doing this, though she'd most likely enjoy it if she knew. Why wasn't there a consent form for such situations? Then he thought about the waitress, her demeanor, frank yet somehow innocent, and that tight little body. He imagined her looking up at him with those big dark eyes as she took him deep into her mouth. He almost came but he stopped himself again. Was he cheating on Christine now, or Haley or, what the hell, Haley's husband, or his own father? Jesus, what about Jennifer? How could he do this to his loving wife? He laughed. *I'm just a happy buffoon with a raging hard-on. Bubububububububu. Sit!*

He got out of bed and stuffed himself into his jeans. Downstairs he searched for something to clean. When he couldn't find anything he hadn't already cleaned twice he decided to wrestle the refrigerator away from the wall. It had become increasingly noisy—a scraping sound that came and went without any apparent pattern—and he didn't feel like calling a repairman, some big hairy dullard who would undoubtedly have decided before arriving, probably before receiving the call, that by gosh the sumbitch needed a new compressor and a fan and a transformer and a capacitor differential and an exhaust pipe and a charcoal filter and a hard drive and a warhead.

Anyway, he'd always had success with mechanical things. He could look at them, see how they worked, find the problems and, surprisingly often, repair them. They were far easier to understand than humans. Sometimes, when someone couldn't get a car started, he'd get in, turn the key and it would simply work. When he was young and something was broken—a radio, a bicycle or a clock, a dripping faucet or a doorknob—he would play around with it for a while and somehow it would work again. And in the last few years, though he lacked any relevant knowledge, he'd solved dozens of computer problems for friends and colleagues.

Covering the upper three quarters of the back of the refrigerator was a vertical grate of thin metal bars through which, from bottom to top, wound a serpentine tube. Beneath the grid was an open rectangle that housed a large black tank and network of wires, several of which sprouted from a small square box. Everything was caked with sticky dust the color of ash. With his father's vacuum cleaner he took off as much of the muck as he could, and then he went at it with a wad of paper towels and his trusty bottle of Formula 409. After spreading newspaper over the floor, he got some tools from the garage. He was about to start disassembling the refrigerator when his cell phone rang. He pulled the phone out and saw Haley's number on the display. Not now. He put the phone down, grabbed a screwdriver and began removing screws and organizing them on the newspaper. A click and a hum. Oops. He followed the cord to an outlet and pulled out the plug. Forty-five minutes and several unanswered phone calls later, parts were spread across the floor and his clothing was drenched with perspiration. He continued working, ignoring the phone when it rang, removing every screw, nut or bolt he found until he wasn't entirely sure he could ever get the thing back together. He stood up and looked at the mess. His life. Then he took a marker and around each item he traced an outline. No. This made sense. There was order here.

In the garage he found a gas can that was about half full. He took it inside and poured a little gas into a bowl, set aside everything that looked electrical and then, one at a time, he carefully cleaned each of the remaining parts, first with gasoline, then with dish detergent and water. By golly, there was real gratification in this. That was greasy; now it's clean as can be. I did that. See? When everything else was rinsed and dry he disassembled the motor. With a toothbrush and a few drops of gasoline he scraped layers of soot from the fan, the grille and the wires, being careful not to let the gasoline drip into the workings of the motor. When he held the motor to his mouth and blew into it a tiny piece of wire insulation shot across the room. Maybe that had been the problem. He stood up to stretch and looked at his watch. He wasn't hungry but he knew he should eat something. Still it would be rewarding to finish this, to get it back together, plug it in and listen as it started up. His phone rang again and without thinking he answered it. "What?"

"Mr. Stoller?"

"Yes."

"Your sister seems to be asking for you."

A chest full of canons. "What?"

"Your sister Hannah is saying your name."

"I'm on my way." He pressed his eyes shut, but there was no way to staunch these tears.

The road, the trees and the buildings rocked and swam before him as he raced to see his sister.

31

She was sitting in the visiting room when he arrived, Eleanor hovering over her like a kindly black blimp.

"I think maybe she'd like to see you, Mr. Stoller," she said, and stepped out of the room.

Chase grabbed a chair and sat facing his sister. "Hannah."

She turned her head toward him, locked her eyes on his. She looked so tired and so sad, but she was actually looking at him, seeing him. She opened her mouth as though to speak, closed it, looked at the floor, then back up at him.

"Hannah, it's me, sweetheart. I'm here," he said and smiled. "I guess you can see that. I'm just . . . I'm so happy you—"

"Not this," she said in a raspy whisper.

"Not what?" He moved closer.

"Not this."

"What do you want? What can I do?"

Her lips began to tremble. "Please."

"Hannah." He reached for her hand. It was like gripping a bird that had just died. "I'm here for you now. Just tell me what

I can do. I'll do anything you want, anything you need. Talk to me, Hannah."

She shook her head, pressed her eyes shut and opened them again. Then, very slowly and clearly, she said, "Let me go." Three swift blows with an axe. Then she said it again and the wailing began, long, strident howls of long-suppressed anguish.

"You don't know what she meant, or if she meant anything at all. And if the change in medication is having an effect, this is all new to her. You can't read anything into what she says, especially right now."

"You didn't see her eyes, Christine."

"She's not herself. She hasn't been herself for years. This could just be a transitional thing."

He was sitting in his car on the shoulder of the road. His hands were trembling and he wanted to scream, to tear out his hair or bang his face against the steering wheel until his skull turned to mush.

"Why don't I come over right after I close up?"

"No."

"I can leave right now if you want."

"I don't want to cry in front of you anymore. I don't want to cry at all. I'm sick of being a fucking crybaby, and I don't want to use you for this."

"Why *not* use me for this?"

"It's not fair to you. I don't want to do that to you and I don't want to bury it under something else."

"You don't have to bury it, but why not allow me, or someone, to comfort you?"

His head felt as though it was expanding. "Because I don't want to feel good."

"Jesus. How does destroying yourself help Hannah?"

"She was . . . she's better than me."

"I don't know, maybe she is, but I still don't see the logic."

"Why is she in there while I'm okay?"

"You're not okay, Chase. I think you can be, I *hope* you can be, but you're not now."

"Well, I'm here, in my nice car, talking on my nice cell phone with someone who . . . talking with you."

"How dare you have anything good in your life."

"It's not that."

"It sounds like . . . it sounds like what your saying is, if she can't come to you, you'll go to her. And I have to tell you, Chase, I care about you—I'm not particularly thrilled about it, but I guess I do—and I see a part of you I never saw before, a part that's raw and vulnerable and . . . maybe the word is genuine, but I really don't want to have to watch while you do everything in your power to sabotage your life. Because you could do that. You have that in you, too."

"I don't know what to do."

"Give her time. And decide that *your* life is worth living, not because you're afraid of dying or because your sister needs you, but because it has value."

"I'm sorry," he said. "I'll call you later."

"Call me, but please stop being sorry."

He leaned back in his seat and closed his eyes. *What do I do now? Where do I go?* He listened to his breathing, felt the steady hammering of his heart. *We're just animals, vulgar pissing farting shitting spitting bleeding drooling fucking slaves to our corporeality, greedy, narcissistic animals with too much information and far too little power. I know what's wrong but there isn't a thing I can do about it. Someone please save my sister.*

32

As soon as he got back to the house, Chase resumed his work on the refrigerator. Although he hadn't bothered to number things earlier, he'd kept related parts together and he had a reasonably good recollection of the sequence of the disassembly. Mostly, the task ahead would require logical thinking and focus. Those were things he could handle. Haley called several more times but he didn't want to talk to anyone now and he had no idea where they stood or how much he really cared. Everything was just too difficult, too complex and changeable. He needed to focus on things he could control. This screw goes in that hole with that washer and that nut—tight, but not too tight. This wire attaches to that contact. This piece must go on first or I won't be able to access the screws for that bracket. Then, after the bracket is in place, the wire harness will fit around the bottom. That's the only way it makes sense. It makes sense. He worked in frantic silence, as though this were all that mattered, all that existed in the world.

He'd pushed the refrigerator back against the wall and was just about to plug it in when he heard the front door close.

"Hello?"

Nothing.

"Aaron?" He turned.

In the kitchen entryway, disheveled and drenched with perspiration, stood Julian, a revolver hanging from his right hand, its long black barrel facing the floor. He was breathing hard, but his expression was one of yogic calm.

An image of Haley's body sprawled on a blood-soaked carpet, arms and legs splayed at awkward angles. "Where's Haley?"

"I have no idea." He swallowed. "But I do know where she was the other night when I was here."

"Are you planning to shoot someone?"

"Someone?"

"Have you ever shot anyone before?"

He shook his head. "I guess it'll be a first for both of us."

"Might not live up to your expectations."

His expression seemed locked in place. "Scared?"

"I think I'm a little too tired and hungry right now to feel the full impact."

"That's too bad." He licked his lips.

"Maybe if you'd let me grab a sandwich and get a good night's sleep we could try this again in the morning." Chase looked around him for something that might serve as a weapon.

"You stuck your dick in my wife and then you were sarcastic and glib."

"I'm sorry I acted that way." What would he do with a knife anyway? Stab the bullet?

"Sorry?"

"I was an asshole and I'm sorry. I really am. I didn't want to hurt anyone. I just—"

"Say it." He raised the weapon.

A sudden chill seized his chest, his face and neck. "I *said* I'm sorry."

"Say, 'I fucked your wife.'" His eyes were glazed and he kept licking his lips and swallowing.

"I don't think so." Chase stepped back. He was shaking. There was nothing humorous about this.

"I want to hear you say it."

"I'm sorry, Julian, but I—"

"Don't say my name." He aimed the gun at Chase's chest.

"Shit." Chase squeezed his eyes shut. "Please don't," he said, and slowly opened them.

"She was a complete wreck when I met her."

"Why? Why was she a wreck?"

"She didn't tell you?"

"No. She didn't tell me anything."

He smiled.

"Why don't *you* tell me?"

"It's a big club. Isn't that what you said?" A single blast of laughter. "Tell me, did your father and grandfather take turns with you, too?"

"What?"

"No big deal, right?"

"Fuck." *I don't know anything.*

"Big club, right?"

"I had no idea. I—"

"I helped her get through all that, and now you come along and destroy everything."

"Do you know what she did when I came upstairs after you left? She was already—" *Fuck.* "She ran out of here like the place was under quarantine. She wasn't interested in anything but you. She wouldn't even look at me."

"That's nice."

"Do you understand? She didn't care about anything but you."

More licking and swallowing. "You mean after you fucked her?"

"Why is this different from the last time?"

"Last time?"

"You said I wasn't the first."

"Did I?"

"You implied it. You didn't shoot *him*, did you?"

"That wasn't going to last. I knew she'd need me when it was over."

"She still needs you."

He shrugged.

"This is an old story, a goddamned pitiful suburban cliché. Husband kills wife's lover then turns gun on self. It always ends the same way and it's just so pointless. A couple people grieve for the appropriate period of time, everyone else talks and wonders for a few days, then . . . then another tragedy comes along—something more compelling, more bizarre or more disgusting—and it's plastered on the front pages and shown over and over on the evening news. The tragic love triangle—they'll call it something like that—is old news."

Julian just glared.

"It's all about the audience. They don't know the people involved and they don't give a shit. They just want to be fed this crap because it makes them all tingly, like a roller-coaster ride or a scary movie, it makes them feel like they got away with something, it makes them feel alive when, really, they've been dead for years. You'd probably make a lot of people happy—people who find child abuse and serial murders entertaining, people who can't be happy unless they're witnessing something ugly—you'd be making a lot of these sick, sadistic assholes very happy for a few days. Is that what you want?"

Julian squinted and swallowed.

"You don't strike me as a murderer." Chase noticed the gas can next to the table. "Is that how you want to be remembered?"

"Like you said, nobody's going to remember anyway."

With his head Chase motioned to a chair by the table. "Would you mind if I sat down?" Maybe if he moved fast enough he could throw the chair at him and then jump him. Probably not, but the slightest chance would be better than standing there waiting to get punctured.

"Uncomfortable?"

"I'm tired and very sad. And suddenly I don't think I'm quite ready to die."

Julian grinned. "Why not?"

"I don't know. I don't know."

"Tell me, Mr. Glib. Why aren't you ready?"

"Maybe . . . maybe because on rare occasions it isn't altogether horrible. Because sometimes there are . . . unexpected moments, and some of them don't completely suck. I'm pretty sure there won't be any surprises when I'm dead. I don't want to die . . . empty. And I don't want to die having been nothing more than . . . than a pathetic jerk. What about you?"

"Me?"

"Are you ready to die?"

"I don't have to follow your little script."

"You wouldn't do very well in prison either." Chase's stomach churned and rumbled. Maybe he could drop to the floor, as though he'd fainted or had a heart attack. Would this guy shoot an unconscious man? What about someone who was vomiting? "I don't feel so good," he said. He forced his tongue to the back of his mouth but there was nothing in his stomach to throw up so he only made himself cough. He could probably wet himself, though that might not be enough. Would this man who was clearly on the edge, if not over it, shoot a man who'd just shit his pants? He tried to relax his sphincter but he was too nervous. Jesus. "I think I'm going to be sick."

"What?"

"My stomach. I think I'm going to throw up. I really need to use the bathroom."

Julian squinted and licked his lips.

Chase bent forward and tightened his windpipe. He wheezed and made gagging sounds. He leaned farther forward. His heart was racing and perspiration was pouring off his head and pooling on the floor. He was afraid to look up, afraid something in his expression would give him away. His head was down to his knees and his hands were pressed to his abdomen. "Oh God," he groaned, and now the discomfort was genuine. The gas can wasn't far from his right hand. No shots had been fired yet but when he moved his head slightly forward he could still see Julian's shoes just waiting there. Something about the image wasn't quite right. He dropped into a kneeling position. The can was within his reach, or close to it. He moaned and glanced up. Julian was still holding the gun, but not aiming it, and he looked confused. "I'm going to throw up," Chase said. Then he looked back down at Julian's shoes, one black and one brown. "Your shoes don't match," he said.

Julian stared down at his shoes and Chase grabbed the gas can and threw it hard. It hit Julian's left shin and he screamed and bent over, still gripping the gun. Chase dove past him into the living room, grabbed the doorknob, yanked the door open and ran outside. A blast as he sprinted toward his car, another as he reached the passenger's side door. It was locked. He turned to look back. Julian was limping toward him, bent over, one hand on his calf, the other gripping the gun.

"God damn it! God damn it, would you *please* not shoot me? *Please*."

Neither man moved.

"I'm asking you to please not shoot me. I'm tired of pain, my sister needs me and I'd really like to try to be . . . better. This just isn't a good time."

"You weren't really sick."

"I was getting there."

"I think you broke my leg."

"I was trying not to get killed. I'm *sorry*. But look at us. *Look* at us. I'm terrified and you're doing everything in your power to murder me. I mean, what the fuck are we doing?" Now he felt like crying or fainting or throwing up. And there was something wrong with his own leg; it felt hot and damp. "Do we absolutely need to play this stupid thing out? Do we?"

No response.

"Because if we do, if we *really* do, I'm . . . I'm just going to sit down right here on the driveway and cry my eyes out until the stupid thing is over."

"My leg." Julian winced. "I think you broke it."

"What did you expect?"

"It really hurts."

"Well for Christ's sake sit down and let me look at it. Let me do one decent thing."

"No." He tried to straighten up. "How can I stop now?" Now Julian looked as though he was about to cry. "Tell me, after all this, after all I've done, how can I stop now? Just tell me that. Cause I just really don't see any way out." There was a frightened child in there. Children everywhere.

"You have a choice. You didn't sign any papers. You can just . . . just stop." Suddenly Chase felt dizzy and cold. "You don't have to shoot anybody. This is something you can choose. You've don't have to play the bad guy. It's a fucking raw deal, and it's not you."

Julian's shoulders relaxed a little.

"Let me look at your leg. Please."

The glaze seemed to be melting. Julian swallowed hard and pressed his eyes shut.

A minute passed and Chase took a step forward. A bolt of pain shot up his leg and he collapsed.

33

"We were in the kitchen talking. I heard a noise and went outside to see what it was and someone shot me. Of course I didn't get a look at whoever it was. You were in such a hurry to get outside after you heard the shot you tripped over the gas can and hit your leg. It doesn't have to be any more complicated or credible than that."

"I don't know. What if they find the gun?"

"Have you had any contact with the local cops?"

"No. Why?"

"I've seen brighter shrubbery."

They sat next to one another on the couch, their injured legs stretched out on the coffee table, Chase's new bottle of Scotch between them. They'd had to hold on to one another to get inside the house and then struggle together to the kitchen, where they collected what was left of the ice, a few dishrags and the bottle of Scotch.

"What if they get a search warrant and go through the house? They could get lucky."

"In that case I guess I must have blacked out because I really can't remember a thing. But they won't find it. They'll get all giddy and go out looking for someone who doesn't exist and this will all be over. How's your leg?"

"It hurts like hell. How's yours?"

"It's awful, but I think I'm getting used to being wounded. I didn't even realize you'd hit me until I tried to walk."

"I'm.... It's not easy for me to say this, but—"

Chase put his hand up. "Don't say it. Please don't say it. Let's just ... let's just forget it."

"How can we forget it?"

"What's the option?"

"I don't know." Julian reached down to adjust the ice pack Chase had made for him. "But nothing's solved. All this ... drama, all this rage and insanity and violence and still nothing is solved."

"You found out you're not a murderer."

"No. What I found out is that I'm a lousy shot. I wasn't aiming at your leg."

"But you had a second chance."

Chase's cell phone rang. The number was Haley's. He pressed the phone to his ear. "Hello."

"Thank God you're okay. I didn't want to come over because ... but I was afraid Julian—"

"Hang on." Chase looked at Julian and wondered what had gone so wrong between the two of them. Had there been any choice for either of them? Was there something they could have done to avoid all of this? Sometimes people found ways to get past the most horrific things. Given the chance could they still somehow work it out? But what about him, what did he want? There was no answer, and suddenly that just wasn't good enough. He held the phone out to Julian. "It's your wife."

"What am I going to say?"
"I don't know. Say you missed."
Julian reached for the phone. A siren wailed in the distance.

34

Haley stepped through the doorway and stopped. Her hands were trembling and her complexion was the color of chalk. Chase was hoping she would ignore him now and go to directly to her husband. Probably they'd find a way to talk later, though he had no idea now what they might say to one another.

I'm awfully sorry my husband tried to kill you.
And I'm sorry your father and grandfather raped you.
Are we good?
Hell yes!

The hole in his leg seemed to have muted any romantic feelings he'd had for her, at least for the moment. But how had all this drama and pain changed things? Were they all different now, were their lives somehow transformed or redirected or would they gradually revert to what they'd been before their lives collided? Was anything powerful enough to permanently alter the basic structure of the selves they'd spent years becoming?

For a moment she just stood there staring straight ahead, her eyes frosted with fear, shame or confusion. Perhaps she wasn't feeling anything at all. She opened her mouth to speak, stuttered, stopped, then tried again. "I'm sorry." She looked at her husband, then at Chase. "I'm sorry." It seemed a general comment, a simple statement of fact.

Chase pointed to the curtain that hung open between their beds. "Would you mind closing this?" he said. "I'm very tired."

"Which one's the gunshot?" Chase forced his eyes open. Standing at the foot of his bed with a clipboard in his hand was Dick Best. He'd lost most of his hair and gained at least twenty pounds since high school.

Chase grinned. "I'll let you have a look if you promise not to put my gonads in a cast."

"Maybe you should just move in." His laugh seemed a little forced. "Did you punch somebody else's car this time?"

"Am I really stuck with you?"

"Unless you'd like to wait for the shift change in . . . ," he glanced at his watch, "about six hours."

Chase pulled the sheet aside and the doctor peeled away the bandages they'd applied in the ambulance.

"The bad news is you're going to live." A smile. "The good news is that cleaning this thing out is going to hurt like hell."

Chase threw the sheet back over his leg. "I think I'll do it myself."

"It won't be so bad."

"The thing with my hand? That was pretty funny," Chase said. "But you screw up my leg and I swear I'll murder you and run off to Mexico with your wife and kids and life insurance."

"Doctor?" The nurse stepped forward. "Should I—"

"Just an old high school pal, Lisa. We're going to get along fine. Now let's get this thing X-rayed and see what kind of damage you did." He stepped over to Julian's bed.

The pain was tolerable most of the time, but the temperature in the hospital, which had been subarctic from the beginning, seemed to be plummeting steadily. Either that or he was dying. He'd been waiting in the hall outside the X-ray room for what seemed like an hour and his patience was exhausted. When the technician, a short Hispanic man with a pencil moustache, finally wheeled him in, he was gruff and hurried, like a short order cook begrudgingly slapping on the grille his fiftieth cheeseburger of the day. Ten minutes later he steered Chase's bedmobile back outside the door and left him there, helpless and shivering in the refrigerated hall. It was another forty-five minutes before anyone realized he was waiting to go back down to Emergency, and by that time the only part of his body that wasn't numb with cold was the wound.

Julian was no longer in the room, but his pants and mismatched shoes were still there. A new nurse came in and, without looking at his face or uttering a syllable, checked Chase's IV. When he asked when the doctor would be back, she glared at him and sighed. "After he's had a chance to look at your X-rays, I imagine."

"When will that be?"

"I have no idea, sir. We're very busy."

"Do you think I could have a couple more blankets?"

She raised her painted brows and retracted her chin. "I'll see what I can do." Her life would be so much easier right now if only he'd had the courtesy to die.

He decided not to tell her how special she was.

Blurry images shattered and faded.

"Chase?" It was Dr. Best's voice.

He struggled to open his eyes. "I guess I fell asleep."

"I'm afraid I have some bad news."

"You really need to get some new material, Dicky."

For the first time, Dr. Best looked into his eyes. "I'm sorry, Chase, but this isn't a joke."

He lifted his head.

"We just admitted your sister."

"What?"

"I'm sorry," he said. "Apparently she . . . ," he looked down at the floor, then back up at Chase, "she tried to kill herself."

Chase grabbed the rail and hoisted himself up. "Where is she?"

"She's two rooms away and she's stable, so you can wait right here until I can have a look at those X-rays."

"No." Gripping the bedrail with his left hand, Chase slid off the bed and put his weight on both legs. The pain was so intense he cried out. Doctor Best caught his right elbow and together they lifted him back onto the bed.

"She's not conscious now and she won't be for some time—she got a hold of a lot of pills—and *you've* lost a fair amount of blood. You can see her as soon as we take care of this. In the meantime, we'll be monitoring her. She won't be going anywhere until they're comfortable with her medication again. She'll be here for at least a couple days."

"Fuck."

"I'm . . . ," he put his hand on Chase's shoulder, "I'm sorry, Chase. But we'll get her through this part. I'll keep an eye on her."

"What about . . . what about my roommate?" Chase motioned to the empty bed.

"He's up in X-ray now but it looks to me like a tibial shaft fracture. I don't expect to see a lot of displacement."

"That's extremely helpful."

"He'll be alright." His smile seemed genuine. "I'll go see if your X-rays are down yet."

Chase took out his cell phone and stared at it. He should tell someone where he was and what happened. Aaron would come, which was worth acknowledging, but once he got there he'd be self-involved and almost entirely useless. He didn't want to lean on Christine. No matter how he couched it she'd have an anxious moment. She'd rush to the hospital and as soon as she was convinced he was okay he'd feel compelled to tell her about Hannah. Why put anyone else through that? It wouldn't change anything, wouldn't help anyone; he'd be spreading the horror without making himself feel any better. And the truth was that he'd done all of this; he'd put himself where he was and he'd given Hannah the power to kill herself. He deserved to suffer alone. He'd earned it through his obstinacy and selfishness and he would pay for it with his guilt. But no. Guilt provided comfort to the guilty. Guilt was proudly presented, to ourselves and to others, as indisputable evidence of our rectitude. *Yes, I did a bad thing, but I wouldn't feel so darned guilty if I weren't a good, caring, morally upright person.* No thanks.

But was there any way to get through this without decimating himself, or had that always been the goal? Then he recalled the moment on his father's driveway when he thought he was about to die. Had his instinctive will to survive just taken hold of him or had he sensed that there was something worth hanging on to? It didn't matter. Living was difficult and yet, unlike Hannah, he didn't want to die. What did he have that she lacked? But his problems were beside the point, and his questions wouldn't help Hannah now.

He sat up, turned to the side and eased his legs off the bed. Gradually he slid down and put his weight on his left leg. Two rooms away. How many steps could it be: twenty, twenty-five?

People survived far worse. It's only pain, and it will pass. He could endure anything for thirty seconds, for a minute. He'd had sex with Alice. A chuckle escaped. He clenched his teeth and took a deep breath, held it. Focusing on the floor, he let his right leg down. His eyes watered and it felt as though a golf ball was lodged in his throat, but he was able to keep a groan from escaping. He grabbed the IV tube and used it to steer the IV stand toward him, then gripped it and tested its stability. Oh well. *Once you start you can't stop. If you do it's over and you've failed again. Find some strength or fake it. Think of something else, anything else.* He tightened his fists until his arms were trembling. *Create a system, a word for each step. Another deep breath. Just go.* He stepped forward. The floor rocked and spun and tears streamed down his cheeks. Huge jaws bearing down, teeth like burning blades tearing the flesh from his thigh. He looked up. The lights circled above him like vultures as he turned toward the first room. An old man with drool on his chin. *Step . . . fucking . . . shit . . . just don't collapse.* At the next doorway he caught his breath and turned again. There on the bed, the corpse of some discarded derelict. *That's not you, not my sister. That's just the tormented stranger who stole her body. Are you still in there? Is there anything left?* He stumbled into her room and grabbed the bed, pulled himself up onto it and slid up next to her and closed his eyes. The monitor was beeping. Shallow breathing. Someone said something, touched his leg. "No," he said. "No."

They lay side by side in the grass gazing up at the stars. She was talking about a boy she'd met, someone special, where they'd live when they got married—they'd be happy, not like Mom and Dad. "You'll be married, too. We can buy two houses right next to each other and we'll share a huge backyard." "There's one!" He pointed. "Darn, I missed it." "Don't worry. There'll be more." They'd live near the ocean, she said. They'd have a vegetable garden and they'd always be close. They'd always be there for each other, just like now. Their children would be that way too, best of friends. But they'd be different. They'd be happy. He turned to look at her. She was older now and she was rising up, her body hovering just above the ground. "I have to go now," she said, her voice echoing. One at a time, her eyes, nose and mouth dissolved, leaving her face blank, empty. Suddenly her body tore apart, shredded, shards of flesh and bone shooting upward, disappearing into the blackness. He screamed.

"What the hell are you trying to do?" Aaron was scowling down at him.

"Where's Hannah?" Someone had stuffed his skull with rags. What had happened?

"She conscious, but not very coherent. What happened to you?"

"I guess I walked into a bullet." Now he remembered someone taking him out of her room.

Aaron sighed and shook his head.

"Sorry for the inconvenience."

"Fuck you."

"Sticks and stones." Then he'd been carted to another room.

"And bullets, too, I guess. What's . . . what's *wrong* with you?"

"I seem to be missing certain filters." He tried to smile. "Thanks for coming."

Aaron scrutinized his brother. "Well, for what it's worth, whoever shot you just grazed the bone."

"I want to see Hannah." At some point Dr. Best had appeared. He just talked and talked about his kids, his voice a soothing monotone.

"Jesus Christ. I'm your brother. I can stand right here and talk to you, and I'll actually know the difference if you kill yourself."

"Okay, Aaron. Go ahead. Talk to me."

"You mean right *now*?" He grinned.

"We're just a laugh a week, aren't we?"

Footsteps. "How are you feeling?" Dr. Dick.

"Lousy."

"Well, you were pretty fortunate as these things go. No serious bone damage anyway. But you'll be using crutches until that thing heals a little. We'll give you something for the pain and you're probably going to need some physical therapy."

"I assume you did the leg with the actual wound?"

"I think so. There wasn't that much to do. Just cleaned it, stuffed it with Hamburger Helper and closed it up."

"Well, thanks."

"Is there any point in telling you how to care for it, or would you just ignore that kind of advice?"

"You can tell *me*," Aaron said.

"Before you do, could you give me some idea how Hannah's doing?"

"Well, she's physically okay." Dr. Best folded his arms and bit his lower lip. "I . . . I can't really comment on anything else."

"Okay, but if you *could* comment, what would you say?"

He sighed. "I'm not an expert in these things, but I suppose I'd say that without some serious intervention, she's likely to try it again as soon as she has an opportunity. From what I've seen, and the little I've been told, she's in pretty bad shape, but I imagine you already knew that."

"Intervention?"

Dr. Best shook his head and shrugged. "I really don't know."

"Can I see her?"

"Sit tight. In a little while maybe someone can wheel you down there in a wheelchair."

"Christine's been asking to see you," Aaron said.

"Would you do something for me?"

"That depends on what it is."

"Tell her I'm fine but that I need to sleep for a couple hours or so. I'll call her when I wake up."

"She's waiting right down the hall."

"Just tell her that, okay?"

Drama, trauma and tragedy were tricky little bastards, and the initial responses to them were seldom to be trusted. Situations like this had a tendency to force people into unnatural positions. They'd make promises they'd soon regret, say things they didn't mean. *You're hurt so I love you.* Emotions get stirred, they boil and bubble and emit a seductive odor, they get greedy and clingy and suddenly they need something, anything, to attach themselves to. We're all susceptible to something, potential addicts waiting for the ideal substance to abuse: alcohol, chocolate, Coca-Cola, gambling, cocaine, love, sex, cigarettes, pain, Law & Order, loneliness, need, pornography, cartoons, funerals, plucking hairs, fast food, doing repairs, poetry, driving, crying, sleep, potato chips, power, hunger, shame, exercise, praise, pity, chess, sunlight, shopping, God, fame, tattoos, painkillers, laying blame, laying blame, laying blame, laying blame, cha cha cha. Distractions and excuses. *Think of colorful balloons and happy children and joyful baboons swinging from Kookamunga trees and . . . what?* This was just another game, something to distract him. *Can you stop? Just stop. Can you make something from the muddle? Just stop. Just be here. Stop and be here.*

He closed his eyes and listened, blocked the endless stream of thoughts. Here, now. No thought. His leg began to throb.

35

Chase sat in the wheelchair gripping his sister's bedrail. Her eyes were closed and her breathing was shallow and faint, but as steady and even as a metronome. Her body, at least, still wanted to persevere.

"I'm so sorry." He surveyed her face. "It's hard for me, too, but I guess . . . I know it's never been as difficult, as painful for me as it has for you. And we're just different, Hannah." Every time he saw her she looked older. "For some reason I still want to go through with this silliness. It seems I'm not quite ready to quit. But I don't blame you. I'm just . . . I guess we're just wired differently. But maybe if you give it a little more time, if you try to adjust to the changes and hang on to me—I'm going to be here for you now—maybe you'll feel differently. All you have to do is hold on for a little longer. It'll get better, and I'll be here with you whenever you need me. I promise. You're going to get through this."

"No." She didn't open her eyes, didn't move at all. Then she spoke in a voice that seemed to come from somewhere deep inside her. "It was . . . it was a dull throbbing, pounding thing, a horrible, slow torture, and now it's sharp as . . . as ice." She turned her head toward him and opened her eyes. "It's stabbing . . . and stabbing, it's a knife and I want to kill something, tear it apart, and it's too close and I have to hear things and see things and *know*, I have to *know* things, awful things." Now she was almost shouting. "The stabbing, you don't know. You don't know." She sat up. "You don't . . . you aren't anybody. I am. I am everybody and inside them and see *every*thing and it's terrible . . . oh you just can't see it. It's like . . . dead and, and, and it . . . it just stabs like sharp like stick it in and twist it and laughs at me, laughs at me because who are *you* to say and it knows I can see it knows and it laughs anyway cause I can't stop it, can *you*? No, nobody can fucking shit and then I get cl . . . I . . . st . . . get stuck in there where it everything happens and they're all so awful, dirty little cunts, *all* of them. Cunts. They hate God, they just stand there jerking off cutting each other apart with . . . and the women are always bleeding, bleeding everywhere, filthy whores bleeding on Jesus on the cross and I'm inside them where it all happens it it isn't I can't stop it. Don't you *know*?" Her eyes were wide with rage, confusion, madness, terror, with something he could never understand. She was panting from the effort.

"Hannah, listen to me. They can raise your medication again. You'll be back the way you were at the—"

"No!" Her face wrinkled up like an old woman's fist and she shook her head. Then her lips began to quake. "Don't make me go back there. *Don't you make me go back.*"

"Isn't it better there?"

"Are you in*sane*? Are you crazy, *mister man*?" She spit out a laugh. "Is suffocating better than drowning? Are you? Are you any better than that? Don't laugh 'cause they can see and I'm in them and then I see, too. Oh yes. Which way do you want it?

You don't want to see what I see. You think I'm crazy." She punched herself in the chest. Then, quietly, she began to sob.

"Hannah."

She smiled at him. "Chase?" Her smile disintegrated. "If that's really you, you can help me. The balloon, the mountain."

He squeezed his eyes shut. After their mother disappeared, when they'd finally accepted the fact that she wasn't ever coming home, they would occasionally talk about where she might be. One day he told Hannah about a dream he'd had the previous night: a hot air balloon drifted over distant snowcapped mountains, gradually shrinking as it faded into the mist. He knew when he woke that their mother had been in the balloon. Hannah only frowned and said, "I envy her." He should have heard her more clearly, understood better.

"I don't want it anymore. No more." She drew a staggered breath. "Please."

He lay back in his hospital bed trying to ignore the steady, dull pain in his calf and thinking about the sister he'd grown up with and adored. Most of what he recalled was just the feeling of closeness they'd shared. There were images of course, but they were mostly static and indistinct. He had to dredge his memories to isolate specific incidents, to see her in motion, to be able to touch her. But there she was, down on her hands and knees helping him with his train set, playing along with whatever scenario he'd devised. Did he recall that or was it something someone had told him? It didn't matter; if it wasn't trains it was something else. She was always nearby. As they got older she developed her own interests, dance and painting and poetry, but most of the time when he wanted to play, their age difference didn't seem to matter, and she didn't seem to care that she was a girl and he was a boy. When her breasts finally began to develop it embarrassed her. She wore baggy blouses and always found something to hold in front of her. She once confessed to him that she'd begun to sleep on her stomach to keep them from getting any bigger, but after a couple months she was complaining that they weren't developing fast enough. She was afraid she'd ruined them, that they'd become clogged, their growth stunted. They could talk about almost anything, probably because there was no one else at home to talk to. One night when he was about twelve and she was fifteen, they ingested an entire box of NoDoz. He threw up and she was so restless and agitated she made him stay up all night watching her do calisthenics and ballet moves, or a manic parody of them. Neither of them would have guessed that she had less than a year of sanity left. The one thing they knew was that they could trust each other. Perhaps he had idealized her, had forgotten or blocked the slights and quarrels; that would make sense. Still, for a long time she was his closest friend, willing to be a playmate, a caretaker or a confidante, whatever he needed, and unlike the elder siblings of his friends in school, she treated him like an equal, sharing with him her successes, failures and fears, allowing him to be a friend to her. What he could never do for her was play the role of a parent, as she sometimes did for him. But there was so much more, hundreds of memories he'd never retrieve. Where were they now when he needed them?

"It looks like you'll be out of here soon."

His thoughts scattered at the sound of a voice. "What?"

"Doctor Best said we could discharge you as soon as we can get you up and walking on a pair of crutches." The nurse straightened his blanket.

"Are you . . . are you sure?"

"Is something wrong?" She frowned.

"I . . . I still feel dizzy."

"I imagine you could use a good meal, a little fresh air and a good night's sleep in your own bed."

"I don't know. I'd like to try the crutches to get used to them, but . . . I don't know, I really don't feel up to going home yet."

"Okay, well. . . ." The nurse sighed and scratched her head. "Let me check your blood pressure and then we'll see what the doctor has to say." She fitted the cuff around his left arm and squeezed the bulb until the cuff was snug. Then she gradually released the pressure. "Okay," she said. "I'll see if I can't find the doctor."

"You must really like it here." Dr. Best grinned.

"I just don't feel up to moving around that much, going up and down the steps at my father's house and all that."

"Between the gunshot and your . . . your sister, I'm sure you're exhausted. I know I'd want to get out of this place as fast as possible, but things are pretty calm at the moment and I don't see any reason to rush you if you really want to enjoy our fine Continental cuisine a little longer."

"Can I just stay right here, I mean, in this room? I'd like to be close to Hannah."

"That shouldn't be a problem . . . unless we get a bus accident or something."

"Thanks . . . I don't know what to call you now that I don't want to be an asshole."

"Just about anything but Dicky would suit me fine."

"Fair enough."

Dr. Best scrutinized him, opened his mouth as if he was going to say something, then left the room.

Chase set the alarm on his cell phone and let his eyes fall shut.

36

The lights were dim as he made his way to her room. A lone nurse sat behind the desk, hunched forward, her arms folded on the counter to cradle her head. The emergency room hadn't been this calm and peaceful since he'd arrived. It was as though the entire hospital had slipped into a coma. He sat down on the chair next to her bed and leaned his crutches against the wall. One of his first assignments as a reporter was a story about a retired doctor who was suspected of murdering his terminally ill wife. An air embolism: that was how the Westchester District Attorney had described the cause of death. Before formal charges could be filed, the man used their gas oven to end his own life. Instead of a suicide note, he left behind a three-page love note to his wife. Chase cried when he read it. If he read it now he'd cry again. He might never stop. Two things can both be true and also be contradictory. He took the tube in his hand and carefully tugged the drip chamber away from the bag. Example: I love my sister, and I am doing this. His heart hammering, he pressed one finger against the bag's open valve and held it there. He looked at his watch: 3:37. The facts don't constitute the truth. He placed the loose end of the tube between his lips. *My breath to stop yours.* When he was five or six years old he'd wake up in the middle of the night and feel the need to be close to someone. Very gently, he blew air into the tube—his hands were trembling. His mother and father had forbidden him to enter their room at night so he'd make his way quietly down the hall and into Hannah's room and crawl into bed with her. But for the distant beeps and hums, the emergency room was silent, and for a minute he imagined there was no one else around but the two of them, that they were children back at home in the middle of the night, that he was about to climb into bed with her. He looked down at her face, so different now from what he recalled, ravaged by all the years of fear and confusion. Perhaps that little girl had escaped, was running around somewhere, laughing now. *I love you. Even now, like this.* She'd say, "Okay, little one. Okay," and pet his head until he fell asleep. His body jerked as he forced back a sob. The remaining liquid moved gradually down the tube. *My breath to your heart.* If he couldn't sleep she'd tell him the story of the two children in the woods, Chance and Hope. The definition of irony. He leaned toward her, pressed his cheek to hers, then kissed her softly. In the morning she'd wake him so he could get back to his own room before their parents noticed he was gone. He wasn't supposed to need this now that he was older. *The person I love the most, the one I've loved the longest. Control.* If he pushed too hard, if he tried to rush it, the catheter might slip out, or her vein might explode from the pressure. *Softly. All I can give you, the only thing you want.* The line where the air and the liquid met approached the catheter and his body quaked. *She wants this wanted this will have wanted this will want nothing more.* Suppressing the sobs was like trying to hold back a breaking wave. *But my sister has been dead for years. My purest love. Am I taking a stranger's life?* Slowly. Would he feel better when this was over? *Murderer. Acting on the pleadings of a lunatic. How can I possibly know what's right?* It moved so very slowly down the tube. *I have nothing else to give you. All of it is wrong. Please move, just a little faster. Let it end. She wants this.* She wanted this. But it just crept through the tube. He pushed a little harder, almost choked stifling a howl, then eased off. *When it's over she'll be gone. I love you. Grief is a ball growing inside me, swelling like a mushroom cloud, toxic, blinding, choking and cold. I love you, Hannah.* Slowly. *Hannah.* Closer. *My gift. I'm so sorry.* Tears push out. He leans closer, looks for his sister again in that distorted face, her eyes creep open, she stares into his eyes—does she see him, does she know, is she telling him something—her eyes fall shut again. Had they really opened or was that only an illusion, fabricated by need? *Who am I now?* It's closer. Almost there. Quiet. *Why must it take so long? Goodbye, my love. Why must it ever end?* So slowly. Footsteps in the hall, a voice. *Please don't stop me.* Almost there. Quiet. The last of the liquid disappears. Gently he breathes into the tube, a little at a time. "It's okay, little one." So very gently. "It's okay." *What else could I do? No more pain, sweetheart, not for you.* "It's okay."

"I love you."

It's okay.

Now the sobs came. And for a long time he remained there resting his head on hers, bathing her face in the product of his grief.

37

"Wake up, Chase."

He opened his eyes. Aaron was standing next to the bed looking down at him, his face unshaven, his eyes swollen and red.

"What time is it?" Chase said. He looked around the room. "What's going on?"

"It's Hannah."

"What?" He pressed the button to raise his head. "What is it?"

Christine appeared in the doorway. "I'm sorry, but I'm not waiting outside this time."

"She's dead, Chase," Aaron said. "She . . . passed away some time last night." Had he been crying, too?

Christine stood next to the bed and clutched his hand. "I'm so sorry."

Chase squeezed her hand and let his eyes fall shut. Now she was nowhere, not happy or healthy, not sad or sick or disappointed or worried, not tired or frustrated or confused or angry or agitated or paranoid, not tortured and terrified, but gone. At least the suffering was over; that was something. That was everything. He looked up at Christine, then at his brother. "It's okay," he said. He wiped his eyes.

"They haven't taken her out yet," Aaron said. "Do you want to see her?"

"No," he said. "No."

"Are you sure? If we're going to have her cremated—"

"She's not in there. I just want to go. Maybe one of you could find a nurse so I can get out of here."

Aaron stepped out of the room and Christine grabbed a chair and pulled it over next to the bed. "Are you really okay?"

"Yeah." He smiled. "I'm okay."

"Well, I know this is a lousy time, but I'd like you to tell me what happened to you." She took his hand again. "No clever quips, no jokes. I'd just like the truth."

"I was shot."

"Well, if that's your entire story I can see why the paper fired you."

Would she be jealous? Perhaps. Anyway, she deserved to know. "I was sleeping with a married woman. When her husband found out he lost it. He's got a broken leg—I threw a gas can at him—and I've got a nice clean hole in my thigh."

"You were screwing this guy's wife."

"I guess you could call it that. We were together a couple times."

"Are you *trying* to get killed?"

"If I am I'm doing a pretty lousy job of it."

"Has this guy been arrested?"

"No."

"Why not?"

"No one else knows what happened."

She rubbed the bridge of her nose. "I don't understand."

"He just went a little crazy."

"A little?"

"He could have killed me and he didn't. He's got enough problems and I really don't feel like making it harder for him than I already have." Chase sat up and slid to the edge of the bed. "Can we talk about this later?"

"I guess that's up to you."

He pulled the crutches toward him, positioned them under his arms, grabbed the handgrips and lifted himself off the bed.

"Aaron tells me you're ready to go home now. Is that right?" Dr. Best looked as though he'd just showered and shaved and was ready to go dancing.

"Yeah. I think I've been here long enough."

"How are you getting around on those?"

"Alright, I guess."

"Good." The doctor glanced at Aaron and then at Christine. "Would you mind giving me a few moments with the patient before I release him?"

When they were gone he pushed the door shut. "Have a seat."

Chase hiked himself up onto the bed.

"It seems your roommate paid your bill."

"That was awfully generous."

"Maybe someday you'll tell me what really happened between the two of you."

"Maybe I will."

Dr. Best looked down at the floor. "I wasn't here last night when your sister passed away. I heard about it when I got in today." He let his eyes meet Chase's. "I'm sorry, Chase."

"Thanks."

"Her condition, her illness must have been very hard on everybody."

"No," Chase said. "It was impossible. But it was much worse than that for her."

He nodded. "Were you two very close, I mean . . . when she was . . . younger?"

"Yes, we were. We were best friends, and I appreciate—"

Doctor Best shook his head. "You know, whenever we lose a patient there are questions." He cleared his throat. "Particularly when we can't identify a clear cause of death."

"Maybe she was just done with life."

"I guess I wouldn't blame her. In any case we may never know exactly why her heart stopped." Again he looked into Chase's eyes, as though he was searching for something. "I guess. . . ," he turned his gaze first to the ceiling, then to the floor, brought his hands together as if to pray and tapped them lightly against his chest, "I guess it doesn't make much difference now."

"No."

"You did . . . you loved her very much, didn't you?"

"Yeah. Yeah, I did." Chase returned his stare. "I would have done anything for her."

He nodded.

For a moment they were both silent.

"I wasn't at all prepared to like you," Dr. Best finally said. "But I saw how you reacted when your . . . when Hannah came in, how much you. . . ." He took a step toward Chase and put his hand on his shoulder. "Try not to dwell on all of this. It's over now. I'm sure you did everything you could for her. I should be able to deal with any questions that arise and you'll be back on your feet and beating up expensive German cars in no time."

"Thanks, Doc." Chase smiled, secured the crutches under his arms and moved forward. He wanted to say something more, but maybe silence was better now. He opened the door and made his way out into the hall.

38

Over pasta at a small Italian restaurant, Chase, Christine and Sarah sat obediently nodding and smiling while Aaron prattled on about his band and his plans to produce and market a CD. When he'd finally tired of the topic, the two brothers discussed their father's house, his furniture and his car, which Aaron said he'd been thinking about keeping for himself. Hannah's name was never mentioned, and Chase had made it clear that he didn't want to discuss his injury or how it had occurred. Aaron asked Chase again if he'd consider staying in town and Chase said he didn't know, that there was a lot to consider. For reasons he couldn't have clearly identified, he didn't want to say it in front of Christine, but the thought of spending the rest of his life in Monroe County was enough to produce in him all the symptoms of food poisoning. In spite of whatever had happened or was happening or might eventually happen between Chase and Christine, Hannah's death had extinguished any desire he'd had to remain here. Even if he thought he could survive in this stifling environment without his sister, there was the problem of work. Certainly that needed to be addressed no matter where he lived—his severance pay would carry him for a while, and whatever inheritance there was would help, but he needed to start thinking seriously about some kind of future—but the limitations here seemed greater than almost anywhere else he could imagine living. The local paper was an embarrassment, even to the locals, and there wasn't another place within twenty-five miles where a journalist could earn a living. He pictured himself hunched over a folding table in a dimly lit trailer sipping cheap bourbon from a jam jar and typing hardware store flyers. *Save Our Soil—Don't Miss March Mulch-Mania Madness!!! Ball Peen Blowout This Tuesday Only—We've Hammered Our Prices DOWN DOWN DOWN!!!!!* And if he wanted to try another line of work, this was not the place to do it. Beyond real estate, miscellaneous food and beverage industry jobs or a life sentence at one of the resorts, there was very little to do. Even if he somehow found a satisfying job or decided that commuting to New York or Philadelphia would be tolerable, the cultural vacuum would siphon the life out of him. But perhaps he was in love with Christine. That complicated things.

Chase tried hard, as he nursed his second glass of wine, not to think about Hannah's death and the role he'd played in it. Still, it was there, just beneath the surface—it would always be there. Seeing the children might help but they were staying with their grandparents for the night. What he really wanted, as the conversation turned to finances, local politics and the coming school year, was to say it out loud, to say, "I killed her," to get the damned thing out of him, to release it into the atmosphere, to let someone else take some part of it from him, though he knew it wouldn't do any good. I killed someone, no, not someone, my dear sweet sad suffering lunatic sister. No one wants to know that. No one should be forced to deal with that.

There had been a moment, just after he'd spoken with Dr. Best, when Chase thought the worst might be behind him. Now he realized how foolish that was. Intellectually he understood why he'd had to do what he did, but it, the act, had done something to him, and he felt colder and more alone than he'd ever felt before. It was as though something inside him was turning rancid, like an untreated infection, and venom was spreading throughout his system. Aaron might offer his God if he knew; Christine, if she wasn't repulsed, would offer her love, or at least her sincere concern and compassion. And Chase, if not for his exhaustion, would already be clinging with profound, heartfelt desperation to a bottle of Scotch, an eager young body or both. Though none of those measures would cure him, drinking and fucking would almost certainly distract him for a while, for minutes or hours, and that was worth something. But it wouldn't be enough and in the end he'd hate himself for having felt even a little better after. . . . *How dare you have something good in your life?* Well, okay, maybe she'd had a point. He wanted a friend but wasn't at all certain what he'd do if he had one. Yes he was. He'd do nothing. Sharing his pain had never provided much comfort, though he hadn't tried it often or with much conviction. The thought of crying was nauseating. He could go out and search for their mother now—apparently no one had ever done that and it might be easier with modern technology than it would have been when she disappeared. *Hey, Mom, great to see you. By the way, I killed your only daughter. Gotta run. Oh, by the way, did you know that Dad sniffed panties?* It might be entertaining, though probably not as entertaining as he once would have thought. He lacked the energy now and, more importantly, the inclination to blame anyone for what had happened to his sister. That, in itself, was a great loss. *Now where do I put the rage?*

From what Julian had said, Haley's childhood had been far worse than any of theirs, and yet she was relatively functional, if not entirely healthy. There were so many indiscriminate forces at work—genes, chemistry, environment, instinct, chance. So much of life was just that, a series of random events, causally unrelated or linked by nothing more than coincidence or proximity. Silly, seemingly inconsequential things could dramatically alter the course of a life: a cloudburst, a lost key, a toothache, a slip of the tongue, bad fish, a broken traffic signal, a difficult bowel movement, an unspoken desire or a poorly phrased thought. Some small percentage of the little that remained after everything else had done its damage was, perhaps, up to us. *Okay, so what? I chose to kill my sister. I planned it and carried it out and here I am drinking cheap wine. I did that with what I had. Aaron did this.* At some point Hannah had lost the capacity to choose. Dying was really the only option left to her, the only thing she could decide. Maybe it was all about taking control in the only way left open to her. Haley had been subject to other, more powerful influences; she'd had far less choice than many, but she was going to find a way to survive, a way to deal with the pain and the scars. There was no logic here. But wouldn't life be better spent searching for those few areas where we have some choice, some control or even the illusion of control, and then taking responsibility for them, doing our best to choose wisely, to fight all the forces that tarnish or corrupt our lives, that muddle our judgment and make us less than we might otherwise be? At least then we'd be living our own lives instead of walking through a script produced impromptu by forces with no stake in our welfare. Of course you could get caught up in the question of what good judgment is, what a better life is and what the right choice is, but that would just be another way to avoid ever having to take responsibility, another way of giving up or walking away. He'd already done that and it hadn't gone particularly well. *I want to feel, to feel love, to feel loved, to believe I matter. To be tricked, if that's what it takes.*

"You're falling asleep." Christine was caressing his face.

"Yes, I am."

She stood up and reached out to help him up. "I'm going to get you home."

When he opened his eyes, it took him a moment to remember where he was. "What time is it?"

"I don't know." She was lying next to him in his father's bed, watching him.

"How long have you been awake?"

"Long enough to go out for a newspaper and breakfast."

"I guess I slept." The cloud was forming again, just above him.

"Is something living in your refrigerator?"

"Not that I know of. Why?"

"It was making noise last night."

"What?"

"I was in the kitchen reading and it was making a sort of scratching sound. That's why I didn't want to risk opening it today."

"It isn't plugged in."

"Well, maybe it was something in the wall behind it. Did your father have mice here?"

"Mice?"

"Yeah, like in the walls or the floor or wherever they live."

"I'm an idiot." He used his arms to hoist himself up. "Shit." He winced.

"Maybe you should take something."

"I am taking something."

"Well, something more."

"It's not that bad," he said. "Shouldn't you be at the store?"

"I might go in later if you can get around on your own."

"I'll be fine." Now he was beginning to feel the full weight of it.

"Are you sure he's not coming back?"

"Who?"

"The husband."

"Julian? No. He's got other things on his mind."

"What about her?"

"I don't know. I really don't know."

"Are you okay?"

"I don't plan to do much."

"I mean about Hannah."

He looked deep into her eyes. What was she doing here with him? Did she really want to know about his sister? "I have no idea how to answer that."

"Why didn't you want to go in and see her? I mean, I know how you feel about death, but she was so incredibly important to you. You could have gotten through it for her."

"She was gone, Christine. She wasn't there anymore."

"Wouldn't it have meant something to kiss her one last time, to look at her face or touch her hand or say goodbye?"

"No."

"I'm just trying to understand. I really want to understand, at least I think I do."

"I don't think I can talk about it right now."

"What are you afraid of?"

"The truth, Christine. Nothing in the world is scarier than the truth."

She sighed and got up.

"Give me a little time. Please."

Chase was lying on the couch with his legs on Christine's lap when Aaron came to check on him and discuss the funeral.

"I thought it should be just the three of us and the minister," he said after taking a seat on the recliner. He turned to Christine. "Or four, if you want to be there. And I'd like to do it here, if that's alright."

"Here is fine, but what about Bradley and Sophie," Chase said.

Aaron did his furrowed brow thing. "They didn't have any relationship with her at all."

"I realize that, but they did meet her and she was their aunt and their father's sister. She was family."

Aaron shook his head.

"I'd also like to invite the nurse who was taking care of her, Eleanor."

"If you really think she'll want to come I guess it's okay with me, but I definitely don't want the kids there."

"Look, I know they're your children, and I respect that, but I think . . . I just think it might be good for them. They met her, and they seemed to like her. And it might help me to have them there."

"I'm sorry, Chase, but I feel strongly about this."

"And I'd really like to keep God out of it," Chase said.

"Excuse me?"

Christine stood up and eased Chase's legs onto the couch. "I don't think I should be a part of this discussion." She leaned down to give Chase a kiss on the forehead. "I'll call you. Or you can call me if you need anything."

When the door clicked shut Aaron said, "You can't keep God out of it."

"He certainly kept a comfortable distance when she was alive. Why should he get involved now?"

"Did it ever occur to you that it was God's choice to . . . to free her?"

"After all that time? I. . . ." *Don't.* "No."

"I'm afraid God is involved, Chase, whether you believe it or not."

"Well, if that's true, why in heaven's name do we need a minister? I mean if He's going to be there anyway, why send some second-rate human representative?"

"Look, I know how much you cared for . . . how much you loved Hannah, and I . . . I understand your feelings about religion, though I could do without the sarcasm, but like you've said repeatedly, she was my sister, too. I don't want to fight with you about this, or about anything, but we need to find a way to make this work for everyone."

"I don't want to fight with you either, Aaron. I don't think I'd survive a fight right now. I know it isn't something we've had much practice at, but isn't there some way we could compromise?"

"If you have an idea I'm willing to listen."

"Okay. You can . . . you can bring your minister, let him perform some kind of brief, informal ceremony, if you'll agree to bring Bradley and Sophie."

Aaron shook his head.

"At least ask them if they'd like to come. Let them decide if they want to be there or not."

"Why is it so important to you?"

"I don't know." Chase eased his head down onto the pillow and closed his eyes. "I really don't. Maybe their presence will be enough to keep me from completely losing control, which I know nobody would appreciate. All I know is that it would mean a lot to me to have them there."

"Okay."

"What?" He lifted his head and looked at his brother.

"I said okay. I'll ask them."

"Prick."

"Asshole."

"Penis face."

"Fuck nozzle."

And then I say Son-of-a-panty-sniffer and then he says Sister killer and we laugh until our brains explode; mirrors and question marks shoot through the air. It might be nice to have a brother I could tell. It might be nice to have magical powers.

The cremation took place at precisely eleven o'clock the following morning and Chase tried not to think about it as he lay on his father's couch thinking of nothing else.

Just before two o'clock that afternoon the doorbell rang. Christine rushed out of the kitchen to open the door and Aaron stepped in, followed by Sarah, Bradley and a generic young man with a receding hairline and a receding jaw. He wore a clerical collar under a wrinkled black suit that looked like something he might have exhumed from the trunk of an abandoned car. Perhaps the outfit was Aaron's concession to informality.

"What happened to Sophie?" Chase was still hoping she might appear.

"She didn't want to come," Aaron said. Sarah turned and walked away.

"Really?"

"Her best friend called and asked her to go on a picnic."

"Okay," he said. He was too weary to fight. He'd have to be satisfied with the anger. No, he wanted to let it go. He wanted to learn to like his brother, to forgive him or at least to try.

He saw the minister standing there with a bible in his hands, heard the somber voice, but the man could have been speaking in some forgotten language. Even when Chase tried to focus, it was nothing more than a jumble of odd vowels and unfamiliar consonants pouring from a face that seemed to take immense pride in its humility and earnestness. Chase wanted to scream at this silly little man for being there, for mumbling nonsense while he sat mourning the life and the loss of a woman he never knew and would never think about again. When the noise finally stopped everyone turned toward Chase.

He had no idea what to do.

"Do you want to say something?" Christine looked concerned.

He stared at her.

"Maybe you should try." A sad smile. "For her."

For a second he forgot his injury and tried to stand. *Shit.* He pushed the pain down. Then he grabbed the crutches and lifted himself up, opened his mouth, took a breath.

"Hannah," he said, and swallowed. "I guess we all live inside ourselves. Maybe we peek out once in a while, but only very warily. Maybe we open up a little now and then to allow someone . . . let someone get closer, to let them see who . . . to let them see us, but it seems we never do anything unless it serves our needs, and. . . ." He closed his eyes and shook his head. "But that's just how we're programmed, I guess, just one of the strategies of survival. It only really works when our needs, when the process of satisfying our needs enables us to get close to someone else, to care for them or give to them.

That's when there is something like magic—you can call it God if you need to, or love—and that's what she . . . what Hannah gave me. She let me give her what she needed, and in the process of doing that I . . . fulfilled some need of my own. And we both did it. There was a time when she took care of me. She was as good as we . . . as people have the capacity to be. And maybe she saved me from the hell that consumed her. But no." He looked around the room. "It isn't quite that. Maybe . . . maybe it's when we care so much about someone that their needs become more important than our own. It isn't that it's unselfish. It's never that. It's just that what you want more than anything is to give someone else what they need, even when you believe it will destroy you, because that's more important to you, more necessary to you than your own survival." They were watching him, waiting. Their faces, their expressions. . . . It didn't matter. "I'm sorry." He smiled at Christine. *Can you, at least, hear me?* It didn't matter. This was only his, only for him. He sat down, closed his eyes. "I guess I'm used to missing her," he said to himself.

A few minutes later there was a knock at the door. A young man stood there with a bouquet of flowers. Chase carried the flowers inside and opened the note that was attached.

> *I didn't feel comfortable coming, but I wanted you to know how much it meant to your sister to have you near her.*
>
> > *With sympathy,*
> > *Eleanor*

For a while everyone lingered, but no one seemed to know what to do or say. They couldn't talk about her full, happy life, since it was neither, and to say she was in a better place would have seemed callous. Could any of them imagine a place worse than the one her mind had devised? So instead of the usual comments, there were stilted exchanges interspersed between long, uncomfortable silences. At one point Chase heard Aaron say something to the priest about how difficult it was to lose two family members in such a brief period of time. The temptation to beat his brother with a crutch was so strong that Chase got off the couch and hobbled outside.

He made his way out onto the lawn and turned to look back at the house where his father had lived. After an awful childhood, the man had married a woman who was probably already insane, a woman who was most likely battling the demons her daughter would ultimately inherit. He'd lived what must have been a lonely, depressing life, a life without emotion or real contact. Yes, that was sad. Had Hannah ever felt loved by anyone, anyone other than a little brother who'd had no choice but to attach himself to her, or had she died not knowing the sweet and terrible power of what we call love? For all his problems, Aaron had at least formed some sort of a family. He loved his children and probably loved his wife, though how deep his feelings for anyone else were wasn't clear. Still, there was some connection, some link to other humans. His life had some semblance of normalcy. Maybe he was the closest one to normal, for whatever that was worth, and the truth was he was trying, doing the best he could beneath the burden of a history that had destroyed Hannah and crippled Chase, whether he recognized that burden or not. It made no more sense to blame him for what he'd become than it would have to blame Hannah. He'd simply found a way to survive. Forgiveness was long overdue.

Maybe Chase's idealized, romanticized version of life was just a fantasy. *I am the idiot. Can I be a happy idiot? No, not happy, but reasonably contented and occasionally fulfilled? Or will I need to continue refilling my leaky ego with flirtations and affairs, with constant reassurances of my value as a person, as a man, as a lover? What will I do when I'm too old or unattractive or angry for that to work? Please need me so I can leave you. Will some minor insult finally ignite the violent explosion that derails my life entirely?* But falling apart would be an act of surrender. *If I'm not ready to die I can't give up. I just wish I knew what that means.*

The front door opened and Christine stepped out. She stood on the doorstep and stared at him. She was beautiful. After a minute she said, "I don't know." A sad smile, faint as the shadow of a windblown feather, appeared to appear and then blew away again. He looked up at the sky, a great gray sea floating upside down, the waves churning to their own sleepy rhythm. When he lowered his eyes Christine was no longer there.

Goodbyes were brief and appropriately subdued, and then he was alone again in his father's house with his bullet hole and his crutches. Christine had left without his noticing. The note on the kitchen table said she was afraid, afraid of getting closer to him, afraid of him, afraid that one of them would let the other down or that what she thought she might be feeling was just an illusion. She wanted to believe in it, but didn't know how to trust. She didn't plan to call or visit, at least for a while, unless he needed something. She cared about him. She was sorry.

The pain of rejection was like a malevolent organism, filling his veins with ice and tearing at his gut. He was trembling, sweating, seething with a sudden rage and terrified of being alone forever. But beneath that there was something else, something light and bubbly; was it relief? Did he really want anyone to be that close? Did he really want anyone at all? Of course he wanted *every*one, but did he want *any*one? And then he laughed. If she were emotionally healthy he wouldn't have any chance at all. At least there was that. He read the note again and like a tidal wave the rage and terror engulfed him once more.

39

For the first couple weeks the physical therapy sessions were agonizing. Within twenty minutes his leg felt as though it was about to split apart and he endured random back spasms throughout the sessions and for hours afterwards. Weary of the fogginess, he tapered the pain medications and when the pain in his leg finally began to diminish he pushed himself harder. The suffering supplanted thoughts that would otherwise torture him. Haley had left a message on his phone apologizing again and asking him to call when he had a chance, but he knew they'd been through too much to reclaim whatever they'd had, if, in fact, that was what either of them wanted. And of course there was her husband. But how could anyone be so insecure and so arrogant at the same time? Sometimes he provided his own entertainment, though it was never without a price. Although he'd come close dozens of times, Chase hadn't called Christine since the day of Hannah's funeral. He still thought about her often, still held on to some vague hope for the two of them, but he had no idea what to say to her and was confident he'd find a way to screw it up if he spoke to her now. He ignored calls from his wife and his attorney and avoided contact with Aaron and his family, though he missed the children more than he ever would have expected. Most of his time he spent reading, searching the Internet on his new laptop and fantasizing about Marianne, the physical therapist who usually worked with him on weekends. She was young and energetic and had the muscle tone of a professional triathlete. On the days when she wore one of her halter tops and the tight spandex shorts that revealed her most beguiling knolls and glens, he found himself using the pain in his leg to fend off his erections and keep himself from reaching out and running his fingers over her perfectly formed fundament. Of course she was aware of her effect on him. It was as though they were electrically charged and the closer she got the more powerful the current. When their bodies touched, a bolt shot directly to his groin. This was not love. This was better. It was pure, undiluted desire and far less daunting than the prospect of some sloppy emotional connection. And the cleanup would be so much easier.

He began masturbating almost every day, sometimes two or three times a day, either thinking of Marianne, looking at pornography on his computer or both. This was something new to him, and it was a peculiar world, where subtlety had no place. He simply Googled the word "pussy" and within a few clicks, presto, he found dozens of websites: Cum Shots, XXX Cum Shots, SpermSuckers, Pornholia, Cornholia, Cumflood, Cum Guzzlers, Ass Bangers, Blowlita, Teen Facials, Cum Geyser, Pink Pussy, Pink Teen Pussy, Wet Teen Pussy, Hand Ejac, Real18, 18Only, College Sluts, Perversius, Goo Clips, Teen Pervs, Dorm Sex, Quick Jerk, Bitch Fuck, Clipped Pussy, Gals With Guts, Screw Tube, Blue Tube, Goo Tube, Chicks With Dicks, Boneprone, Amateur Blowjob, Handjob Video, Schoolgirl Sex, TitJobs, AllJobs, XXX Hoes, Creampie mpegs,

Dirty Hoes, Busty Hoes, Unshaven Pussy, Porn Addict, Filthy Hoes, Fat Ass, Twatalot, Fat Ass Filthy Hoes, Mouth Splooge, TitCum, Sperm Flood, Filthy XXX Hoes, Family Facials, Daddy's Pet, Solo Girls, Uncle Gush, Russian Pussy, Slut World, Doggystyle, Jerk Now, Fistfuckers, Ass Puddle, Faces Loaded, Butt Spackle, Yank My Crank, Dirty Virgin, Jizz Clips, Hairy Fat Ass Filthy Hoes. *Yum.*

   His manic search for inspiration and stimulation led him to photographs and video clips of women in a vast range of ages, sizes and shapes, from the startlingly attractive to the hideous, the crippled and the deformed. He had to navigate away from links to "live shows" and ads for sexual aids and videos of bestiality. The process was daunting and occasionally repugnant, and much of what he saw before he learned to sift through the detritus turned his stomach and drained the blood from his heads. All he really wanted was a little nudge of arousal, photos or videos of attractive women touching themselves, giving gentle but passionate blowjobs or handjobs or enjoying apparently voluntary intercourse with another normal human, maybe a couple women together to add some spice. He didn't need shackles or complicated lingerie or, dear God, pregnancy, and he had no desire to see additional men; the less he saw of the man the better. He just couldn't seem to fantasize that he was the one who was receiving the blowjob on his screen if the man in the video had fur on his palms and a swastika tattooed on his blubbery gut. Maybe he lacked creativity as a sexual partner, perhaps he was boring and uninspired, though there were moments when he wasn't sure what he'd do if his father's panties were still accessible. *My father's panties.*

   When he was strong enough to pedal a bike he went to one of the local bike shops and bought a six-thousand-dollar racing bike and over five-hundred dollars' worth of cycling clothing and accessories. Why not?

He started with short, easy rides—just five or ten miles at a time—and gradually increased his distance and his pace. He was getting stronger and faster, and soon, disturbed by the realization that he'd become familiar enough with several of the porn models to be able to identify them based on a momentary glimpse of a chin, a couple fingers, an ear, a nipple or a tattoo, he transferred some of his obsessive inclinations to the bike.

It wasn't long before he was riding four or five days a week, doing hill repeats on Fox Town Hill and intervals along Route 209 between Stroudsburg and Snydersville. The limp was diminishing and his body was getting stronger and tighter and finally on a Saturday morning late in August he shyly asked Marianne out. She smiled and flashed her dark brown eyes and said she was tempted and honored but that her boyfriend probably wouldn't appreciate it. He promised not to tell, but that wasn't enough to sway her.

In spite of all the distractions, he continued to think about Christine much of the time, but for reasons he couldn't name he still couldn't bring himself to act. Hannah, of course, was with him day and night. Even more unsettling than the memory of that night in the hospital were the dreams. Sometimes, in the middle of the night or just before dawn, he awoke wrapped in a tangle of sweat-drenched sheets and blankets with a sense of dread so palpable he couldn't stop trembling, though often there were no images or recollections to justify the feelings. The dreams he did remember were vivid and agonizingly concrete. Hannah, younger and healthier, a shiny silver wire tied around her neck, smiling and saying, "Come on, Chase. Now *you* can pull harder than that." Hannah pulling back her blouse, revealing a chest that was split open, her heart pumping loudly.

The heart expands, bubbles, her face contorts and she screams as the swollen organ bursts. Hannah dressed in a pure white wedding gown, lifting the veil. She coughs up a little blood, then a little more, a dark clot, a thick spray of excrement. Huge rats covered with bile pour out of her open mouth. She melts into a heap of body fluids and gurgling organs. Then a little girl says in a sweet singsong voice, "Thanks for killing me." He knew now that there would be no answer to the question that haunted him. What he'd done might have been an awful, unforgivable mistake or a tender, selfless act of love. All he could do was try to find a way to live with it, try to convince himself to trust his instincts, which far too often had proved entirely unreliable. Perhaps, if he could find a way to feel good about what he'd done, he could begin to reclaim his life and move forward, or, for that matter, in any direction at all. Shock treatment might be of some value. A convincing lie might help. A credible God would be a great comfort now. Pornography had already begun to lose its appeal.

Perhaps it would help to tell someone. There was so little to lose. It was time.

40

He was waiting for a response, a rebuke or a renunciation, waiting for her to stand up and walk out or for her head to pop open and a nest of snakes to slither out to devour him—Satan had always been a more credible character than God—but Christine just sat motionless at the far end of his father's couch wearing something resembling a grin. And when he looked closer he saw that there were tears, too, though just enough to make her eyes glisten. Perhaps he should have led up to it gradually instead of blurting it all out in one desperate breath. No, if he'd done it any other way he would have fallen apart. He should have just shut up and kept it to himself. But it was too late.

"Do you think you could say something?"

"I'm so sorry."

"Sorry. . . ."

"For her." She shook her head, sniffed, wiped her eyes. "And for you, Chase. I can't even imagine. . . ."

"Don't try."

"What made you decide . . . why did you tell me?"

"I guess I wanted . . . well, I wanted you to say I did the right thing. Or to say I was a vile murdering wretch. I need some perspective and I don't trust anyone else. And I needed to say it out loud."

"I can't tell you if it was right or wrong. You're the only one who knows that."

"But I *don't* know. That's the problem."

"You had to make a horrendous, impossible choice. Somehow you made it and acted on it. You wouldn't have been able to do it if you hadn't been certain it was the right thing to do."

He shook his head. "That's not exactly what I was looking for."

"But nobody else can ever know what you know about it or understand how you . . . how you got there. It doesn't matter what anyone else thinks."

"It matters to me. I can't seem to find it on my own."

"Okay," she said and looked down at her hands, fingers intertwined on her lap. "I've always liked you, Chase. I've always been fond of you, in spite of our peculiar, awkward, contentious . . . relationship . . . relationships. Recently I've been thinking that maybe I'm in love with you, or that if I allowed myself to I could be, although that word—love—it carries a load of baggage and gets everyone in trouble. But—and I don't mean to be cruel—but I would never have said that I . . . that I admired you." She looked into his eyes, studied his face. "Not until today."

He swallowed. "Well. . . ."

"I guess that doesn't help much."

"It means a lot. It does. I'm just not sure it'll make it any easier to live with."

"You risked a lot to help Hannah, far more than most people would have risked for someone they loved."

"Maybe most people have more to lose than I do."

"Maybe." She was examining him, squinting as though her vision had suddenly blurred. "No. I don't think so. I think you're finally growing up. Just don't let this destroy you."

But it had destroyed some part of him. There was no question about that. "Yeah, well."

For a few minutes they were silent. Chase surveyed the living room. He could never live here, in this house. He sat up and turned toward Christine.

"I'm going to do what I can to help Aaron with the mess my father and Hannah left behind. He's been dealing with everything and, as much as I hate to admit it, it really isn't fair. And I'm going to take care of all the crap I've been so vigorously ignoring. My divorce, my life."

"Makes sense." A tight-lipped smile.

"I'm going to have to go back to New York pretty soon, at least for a while."

She nodded. "At least."

He slid closer and reached for her hand. "Do you think we could make love?"

She winced. "What if it isn't any good?"

"I don't think there's much chance of that, though that would certainly make things easier."

"What if it is?"

"I don't know."

In the morning Chase listened to all the messages he'd been avoiding. The majority were from either Jennifer or his attorney, each reminding him with increasing urgency that there were critical issues to resolve, documents to fill out and file, blah,

blah, blah. He called David and told him to schedule a meeting some time the following week with Jennifer and her attorney and, hey, what the heck, she could bring the prick whose mutant child she was carrying if she felt like it. Then he called Aaron and said he wanted to help with the estate, with the paperwork and the sale of the house, the furniture and the car. He'd be dealing with his divorce in New York for a while, but would find a way to make himself available for whatever needed to be done. Aaron sounded appreciative but was unwilling to give up what he apparently perceived as an indispensable and potentially eternal wellspring of praise and pity, though he was happy to let Chase deal with anything related to Hannah's death. In the absence of any evidence to the contrary, Chase decided to view the latter as an act of generosity. When he asked to speak with the kids, Aaron put them on separate extensions. They sounded interested in his imminent departure, even a little upset at first, but after a minute or so they found other things to occupy them. Anyway, he'd see them at least one more time before leaving. Chase was about to end the call when Aaron asked him if he would like to have Hannah's ashes. Without thinking Chase said yes. Aaron offered to drop them off the next day and Chase broke down. He forced out a goodbye and hung up.

When he'd recovered, he dialed Haley's number. Hearing her voicemail was a relief.

"Hi, Haley. It's Chase." *Gosh, how's it going?* "I guess it's obvious that I don't know what to say, but I feel like I need to say something. I like you." *Wanna go to the sock hop?* "I care about you, but I think we both know there's no way to continue whatever we began together. It's sad, I mean to me it's sad—I really have no idea how you feel—but anyway, shit, I'm sorry. I'll always care about you, and I wish you the happiness, the life you deserve. If things had been different maybe . . . what? Maybe things would be different. Blah blah. Fuck me. There is no way to do this and I'd erase it and start over if I thought I could do any better. I really hope you find some way to be okay and to know you deserve to be okay. You can call me if you want to, whenever you want to. If not, thanks for . . . thanks for making me feel. I'm sorry. I'm sorry I didn't know you better."

He didn't expect to hear from her, and that was mostly okay.

Dr. Best sounded happy to hear from him and immediately agreed to have a quick lunch with him providing he didn't mind eating bad pizza in a greasy pizzeria run by a couple shady Turks with hostile attitudes and world-class body odor.

They each ordered two plain slices and then took a booth in the corner farthest from the counter.

"What can I do for you, Chase?"

"I wanted to thank you."

"For what?"

"I think you know."

"Just doing my job."

"Not quite."

Dr. Best shrugged and took a bite of his pizza.

"Didn't you ever want to leave the Poconos?"

"I don't know. I thought about it when I was younger, like everybody else, but I'm doing pretty much what I always wanted to and my entire family's within twenty miles. The area's a little backward in some ways, and by the end of summer every year I've had more than enough of the tourists, but we get the same books and movies you get in the city without all the noise and pollution." He sipped his Coke. "All things considered, I'm not sure there's a place I'd rather be."

"That must be a good way to feel."

"Are you thinking about moving back?"

"Not really."

"That's a shame. I think I'd actually enjoy having you around."

"That's an awfully nice thing to say." Chase looked down at the table.

"I don't socialize much. It would be good to have a friend who's spent a little time on the outside."

"I'm not sure what I'm doing, but I think I'd suffocate here. And I don't think I could afford the medical bills."

"You might have a hard time getting used to the pace, and some of the attitudes would probably get your dander up, but you'd find some like-minded people to piss off." He smiled. "We're not all ignorant and uneducated."

"Yeah. I can see that." Chase leaned in. "Now, didn't you used to be an asshole?"

"Probably, yeah. I'm sure you'd find a few people who think I still am. But, you know, the older I get, the more I realize how little I know. I think maybe that makes me a little easier to get along with."

"Really? I still know everything."

Dr. Best smiled. "I assumed you did."

"It looks like I'm going to be going back and forth between New York and here for a while. If it's alright, I'll call you next time I'm in. Maybe we can have a drink?"

"I'd like that a lot." He sat back and scrutinized Chase. "Now, why don't you do me a favor and tell me what really happened to you and your friend?"

"Well." He sighed. "Given our early history, this could be a little awkward."

"For you, I hope."

"What the hell. I was . . . dating his wife and—"

"Dating or screwing?"

"I really did like her. I was quite smitten, or thought I was."

"Okay."

"Well, he found out about it somehow and came after me."

"Why didn't I think of that?"

Chase shrugged. "I was in my father's kitchen reassembling the refrigerator when he walked in. Of course he had a gun, this being Pennsylvania and the land of the eternal flannel shirt, though he wasn't actually wearing a flannel shirt at the time. Anyway, he was pointing the damned thing at me and acting fucked up enough to almost literally scare the shit out of me. It was starting to look as though he might have the capacity to kill me, so when I saw what I thought might be an opportunity to get out of there, I grabbed it. I . . . I distracted him by telling him his shoes didn't match, which, by the way, they didn't, and then I threw a gas can at him, hit him in the shin and ran out of the house. He came limping after me and fired a couple shots. One of them hit me, though I didn't realize it until a few minutes later. Afterwards we sat side by side on my father's couch self-medicating with my expensive Scotch and singing songs together while we waited for the ambulance."

"Okay. If you don't want to tell me that's fine."

Chase laughed. "So is it Dr. Best, Dick or Richard?"

"My friends call me Richard."

"Okay."

"So Dr. Best will be fine."

Chase pushed his paper plate away. "This pizza sucks."

"All part of my new weight loss plan."

Chase drifted from room to room, straightening up and beginning to organize his things for his trip home. He didn't want to do a final housecleaning until the day before he left so there really wasn't much to do. But as he toured the house he had the feeling he was forgetting something. He went out to the garage and puttered around, then came back inside and sat on the couch. He thought about the day he and Julian had sat there waiting for the ambulance. Then he remembered the gun. He went into the kitchen and pulled the refrigerator away from the wall. Crouching down, he reached one hand in and felt around. Nothing. He slid the refrigerator a little farther from the wall and wedged his head in to look. It was too dark to see anything so he pulled the plug and shoved the refrigerator out far enough to let some light in. No gun. His stomach did a free fall. The room lurched and swayed. He grabbed his phone and dialed Haley's number. Her message answered and he ended the call. Maybe Julian had taken the gun back to wherever he'd gotten it. Maybe he'd come to get it when Chase wasn't home. Maybe he was perched on a rooftop somewhere picking off strangers. *Fuck*. He reached in as far as his hand would go and felt around. In the far left corner he found a sheet of paper. He pulled it out and unfolded it. It was a note.

> *Chase—*
> *I didn't want you to be stuck with it and I didn't think I could face you so I came in and got it when you were out. I will dispose of it properly. It won't be easy given my anger and her history, but Haley and I are trying to work things out. I still get upset when I think about what you did and maybe I always will, but I realize that doesn't justify what I did. I do hope you're healing quickly and that someday you'll forgive my actions.*
> *—Julian*

Thanks. He wrinkled up the note and smiled.

41

The following morning was sunny and cool and Chase wanted to take one last long ride in the mountains before getting back to his life. He went out early, with no particular route or destination in mind, and headed in a direction he hadn't ridden before. He didn't like riding with a backpack on, but he couldn't think of any other way to take her with him. For a couple hours he just pedaled, thinking about nothing, focusing on the moment, on the feeling of being on the bike. When he finally sat up to look around him, he was gliding through Pen Argyl, a terminally drab, atavistic town that seemed to subsist in spite of itself. On what was apparently the downtown section of the main street, he slowed to get a better look at his surroundings. On the left was an Italian restaurant that appeared to be constructed of cardboard and plastic, on the right an appliance store with a display window full of dusty washers, dryers and boxy television sets that might easily have been a couple decades old. The place was in a state of suspended animation. About a quarter mile farther on he stopped at a traffic light to get his bearings. After a minute of uncertainty he followed the road around to the left, past the public swimming pool and a playground. A few minutes later he saw the sign for Bangor and knew he was going the right way. About ten miles ahead on Route 191 between Bangor and Stroudsburg was a long descent, a couple sections of which were very steep, with a series of winding switchbacks that would be invigorating on a bike. The final mile and a half or so was a steady, dangerously steep drop that terminated at the stop sign where Route 191 intersected with 611. Chase remembered the stories he'd heard about that hill. In one of them, the brakes on a Volkswagen van locked up halfway down, in another one, an oil truck's brake pads ignited just before reaching the intersection. He'd made it this far. If he could endure the long gradual climb out of Bangor and past Roseto, he'd have earned the switchbacks and the exhilaration of that final descent.

On the narrow road between Pen Argyl and Bangor, a truck driver slowed to call him an asshole, then ground his gears before chugging off. A few minutes later, a man traveling in the opposite direction yelled something Chase couldn't decipher; it sounded like someone hacking up bile with a few hostile words mixed in for good measure. They seemed to be trying to make a point, challenging him, testing him, reminding him not to become too comfortable. Chase shifted into a higher gear and increased his cadence. As he approached Bangor, the road surface suddenly became rougher, as though some weary road crew had just quit in the middle of the job and gone home. Gravel was scattered everywhere and he had to reduce his speed and snake back and forth to avoid all the potholes. Bangor had always been a depressed town but now it looked as though it had given up and committed a swift, violent suicide. The buildings in the small downtown area were in varying states of disrepair, some were boarded up, others looked as though they were caving in or leaning on each other for support. Most of the storefronts were vacant. Sitting on scattered doorsteps were men, young, middle-aged and elderly, staring ahead, expressionless, like weary specters with no one left to haunt but each other, but without the energy to bother. It was frightening and he grew increasingly uncomfortable.

Between Bangor and Roseto, a red Ford pickup truck charged by him, then veered to the right and skidded to a stop. The passenger, a boy who looked as though he was about ten years old, gave him the finger before the truck sped off. A little farther on someone in an old Dodge Dart threw a bottle out the window at him. It missed him by several feet, but the message made contact: he was just a bug at their picnic. From Roseto to the beginning of the winding descent was a steady climb, and Chase struggled to find the right gear. He'd allowed the antagonism to derail his focus and now he could feel everything. His legs were on the verge of cramping, his hands were sore from holding the handlebars, the muscles in his neck and shoulders ached and his back was hot and itchy from the backpack. A couple miles past Roseto, the grade increased and he downshifted and moved back in his saddle. *Just keep pedaling. Find your rhythm.* If his cadence was right and he was breathing evenly he could go forever. In the proper state of mind the pain was manageable, sort of a familiar companion, and when everything was right, there was joy in this, euphoria in the steady movement, the constant effort and forward motion. This causes this. Push the pedals and the bike moves forward. When the crest was in sight the grade increased again and Chase downshifted. Using his shoulders and arms to steady the bike against the thrust of his legs, he stood up and rocked the bike back and forth. Breathing hard, his heart pounding, he approached the crest and downshifted again. The road leveled and he sat and shifted into the big chainring. The bike lunged forward, perspiration stung his eyes, something moved in the bushes up ahead. A second later a deer loped across the road and disappeared into the forest. He wanted to call Christine now—*maybe I'll be okay, maybe.* . . . But stopping was unthinkable. The descent began and he shifted into his smallest cog and went into a seated sprint. The road swerved hard to the left and he nearly lost control. Then he remembered countersteering. He extended his right leg and angled his left knee out, pushed the left side of the handlebar forward and, keeping his eyes focused on the road ahead, he leaned the bike hard to the left and followed the curve to a short straight stretch that was followed by a sharp right and another steep drop. Within seconds he was going forty-five miles an hour, tucked in tight to keep the wind from slowing him and grinning so hard his face hurt. His chin was almost resting on the handlebar and his shoulders throbbed as he made a few gradual turns, then soared down another straight stretch. He steered wide around a badly banked right, almost sideswiping a big brown Oldsmobile that was struggling along, coughing and belching, billows of blue smoke stumbling up the hill after it like a drunken ghost tripping on its own ghostly pants. A steep descent past a small tavern on the left, then the road leveled out. He sat up and checked his maximum speed on the computer: fifty-six miles per hour. He hooted like an Apache in a 1950s western. Then he looked up and saw the climb he'd somehow put out of his mind, a long steep ascent to the plateau before the final descent.

He was exhausted and the hill ahead looked like an endless wall. As the ascent began he reached down for his water bottle, brought it up to his lips and took a long slug. After wiping his lips with the back of his hand, he replaced the bottle in its cage, downshifted and slid back in his saddle. Okay, he was climbing now. He found a comfortable cadence and steadied the rhythm of his breathing. If he pushed too hard a gear now he'd burn himself out before he made it halfway to the top. Too easy and the climb might take too long to survive. The grade increased rapidly and he had to concentrate to coordinate the tempo of his pedal stroke with his respiration. *Relax your arms and breathe, fill your lungs, now push it all out. Keep your rhythm, rinse, repeat.* His legs were threatening to cramp now and the bottoms of his feet were throbbing. He knew that he hadn't been drinking enough. Every stroke was a new battle, but he couldn't focus on that. He wasn't sure he could keep it up much longer, but when he tried to pedal faster his legs sent out warning spasms that felt like jolts of electricity applied with a mallet. He grabbed the brake hoods and stood up, using his arms and shoulders to rock the bike, trying to get the lactic acid out of his legs. Only two or three minutes more. Put the pain out of your mind, keep pushing, turning the crank, moving forward. Just as he was approaching the crest, he sat, shifted to a higher gear and sprinted the remaining distance to the plateau. When it finally leveled out, he downshifted, relaxed his arms and pedaled lightly until his breathing had calmed. He was smiling. And the final descent was just a couple hundred yards ahead. Despite his physical exhaustion, or perhaps because of it, he was energized now. Maybe it was a simple chemical reaction, or the fact that his thoughts had been nowhere else but exactly where he was. It didn't matter. He clipped out of his right pedal, slowed to a stop, leaned to the side and planted his foot on the ground.

At the bottom of the mountain was real life, everything he'd been avoiding: his pregnant wife, their divorce, his brother and their father's house and his unemployment and all his foolish mistakes and Christine and his sister's memory, the memory of her death and the nightmares, insistent, debilitating. It was all there waiting to pounce like some ravenous predator. The road was straight and he could just about make out the intersection at the bottom where he'd have to stop. The bike was new so there was little chance of a brake cable snapping. If he rode the brakes and overheated the rims he'd risk blowing a tire, but he knew better than that. All he had to do was sprint up to speed, tuck in tight, shoot down the hill like a dive-bomber and start feathering the brakes in time to make the stop sign. Perhaps the stories about brakes locking up or igniting were invented, but in the years he'd lived there that intersection had been the site of at least one fatal car crash.

Chase guzzled what was left in his water bottle and clipped his right shoe into the pedal. He grabbed the bars and took a deep breath. *Okay.* But something was holding him back. Why couldn't he just stay right here, away from all his problems, high above them? Or just turn around and go back to Bangor? The entire town had apparently given up, why couldn't one world-weary victim of life do the same? It wasn't as though he couldn't continue to function, but he knew now that some part of him had been destroyed. At times he could feel its absence, like the memory of a wound sustained in a dream, or a childhood injury that might never have occurred. He could find an untenanted doorstep and sit down, buy a brown shirt and fade into the background. I'll be a brick. There had to still be a bar or two within walking distance, somewhere to get a burger and fries, maybe sit down and eat with a homeless man who resembled an old friend. Or he could just squint and pretend. He could dot his T's and cross his eyes. He could live on peanut butter, tuna salad and Budweiser. Develop a stutter or a lisp, maybe both, so people wouldn't think he was haughty and shun him, or *thun* him; he wouldn't want that. Maybe a couple twitches in honor of his mother. And a pet rat. Everyone should have a pet. They could whistle tunes together and cuddle up in the alley at night. He could get the rat a pet mouse and the mouse a pet cockroach and the cockroach a pet fly and the fly a pet flea and the flea a pet peeve. He could be a pick-up artist for sanitation and drive a hard bargain. He could solve riddles, write poetry and smoke insulation in a real corncob pipe. He could chew the fat and exercise restraint. He could pilfer a flannel shirt from Kmart. He could swallow lies and regurgitate old ideas. He could measure his words and weigh his options. When he ran out of money he could beg to differ. Sell his eyebrows to the needy at a substantial discount. He could let the cat out of the bag and pass the buck. He could ignite the flames of passion and extinguish hopes. He could tilt his head to tip the bartender, turn his underwear inside out when it got dirty, brown in back, yellow in front. He could cash in his chips and buy the farm, upset the apple cart and spill the beans. He could open a wine bar in East Stroudsburg. He could pay through the nose and take it like a man. He could find God. He could lose his way. He could cast a long shadow. He could just stand here where it was lush and green straddling his overpriced bike until the danger passed or he collapsed and expired. He could sell himself short, but no, he'd already passed that intersection. *Enough.* Enough. He pushed down on the right pedal, sat on the saddle and clipped his left foot in. Then he shifted to his highest gear and stood up. Howling like a burn victim in a sandstorm, he powered the bike forward. *Use the anger. Produce something, something of value. Get it out.* The descent began and in a less than thirty seconds he was going too fast to pedal even in his highest gear. He tucked down low and brought his hands close together on the handlebar. The wind whipped over him, filling his ears with white noise, blocking out the last of the nagging clamor in his head. Roadside vegetation and litter rushed by in a hurry to get somewhere back there where he'd stopped or far beyond. He brought his knees in and rested his chin on his knuckles and pulled his elbows in. It felt as though some powerful force had shoved him forward. The road beneath him was racing past now, a dark-gray haze. Bye bye. He squeezed the top tube with his knees to steady the bike and sat up just enough to ride with both hands off the bars. Keeping his eyes on the road ahead, he reached his right hand back to release the buckle on the backpack, slipped his arms from the straps and brought the bag around in front of him. *Keep it steady, sport.* After extracting the urn he tossed the backpack. A strap slapped his wrist, grabbed it, yanked (*careful!*), then let go. The urn was heavy and a little cumbersome. *Don't think. She wouldn't mind.* He removed the top and jettisoned it into the brush. *This is for me.* Then he grabbed the handlebar with his left hand, held the urn out in his right and turned it upside down. The ashes cascaded out, a final exhalation. It was over in seconds, too fast. There was nothing more to say. He gave the urn a heave, grabbed the bars close to the stem and ducked down tight, knees and elbows in, back flat. The bike shot forward. *I'm a missile. A bomb. I'm great and awful and so many shades of gray. Or maybe I'm not that special. Well. . . .* He glanced up. The stop sign was hurtling toward him, quivering on its post like a nervous lollipop, the busy intersection just beyond it. Everything was shaking, trembling. Earthquake. The fucking sign was heading straight for him. *No,* you *stop!* Closer. *Construct from the rage, from the despair, something . . . what?* He moved his hands to the hoods and squeezed the levers, released, squeezed. The bike slowed, but it wasn't enough. *Shit.* He gripped the brake levers and squeezed as hard as he could. The wheels locked and the rear wheel skidded out to the left almost catapulting him into the road. He released the pressure and regained his line, then squeezed hard again and skidded to a stop. He twisted his foot out of the pedal, leaned over and nearly lost his balance. He laughed at himself, at everything. He laughed until it hurt.

Well . . . okay.

Okay.

He was tired now, but he didn't have too far to go.

About the Author

Grant Jarrett grew up in Northeastern Pennsylvania and currently lives in Manhattan, where he works as a writer, musician, and songwriter. He has written for magazines including FOW and Triathlon, and is the author of *More Towels,* a coming-of-age memoir about life on the road. He is an avid cyclist and a reasonably competent flosser. *Ways of Leaving* is his first novel. Learn more at grantjarrett.com or connect on social media.

Twitter: @grantdjarrett | Facebook: AuthorGrantJarrett

About SparkPress

SparkPress is an independent boutique publisher delivering high-quality, entertaining, and engaging content that enhances readers' lives. We are proud of our catalog of both fiction and non-fiction titles, featuring authors who represent a wide array of genres, as well as our established, industry-wide reputation for innovative, creative, results-driven success in working with authors. SparkPress, a BookSparks imprint, is a division of SparkPoint Studio, LLC. To learn more, visit us at www.sparkpointstudio.com.

CPSIA information can be obtained
at www.ICGtesting.com
Printed in the USA
FSHW011148200119
55146FS